Nilanjan P. Choudhury's debut novel, a mythological thriller titled *Bali and the Ocean of Milk*, was a (very) brief bestseller. His subsequent writings include *The Case of the Secretive Sister*, a detective caper set in Bangalore, and *The Square Root of a Sonnet*, a pioneering play on the history and science of black holes; both of which received wide critical acclaim. He confesses to having studied at IIM Ahmedabad and IIT Kanpur, and hopes that this will not be held against him. He grew up in Shillong and now lives in Bangalore with his family. He can be reached at www.nilanjan.net.

SHILLONG TIMES

A Story of Friendship and Fear

Nilanjan P. Choudhury

SPEAKING
TIGER

SPEAKING TIGER PUBLISHING PVT. LTD
4381/4, Ansari Road, Daryaganj
New Delhi 110002

First published in India by Speaking Tiger in paperback 2018

Copyright © Nilanjan P. Choudhury 2018

ISBN: 978-93-88326-05-6
eISBN: 978-93-88070-48-5

10 9 8 7 6 5 4 3 2 1

Typeset in Sabon Roman by SÜRYA, New Delhi
Printed at Gopsons Papers Ltd.

For Baba, Ma and Buri,
in memory of the wonder years

'You have to begin to lose your memory, if only in bits and pieces, to realize that memory is what makes our lives.'

—Luis Buñuel

'Cities, like dreams, are made of desires and fears.'

—Italo Calvino

'This city knows my every first thing
The more I struggle to escape from it
The stronger are the memories it brings.'

—Kabir Suman

CONTENTS

INCIDENT AT JACOB'S LADDER

DEBU WAS FOURTEEN when he first heard the word 'dkhar'. He was walking back home from school, preoccupied with the dilemma of whether he should spend the last one rupee of his pocket money on chana masala or on sour berries. It was not an easy choice. The chana masala tasted better, but a larger quantity of sour berries could be had for the same money. The ten and twenty paisa coins inside his trouser pocket jangled agreeably as he stepped into Don Bosco Square. Lost in thought, he walked past the grey concrete statue of Don Bosco, who seemed to be in an equally pensive mood. A few minutes later he arrived at Jacob's Ladder—a steep flight of steps that twisted down the slope of a low wooded hillock.

Like most days, Jacob's Ladder was empty. Not many people used it owing to the sharpness of its incline. But it was the shortest way back home and Debu's preferred route, inspite of his mother's orders to stay away from lonely roads. He was halfway down the steps when he heard someone yelling at him from behind.

'Hey dkhar!' the voice said.

He turned around to see three boys standing at the top of the hillock, their dark silhouettes framed against the buttery sunshine of an early summer afternoon in Shillong. He squinted at them. They did not look like anyone he knew. Must have mistaken me for someone called 'Dkhar', he said to himself. Poor fellow, he thought, to be saddled with such a weird name.

The three strangers began running towards him. He could not make out their faces clearly, but they looked like Khasis.

'We need to talk to you,' they said. 'Wait for us.'

Debu was unsure what to do. On the one hand, it was clear that they were keen to meet him. Perhaps they had some urgent business with him, and he was curious to know what that might be. On the other hand, his mother had repeatedly warned him to come home straight after school—no looking left or right, no stopping here and there, no eating this and that, and most importantly, no talking to anyone and everyone—especially not strangers and Khasis.

The trio was closer to him now and he could see them clearly. They were older than him, probably eighteen or nineteen. Their lips were stained red with kwai juice—the local betel nut and leaf. They were smiling at him—cold smiles that stopped short of their eyes.

'Hey, dkhar!' they yelled again. 'You going home? Come with us, man. We'll take you home.'

They broke into a sprint now. As they loped towards him, eyes glistening in the summer sun, a chilling thought occurred to Debu. What if they were after his pocket money? Or his school bag? It was a recently purchased khaki-coloured satchel, and he was rather proud of how smart it looked. What if they thrashed him and took it away? They looked like the sort of boys who thrashed other boys. Of course, they might be completely harmless also. But why take a risk, especially when his mother had repeatedly warned him to stay clear of strangers? Better safe than sorry, he thought, and clutching the coins inside his pocket, he broke into a half-run.

The boys stepped up their pace. 'Hey, think you can run away from us?' one of them said.

'Why are you here? What are you doing in our country?' said another.

'Yeah. Go back to your own country and eat your rotten fish, dkhar bastard,' the third shouted.

By now, it was beginning to dawn on Debu that 'dkhar' wasn't someone's name but an insult of some sort. One that could not be taken lightly by any self-respecting fourteen-year-old. A suitable retaliation was called for. But the enemy outnumbered him three to one, and it would be foolhardy to get into a physical fight. Better to hit back with a few stinging counter-insults and make a run for it, thought Debu. He delved into his limited stock of invectives. Most of them concerned the offspring of pigs and dogs, going along the lines of: 'shaala shuworor bachcha,' 'halar hala kuttar bachcha,' and so on. But compared to the raspy, guttural ring that 'dkhar' had about it, they all seemed rather tame, musical almost.

The most venomous abuse he could think of was one that his father was prone to use on the rare occasion when he was really furious—'phungir-bai'. He had no idea what it meant and his attempts to find out had been greeted with a curt dismissal from his father. In any case, there was no need to know what it meant. It sounded adequately indecent and there was a nice explosive feel to it. It would do for now.

He spun around and threw what he hoped was a dirty look at his assailants. 'Halaar haala phungir-bai!' he shouted at the top of his voice. And without further ado, he fled down the steps of Jacob's Ladder as fast as his legs would carry him.

'Bengali bastard! Stut liah!' the boys yelled back as they pursued him down the hillock.

They were good runners. The gap that separated them from Debu was rapidly shrinking. It was only a matter of minutes before they caught up with him. The weight of the books inside his school bag was slowing him down. He could hear them panting behind him. The sweat streamed down his forehead, trickling into his eyes and lips. He felt himself growing tired, slowing down as he laboured past the final bend on Jacob's Ladder.

He knew that he wasn't far from the main road now. The thought gave him hope. Bomfyle Road was home to several government offices, most notably that of All India Radio. It was far less lonely than Jacob's Ladder and there was a chance that the boys might not attack him if there were people around. With a desperate effort, he put on a final burst of speed and hurtled onto Bomfyle Road. To his relief, there were several people ambling along the pavement near the entrance of the

All India Radio station. He sneaked a quick look behind to
see if their presence had induced the boys from calling off
their pursuit.

But their resolve only seemed to have hardened. A squat,
thickset fellow with close-cropped hair that stood up like a
porcupine's spikes, had shot ahead of his companions. He
was racing towards Debu, his arm stretched out. A few more
strides and Debu's neck would be in his grasp.

There were only two choices now—turn around and fight,
or surrender and beg his way out by appealing to the hitherto
undiscovered humanitarian impulses of his pursuers. Either
way, he didn't rate his chances of survival very highly. Only
god could save him now, Debu thought in despair.

He uttered a silent prayer that if he managed to escape
unscathed today, he would perform a grand puja at the Shani
Mandir in Police Bazar. The temple was held in high regard
by the people of Shillong, on account of a popular belief
that Shani Dev himself paid it the occasional visit. He was in
desperate need of an ally and who better than the powerful
Lord Shani, whom even his mother feared?

O, Lord Shani, save me today, and I will sacrifice one
full year of my pocket money for your puja, Debu muttered
under his breath. At ten rupees a month, this would amount
to one hundred and twenty rupees. A handsome offering by
any standards, thought Debu. Surely enough to earn him the
blessings and protection of the gods, even one as grouchy as
Shani.

The very thought gave him fresh hope. He raced ahead
with renewed energy and opened up a respectable gap between
himself and his pursuers. They seemed to be slowing down.
Perhaps they were getting tired or simply giving up. In any
case, it would appear that Lord Shani had heard his prayers
and he might get away after all. His investment was showing
a return already.

On second thoughts...perhaps he had been a little too

hasty...a little too generous for his own good. It would be torture to live through one whole year without any pocket money. Besides, one hundred and twenty rupees was a lot of money...too much money, in fact—nearly the price of a new Asterix comic. Better to make it a hundred. But even that seemed a little excessive. After all, he wasn't some rich Marwari kid. Eighty would be quite enough. Or maybe even sixty. Yes, sixty rupees would be perfect. Sixty for god and sixty for himself. 50–50: an equal partnership. Sixty it was—he made his final decision.

He was feeling quite pleased with how cleverly he had extricated himself from the hole he had dug himself into, when he felt a whirr near his ear—like the sound of a dragonfly whizzing past. A fist-sized rock crashed in front of him, splintering against the stone pavement. As he spun around, a second rock came flying at him and struck him on the right knee. A stinging pain sliced through his leg and he fell to the ground, squealing in agony.

'Thought you could get away from us, dkhar?' the boys laughed. They were advancing towards him, rocks held in their hands.

'Not so easy, shih kmei,' said one of them. 'We got you now.'

'And we will not let you go,' his companion sang out in a falsetto.

'Bismillah! No, we will not let you go,' all three sang in unison, the words spat out quick and hard, like the rat-a-tat of machine-gun fire. Debu's mouth turned dry with fear. They were ambling towards him, casually tossing the rocks up in the air like cricket balls.

Debu looked around desperately for help. But the road was deserted. The few pedestrians that he had seen earlier seemed to have vanished. There was no hope now. Even ten years of pocket money could not save him from his fate, he thought. They would reach him any minute.

'Mamma mia, mamma mia,' the boys were shrieking behind

him. 'Wanna go back home to your mama? Wanna go back home to Bangladesh?'

Ignoring the pain in his knee, he somehow willed himself to stand on his feet. If he was going to get thrashed, so be it. He would go down fighting. He seized the strap of his tiffin box, steeling himself to swing at his attackers when the moment came. His heart hammered against his ribs as he faced them, ready to make his final stand.

And at that moment, when all seemed lost, the answer to his prayers appeared out of nowhere. A snub-nosed blue and yellow city bus emerged from behind a sharp bend on Bomfyle Road, chugging towards him. It was as if Lord Shani himself had sent his vaahan to Debu's rescue.

The bus was looming behind the boys but in their excitement, they had failed to notice it. Any moment now, and it would overtake them. This was his only chance. Debu waited dry-mouthed for the bus to reach him. His pursuers were barely a few steps away when the bus passed by. Debu leaped onto the footboard and grabbed the handrail.

The bus shot forward, taking him to safety. Debu could not believe that he was getting away after all. An overwhelming feeling of relief washed over him. It was only now that he realized he was shivering feverishly. The footboard seemed to be wobbling below his feet. The conductor and the other passengers were giving him strange looks. He tried to avoid their gaze and gripped the handrail tightly to stop himself from toppling over, when he felt a ferocious grip on his forearm.

The boy with the porcupine hair had latched on to Debu's arm. He was running like a maniac alongside the bus, matching its speed. His companions followed, hot on his heels. Debu hung onto the rail for dear life but his grip was nearly prised open as porcupine boy gave it a powerful yank. It was all over, thought Debu. He would be dashed to the ground and crushed under the wheels of the bus—dead at fourteen and nothing to show for his brief existence, apart from an empty tiffin box and a rupee in his pocket. At best, they would mention his name on the All India Radio news that night, because he had died in front of their gates. And that would be it—a sorry end to a short life.

His mind blanked out in terror.

And then, some long-lost survival instinct took over. Without quite understanding what he was doing, he found himself seizing his tiffin box and slamming it hard into the boy's face. It caught him on the nose and he staggered back with a cry of pain, releasing his grip on Debu's arm. The bus sped away and at last, Debu was free of his assailants.

Only after there was a healthy distance between them, did he dare to sneak a look behind. Porcupine boy was on his knees, clutching his nose, screaming. And despite the roar of the bus's engine, Debu could hear what he was saying.

'Bangladeshi bastard! We'll kill you. Bloody dkhar! Next time, we will kill you!'

THE FOREIGNERS

DEBU GOT OFF the bus at Police Bazar. It was Shillong's high street—home to many of its iconic shopping destinations like Lila Brothers, Radharani Stores and Ratna's Mascot. It was early evening and the place was bustling with office-goers finishing the day's shopping on their way back home.

Police Bazar had always been too noisy and crowded for Debu's liking. But today it seemed like a haven of peace. He felt grateful for the warm, safe embrace of the hordes of people thronging about him. He stopped for a breather and treated himself to a rupee's worth of chana masala. It helped him calm down and, after a while, he felt that his legs were steady enough to walk back home.

Home was a wattle and daub Assam-type cottage with a red tin roof and a small garden on Upper Jail Road—a residential colony that had sprung up around the high walls of the Shillong prison. Once in a while, a police van would arrive at the gates of the prison and deliver its consignment of sullen-faced convicts, hands tied behind their backs. Debu would watch with a fearful fascination as they disembarked from the van and slouched to their new lodgings at the far end of the prison grounds.

When he was about eight years old, Debu used to have a recurring nightmare. He would dream of the prisoners breaking out of jail and sneaking into his bedroom in the dead of night. Grinning evilly at each other, they would pounce on him and swiftly bundle him inside a thick blanket that muffled his cries. They would then spirit him away to some nameless place, where they would commence to torture him in a variety of unspeakable and embarrassing ways. Why me, why me, what have I done?—he would yell in his dream. But he would never get to know the answer, for he would always wake up at that point, quaking in fright. It was a fear that gnawed at him for weeks on end, until one day, his father came to know of it. Debu's father sat him down for a man-to-man chat. There is nothing to be scared of, he assured Debu. Jail Road prison is the second-most secure prison in the whole world. Which is the first? Debu asked. Alcatraz, his father whispered into his ear, in a voice filled with dread. It was a most terrible prison where only the most blood-thirsty and dangerous criminals were sent. It was located on a desolate island in the middle of the Pacific Ocean—and no one had ever escaped from it alive. The few who had tried had been shot or drowned, or eaten alive by sharks.

Jail Road prison was equally secure, his father went on. Of course, it was not surrounded by an ocean or patrolled by man-eating sharks. But no one in living memory had ever escaped from it. And even if someone did (which they never would), his father said nonchalantly, there was nothing to worry about. Why not? Debu asked. Because, his father replied, the police were very clever. Much cleverer than the chors. That is why they had built Police Bazar right next to Jail Road. Every inch of the locality was bristling with policemen. But most of them were plainclothesmen, which is why no one noticed them. Any prisoner foolish enough to attempt a getaway would be caught at once and thrown right back in. We are lucky to have so many policemen here in Jail Road to protect us, his father said. It is the safest place in the whole world—after Alacatraz.

That was one of the things that Debu really liked about his father—the way he could make his fears go away with a simple chat. So, when he arrived home that evening, it was very comforting to see his father seated in his usual chair on the verandah, sipping on his tea and puffing at a cigarette.

'How come you are home so early today?' Debu asked.

'Business is bad,' his father shrugged. 'The farmers are all busy at the Shad Suk Mynsiem dance festival. No point in keeping the shop open.'

Debu's father, Mr Dutta, owned a small pharmacy in Iewheh, which in Khasi meant big market. True to its name, it was the biggest market in Shillong, much bigger and far more rustic than its urbane cousin, Police Bazar. Farmers from the nearby villages came here to sell their produce—vegetables, poultry, beef and pork. They were simple, hardworking folks, largely untouched by the complexities of urban life. They would often drop into Mr Dutta's shop for a quick chat over a kwai.

The farmers were pleasant company but poor customers. They were blessed with robust health and hardly ever fell ill. And even when they did, they needed a fraction of the medicines that a city dweller might need to get well. It wasn't easy running a medicine shop in Iewheh, and Mr Dutta had to work hard to make a living. He did not earn a great deal but was happy to make enough to take care of his small family.

Indeed, it was a matter of some pride for Mr Dutta that he could afford to send Debu to St Edward's School. It was Shillong's best convent school for boys and had acquired quite a reputation for itself across the entire Northeastern region. St Edward's attracted students from states as far away as Tripura, Manipur and Nagaland, and counted among its distinguished alumni an assortment of Generals, Admirals, Ministers and IAS officers. But its two most famous products were the actors Utpal Dutt and Victor Banerjee,who had studied there briefly. But its most famous products were two Bengali actors, who had studied there briefly. They had gone on find fame and fortune through their memorable roles in the films of Satyajit Ray as well as in Bollywood. They were often held up as inspiring examples of what a hardworking and ambitious Edwardian could achieve if he set his mind to it.

Debu's mother hoped that her son too would reach great heights someday—although preferably not as an actor. Such careers were too exotic and uncertain for Bengali middle-class people like them. Mr Dutta however, wasn't too worried about

Debu's career. The boy seemed to be serious enough about his studies and usually stood first or second in his class. If he kept it up, he would do all right in life.

'So how are things at school?' asked Mr Dutta.

'Okay,' Debu replied.

'You are looking a little out of sorts today,' Mr Dutta said. 'What's the matter?'

'Yes, some boys—' Debu began, but came to an abrupt halt. If his parents came to know what had happened, he would almost certainly not be allowed to travel alone anymore. Until recently, Debu's father had dropped him to school on his scooter and brought him back home in the evening. But of late, most of his school friends had started making the journey on their own—by bus or on foot. They lost no time in ganging up on Debu and ragging him for being such a sissy, a mama's boy, who was too scared to go out alone. It soon became quite unbearable and Debu took up the matter with his parents.

But it was no use. His mother especially could not abide the idea of her only child roaming around the streets of Shillong without adult supervision. The roads are full of dangers, she said ominously, and teenage is the time when boys like you are attracted to dangers. What these were, she did not spell out. She only hinted darkly at two particular perils that she believed were the Scylla and Charybdis of wayward teenage boys. These, in their order of danger, were: girls and drugs. There was no knowing when some young boy would fall into the hands of these twin menaces. Debu had tried to assure his mother that he would stay miles away from both, but this only made her more skeptical.

It took weeks of begging, threatening and sulking before Debu could finally manage to convince his parents that he was perfectly capable of going to school by himself, and that he should be given the chance to do so. It had been a hard-earned privilege, and he wasn't going to give it up so easily.

Even the possibility of getting beaten up seemed to be better than the certainty of being teased by his classmates—if he was seen coming to school riding on his father's coat-tails. More importantly, he loved the sense of freedom and space afforded by his walks between home and school. It was a welcome relief from having some adult or the other badgering him all the time.

But the afternoon's incident had shaken him badly. He felt the need to talk about it to someone, although he would have to be careful not to reveal everything. 'Baba,' he resumed hesitantly, 'something happened today on the way back from school.'

'Yes?' said Mr Dutta.

'Some boys were calling me dkhar,' Debu replied. 'What does it mean?'

Mr Dutta did not reply. He puffed on his cigarette and silently watched the smoke curl upwards. After a while he said, 'These boys...they know who you are? Where you stay?'

'Don't think so. Never saw them until today.'

'I see. Make sure you stay away from them.'

'Yes, that I will. But you're not telling me, what does dkhar mean?'

His father stubbed out his cigarette in the ashtray and said, 'It's the Khasi word for foreigner.'

'Foreigner? Wow!' Debu exclaimed. 'You mean like those people in English movies?' He had recently seen a film called *Dr. No*, which had some extremely good-looking people. The lead actress, in particular, had been permanently etched into his memory. Most of the English movie actors he had seen so far were really handsome—so much better looking than the baby-faced Hindi and Bengali film stars that his mother seemed to be enamoured by. Maybe that's why those boys were after him...maybe they were crazed with jealousy that he was so handsome and they were so ugly.

But this seemed a little far-fetched. With his round face,

skinny build, hair glistening with oil and large eyes framed by oversized spectacles, he looked like the quintessential Bengali good boy—not some Indian avatar of Sean Connery.

'But why would they think that I look like a foreigner?' Debu said. 'I don't have white skin or yellow hair.'

'Obviously not. You are no Englishman. They called you a foreigner because you don't look like *them*.'

'Them? You mean Khasis?'

'That's right.'

'Thank god for that. Who wants to look like a Chinky?'

'Chinky?' Mr Dutta's eyes narrowed. 'Did you just say Chinky?' There was a sudden chill in his voice.

'Yes...umm...I...mean...no. I—' Debu mumbled, startled by his father's reaction.

'Chup! I heard exactly what you said,' Mr Dutta snapped. 'Where did you learn such things?'

'But so many people say it,' Debu protested. 'My friends in school, in the—'

'You are not everyone. You are my son,' Mr Dutta said. 'I have tried to raise you with some values, I have tried to provide you the best of education and this is what comes of it? If I ever hear you uttering that word again, I'll give you such a thrashing that...anyway, never mind. What you must understand is that it's insulting to call Khasis by such names.'

Yeah right, Debu said to himself. He couldn't call them Chinkys, but they could call him dkhar. They could stone him to death, but that wasn't insulting was it, he wanted to ask his father. But he held back, reminding himself that it was in his own interests not to reveal anything to his parents.

'They call us dkhar. We call them Chinkys. Where will all this end? It's 1987 for god's sake! Forty years since Independence. And we are still fighting with each other like cats and dogs! I don't know what will happen to this country,' Mr Dutta ran his fingers through the small patch of hair on his otherwise bare head. He was a short man in his late forties with a thick moustache that had grayed prematurely, and an incipient potbelly that seemed to be unsure of how much further it should grow.

'Can I ask you a question, Baba?' Debu asked meekly. It was unusual to see his father in a bad mood. He was an easy-going man, with a gentle manner and a ready smile which caused the crinkles around his eyes to fan out like sunrays.

'Yes?' said Mr Dutta.

'Why is it wrong to call them Chi—' he stopped. 'I mean calling them...calling them...whatever I shouldn't be calling them. After all, they *are* from China, aren't they?'

Mr Dutta threw up his arms. 'For god's sake, who has been telling you this rubbish! Khasis aren't Chinese.'

'But they look like them—you know...slit eyes, no hair on their faces...and the other day, Subhashish's father was saying that they eat snakes, just like the Chinese and also—'

'Nonsense! Total nonsense!' Mr Dutta said as he flung his cigarette into the garden with a snort. 'Eat snakes! I don't know who this Subhashish character is and why his father has been poisoning his ears with these rubbish stories! It is such third-class people like him who are destroying this place,' he fixed his gaze on Debu. 'For the last time, Debu, let me tell you that no matter what Khasis look like, they are not Chinese. They are Indians. As Indian as you or me. Do you understand?'

'But if we are all Indians, then why were they calling me a foreigner?' demanded Debu.

'They didn't mean it in that way,' his father said with a sigh. 'They were calling you an outsider.'

'An outsider?' Debu said. 'But why? I am from here, aren't I? I even remember going to Tiny Tots nursery in Dhankheti when I was five years old. And you told me that I was born here.'

'Of course you were born here, right here in Shillong—in Roberts Hospital,' said Mr Dutta. A smile came over his face.

'It seems only yesterday that the nurse brought you to me and I held you in my hands for the first time—a little pink bundle wrapped inside a white blanket. Such a sweet baby you were—always smiling. I still remember your first day out. You were four months old and we had gone to Lady Hydari Park. You were—'

'Yes, yes Baba, I know all that,' Debu cut in. He had heard the Hydari Park story many times before. It was one of his father's favourites, and usually led to the recounting of several other amusing and, mostly embarrassing, episodes from Debu's childhood. 'Those boys also told me that I should go back to Bangladesh. Why?'

The lines on Mr Dutta face deepened, making him look much older than he was. 'Have you heard of Winston Churchill?' he asked after a pause.

Debu groaned. That was the problem with his father. He loved giving gyan whenever he got a chance. 'Yes, of course I know who Churchill is. He stopped Hitler and won World War II.'

Mr Dutta shook his head. 'No no, that was Stalin. I don't know why schools are still teaching you these colonial versions of history.'

'For god's sake, Baba! Will you please come to the point! What has Churchill got to do with Bangladesh?'

'Patience, patience,' Mr Dutta wagged a finger at him. 'Churchill was a great man and he said many great things. Like, once he said, "You will never reach your destination if you stop to throw stones at every dog that barks."' Mr Dutta beamed at Debu.

'But they were the ones throwing—' Debu replied indignantly, but realized that it would unwise to tell his father about the stone-pelting.

Mr Dutta's eyes narrowed. 'Throwing what?'

'Umm...nothing, nothing!' Debu hastened to explain. 'They were throwing...umm...dirty looks at me. That's all.' He tried to steer the conversation back to safe waters. 'But what does Churchill have anything to do with this?'

'You young people think you are so smart,' his father said irritably. 'Never want to learn anything. What Churchill is saying is that one should not give so much importance to what people say. Those boys were talking nonsense. You should not bother about them.'

'Okay, fine! But what if they bother me?' Debu said.

Before Mr Dutta could reply, a voice called from inside: 'What are you two doing phus-phus in the verandah for so long? If you have no work, then come inside and help me. The house is a mess.'

'There, see what you have done,' Mr Dutta muttered. 'You've gone and upset your mother.'

'Me? What did I do?' Debu protested. 'I was only asking—' he stopped mid-sentence as his mother swept into the verandah.

Mrs Dutta had the sort of demeanour which immediately made it clear that she considered life to be A Serious Business, and that she expected everyone else to Take It Seriously. She was tall and bony, and the severe cotton saree draped over her gaunt frame accentuated her angularity. She had a long nose that was adept at sniffing out lies, and piercing eyes that would have been the pride of a medieval inquisitor.

'What is there to talk so much about?' she asked Debu. 'Go inside and change out of your school clothes.'

'No, Baba has to tell me first,' Debu replied. 'Why did those boys tell me to go back to Bangladesh?'

'What boys?' Mrs Dutta said. 'What are you talking about, Debu?'

'Arre, it's nothing to worry about,' Mr Dutta said. 'Just the same old story. Some boys were teasing Debu today—they were calling him Bangladeshi.'

'And I want to know why,' Debu said.

'Look, Debu, it's quite simple. We are Bengalis,' said Mr Dutta. 'And there are some people here who claim that all

Bengalis are from Bangladesh. They say that we came here illegally.'

'Oh. And did we?' asked Debu.

'Of course not. I told you. You were born in Shillong,' Mr Dutta replied.

'Yeah, yeah—that I know. I was asking about you, Baba. Did *you* come here illegally?'

'What is this nonsense!' Mrs Dutta exclaimed. 'How dare you ask your own father if he is illegal? One tight slap I'll give you.'

'No, no let him be,' Mr Dutta said. 'How can you expect him to know these things? It's good that he's taking an interest in the family history. Listen, Debu,' he lit up another cigarette, 'our family has been living in Shillong since 1935, over fifty-two years now. It's true that your grandfather grew up in what is Bangladesh today. But, at that time, it was part of undivided Bengal, of India. You, me, my father, we are all Indians—by birth. Satisfied now?'

'Yeah, I guess,' said Debu. 'Accha, Baba, do we eat rotten fish?'

'What sort of question is that?' Mrs Dutta snapped. 'We may not be rich like Tata-Birla, but your father is still not so poor that he has to buy rotten fish. Did those teasing boys tell you that?'

'Yes.'

'They were Khasi boys, right?' asked Mrs Dutta.

'Yes.'

'I knew it! What else can you expect from these people? Rotten fish, indeed.'

But Debu was not convinced. 'What about that thing you sometimes cook on Sundays, the one with that horrible stink—isn't that rotten fish?'

'It is NOT rotten fish you stupid boy. It's shutki! Dried fish. There is a world of difference between the two.'

'Smells quite bad, if you ask me.'

'Dried fish *can* smell a little strong, I admit,' Mrs Dutta said. 'Takes a person with taste to appreciate it. And we can't expect that from these uncivilized Khasis. You think these tribal fellows are capable of understanding fish? Do you know what they eat themselves?'

'What?' Debu asked.

'Pigs and cows!' replied Mrs Dutta. 'If you go to Iewheh market, you can see it for yourself—huge hunks of meat hanging from hooks in the butchers' shops, dripping with blood. Pigs, cows—god only knows what they are.'

'Really? They have full cows hanging from hooks? Like goats in the Jail Road mutton shop that Baba goes to on Sundays?' Debu asked.

'Aiieee, chup! Don't talk of things you don't understand. Mutton is different. But cows and pigs? Chhee chhee. I have even seen them carrying dead pigs on their backs. Even the thought of it makes me feel like vomiting. And these people are mocking us about rotten fish. Some nerve they have, don't you think!' Mrs Dutta turned to Mr Dutta. 'Here, I'm talking to you,' she tapped him on the shoulder. 'What do you have to say about this?'

Mr Dutta wasn't expecting his wife to ask him for his opinion. She rarely did. 'Me? Umm...yes,' he finally managed to say.

'Yes? Yes, what?' Mrs Dutta said. 'Is that all you have to say? How can they insult us Bengalis like this?'

'I don't know,' Mr Dutta shrugged. 'They are just boys. They don't know any better. Does it really matter what they say?'

Mrs Dutta threw up her hands. 'Oh, you are hopeless. Nothing matters to you. But I am telling you one thing. This town is going to the dogs. I feel scared every time Debu leaves home. One day, these Khasis will thrash him and break his bones. You mark my words.'

'Ah, you worry too much,' Mr Dutta said. 'The Khasis

are good people. It's just a few hot-heads who are trying to stir up trouble.'

'I don't know what you see in these uncivilized tribals, these junglees,' Mrs Dutta said. 'Have you forgotten what happened in '79? I'm telling you, we should move to Calcutta before it's too late. It's the only place in India where we Bengalis are safe.'

'Calcutta?' Mr Dutta shook his head. 'You must be joking. It's so hot and dirty and crowded. Plus the load-shedding! We are lucky to be living here—in the Scotland of the East. Leave Shillong? Forget it!'

'Don't be so sure,' said Mrs Dutta. 'You may have to eat your words someday.'

'Listen to me, Debu's mother. You are worrying unnecessarily. You did not grow up here like I did. You came here only after your marriage. You don't understand this place. You don't know the people here,' Mr Dutta said. 'But I was born and brought up here. I know my Shillong like the back of my hand. It will all be fine.'

'Okay, whatever you say. When have you ever listened to me?' Mrs Dutta said. 'But if something happens to us, then don't say at that time that I didn't tell you,' she marched out of the verandah, her slippers flapping angrily against the wooden floorboards.

'Arre baba, don't worry so much,' Mr Dutta called out after her. 'Nothing will happen to us.'

BORDER CROSSINGS

LATER THAT EVENING, after dinner, Mr Dutta was sitting in the verandah, the smoke from his cigarette curling upwards into the clear, cool night sky. The day's work was done, dinner had been skirmish-free, and a hush was falling over the neighbourhood as it prepared for sleep. One by one, the lights in the nearby houses were switched off and soon, all that could be seen were the stars sparkling beyond the dark silhouettes of the pine trees, and the reflection of the full moon in the Umshyrpi river. The strains of a Hindi film song drifted from the old Murphy radio which Mrs Dutta listened to every evening before turning in.

Debu came and sat down next to his father. 'What's Bangladesh like, Baba? Have you ever been there?' he asked.

'Of course,' replied Mr Dutta. 'Every year, my father would take us to our ancestral home in Bangladesh. Even after moving to Shillong, he could never forget the land of his birth. For one month every year, we would go stay in the village in which he had grown up—Singerkach village in Sylhet district. It was like the annual holiday for all our ten brothers and sisters.'

'You had ten brothers and sisters! How did so many people stay together?'

'It was crowded but fun. You wouldn't understand. Sometimes, I feel sorry for you that you're an only child. But your mother's health—' Mr Dutta broke off with a sigh. 'Anyway, never mind. In those days, my father used to take us fishing on the Surma. It's a huge river—big as the sea. I remember there was a storm once and our boat nearly capsized.'

Debu's eyes widened. 'Wow! Did you fall into the river?'

'I didn't. But your uncle, my youngest brother did. Luckily, my father was able to catch him by his dhoti and pull him out. Otherwise, it would have been ta-ta bye-bye for him. Those days were great fun. During the monsoons, the river would flood the paddy fields. And little fishes would swim through the rice stalks. We would try to catch them with our bare hands, but they would slip through our fingers. Once in a while though, we would manage to catch a few. We would bring them back home where my mother would fry them in mustard oil and serve them to us for lunch. Since there were so many of us, there would hardly be much to go around. But whatever we got tasted delicious and we would feel as if were at a king's banquet. Those were wonderful days.'

'I wish grandpa had stayed on there. Then I could also have caught fishes in paddy fields instead of going to school. Why did he have to move to Shillong?'

His father gave a wry smile and patted his stomach. 'The reason why everyone has to leave home one day. To get a job.'

'I'm not going to go anywhere for a job. I'm going to stay right here in Shillong.'

'I hope so. But as you know—man proposes, god disposes. My father also wanted to stay in Sylhet but he couldn't. He owned some land there on which he grew rice. But the income wasn't enough to support our large family. In those days, Shillong used to be the capital of undivided Assam. The British government had many offices here. Thousands of Sylhetis used to come to Shillong from Bangladesh, looking for employment. Your grandfather was one of them. But he wasn't among the lucky ones who could manage to get a job. In the end, he had to set up a small medicine shop and somehow make a living. We never had much money, but we never wanted for anything either. Life was going along fine, until one day we came to know that India was going to become a free country. Everyone was very happy. But not for long. A terrible thing was about to happen.'

'What?' asked Debu.

Mr Dutta's face darkened. 'Partition. The big men sitting in Delhi decided that the country was to be divided into two parts—India and Pakistan. They decided that the eastern part of Bengal, which is called Bangladesh today, would go over to Pakistan. Like millions of people, my father now had to make a choice—India or Pakistan? The peaceful pine-covered hills of Shillong or the majestic rivers of Sylhet? He loved both equally. He thought he belonged equally to both places. But now he had to choose one country over the other, one home over another.'

'And he chose India?'

'Yes. Like most other Hindus, my father also chose India. Which meant that he had to give up everything that he had in Bangladesh. Land, house, relatives, friends—with the Partition, they all vanished. Overnight my father became an outsider in Bangladesh, the land of his birth. And for the rest of his life, we had to hear stories of all that he had lost. Day and night he would puff on his hookah and complain bitterly—'Three bighas of land, five cows, a mango orchard, a pond full of sweet-tasting fish. All gone! All gone because of Gandhi and Jinnah!'

'But I thought Gandhi was a great man. He is called the father of the nation. We learnt that in school.'

'You're lucky that your grandfather isn't around. He would have given you a tight slap if he heard you say that. "Father of the nation, indeed!" he used to swear. "What kind of father cuts his own child into two? Butchers of the nation—this Gandhi and Jinnah!" he would say. Poor man—the Partition had broken him and he blamed whoever he thought was responsible.'

'Did he take you to Bangladesh after the Partition?'

Before his father could answer, Mrs Dutta's voice called from inside. 'Debu, what is going on? It's getting late. Go to bed now.'

'Just five more minutes,' Debu replied. 'We are talking of important things.'

'What important things?' Mrs Dutta asked.

'The father of the nation. History, geography,' Debu said. 'Baba is helping me with my studies.'

'Okay, then finish quickly and come to bed,' his mother said.

'Maybe you should go now,' said Mr Dutta. 'It is getting late.'

'No, finish your story. What happened after Partition? Did you ever go back to Bangladesh?'

Mr Dutta sighed. 'No. Our house, property in Bangladesh—everything was now occupied by our Muslim neighbours who had stayed behind. There was nothing to go back to. And so, Shillong became my father's permanent home, and his exile. He died here, dreaming of the boats sailing on the Surma. But we were children and such things didn't bother us for too long. We were very happy to be growing up in Shillong. We may not have had much money but we had lots of fun. Things were different in those days. Parents were too busy with their work to bother about the children. So we would go roaming in the hills, have picnics in the woods, eat wild berries plucked from the bushes. In summer, we would go swimming in Crinoline Falls, play football, catch fish in Ward's Lake.'

'Catch fish in Ward's Lake? That's not allowed. I've seen the signboards. Didn't the guards catch you?'

'They would try. But we were too clever for them. You see, we had invented car fishing.'

'Car fishing?'

'Yes, car fishing. First, we would make a fishing line from a really long rope. Then we would sneak into Ward's Lake and drop the hook end of the line into the lake. The other end was already tied to the bumper of a car that had been parked outside the lake. Then we would go back to the car and wait for the fish to take the bait. The moment we felt a tug on the line, my friend would start the engine and off we'd go. The car would pull the line out of the lake and if there was a fish caught on the hook, it would be dragged behind us. If a guard saw us, he'd give us the chase. But we would drive off at top speed and he could never catch us.'

'But where did you get the car from?'

'Our next-door neighbour, Mr Warbah, was a car mechanic. There would always be some car or the other in his garage, He had three sons and they were my good friends. His wife was a great cook. I used to love eating the jadoh she made.'

'Jadoh? You mean that pork and rice thing they eat? Chhee! You eat pig meat, Baba?'

'Don't give your chhees and chhaas. Jadoh is delicious. You should try it sometime. But don't tell your mother. She'll throw you out of the house.'

'Of course I'll throw him out of the house! And you as well!' came a voice from behind. Mrs Dutta was standing in the doorway, a thundercloud on her face. 'So, this is what you have been teaching Debu all this while? How to eat pork? Chhee, chhee, chhee.'

'No, no,' Mr Dutta tried to explain. 'I was just telling him about my childhood and all the things that I did—that he shouldn't do.'

But Mrs Dutta was in no mood to listen. 'What will you teach him next?' she barked. 'Wear leather jackets and do jhang-jhang on the guitar?'

Debu's eyes lit up in excitement. 'Baba used to wear leather jackets and play the guitar? Really? Wow! That's so cool.'

'No, not your father!' Mrs Dutta exclaimed. 'I'm talking about these tribal boys. That's all they do the whole day—eat, drink and play guitar. And if you don't study hard and get out of Shillong, that's what you'll end up doing as well. You'll become just like them. I feel ashamed even to think of such a thing. Chhee chhee.'

Debu couldn't see what was so chhee-chhee about it. It sounded like a pretty good life.

But his mother had other ideas. She looked sternly at him and said, 'There is no future in this place. You must leave Shillong and get a good job in India as soon as you can. You are not a child anymore. You are in class nine. Next year, class ten. Then college. It's high time that you started thinking seriously about your career.'

'Career? Like what?' asked Debu. He and his friends rarely discussed careers. Careers were thought of as exotic, endangered species that only the luckiest or most determined of seekers could find. He had often heard his parents discussing how so-and-so's son or daughter had turned thirty and was still jobless, despite having completed all sorts of degrees and extra courses—secretarial, typing, stenography and even computer training. In the India of the eighties, jobs were few and far between and the career prospects for most young people were dismal—even more so in the far-flung hills of Shillong. But Debu's mother was not one to be deterred by such inconvenient truths.

'There are so many good careers these days—engineer, doctor, bank officer,' she was saying.

Debu nodded dutifully. Of late, he had been gorging on Sherlock Holmes, Father Brown and Feluda, and had reached the conclusion that out of all possible career options, being a detective was best suited to his temperament. There was no way he would become a doctor or an engineer, and wild horses could not drag him to become a bank officer. Even the very thought made him feel sleepy. But he did not say anything to his mother and tried to look interested as she continued her lecture.

'These are all good, respectable careers,' Mrs Dutta declared. 'But if you ask me, I would like to see you becoming an IAS officer.'

'What's that?' asked Debu.

'An officer of the Indian Administrative Service—it is the most prestigious job in India. Let me show you,' she picked up a copy of the local newspaper and pointed to a picture on the front page.

It was a black-and-white photograph of a thin man with a wispy moustache, attired in a loose, ill-fitting suit and a striped tie. His eyes bulged out from behind the thick lenses of his rectangular, plastic-framed spectacles, faintly reminding Debu of a frog that he recently had to dissect in the biology lab. The man seemed to be delivering a speech and his forefinger was held upright, as if admonishing his audience. Debu took an instant dislike to him.

'Look at this man. Don't you want to become like him?' his mother said.

You think I'm nuts, Debu wanted to say but he held his tongue and asked, 'Who is he?'

'You can read for yourself. It's mentioned below the photograph.'

'District Magistrate, Shri M. Venkataraman, speaking at the Annual Day function of the Potato Research Institute,' Debu read out. 'What's a District Magistrate? Some sort of farmer?'

'No, you stupid boy! A District Magistrate is an IAS officer. He is the most powerful person in any place of India. He is a VIP. He goes everywhere in a government Ambassador car with a red light and security guards with guns. Everyone respects him.'

'Why? What does he do?'

'I told you. He's a VIP. He does very important work.'

'Like what?'

'Like...umm...signing files, attending meetings, passing orders. But this is not the time to worry about unnecessary things, like what IAS officers do. First you become one yourself, then you can find out what they do. Not that it will be easy getting into the IAS. Every year lakhs of people try but less than one hundred finally succeed.'

'Sounds hopeless. Maybe there's no point trying?' Debu ventured hopefully.

'Don't talk nonsense. Of course, you have to try. Do you think we have put you in the best school in Shillong to swat flies? No. It is so that you will try to make the best possible career for yourself. And that is the IAS. But since it is so difficult and so risky, you will also need to have a fallback plan, just in case IAS does not work out.'

Mr Dutta shuffled uncomfortably in his seat. 'Aren't you making too many plans too early?' he asked.

'Someone has to. And I'm sure it won't be you. You don't have the time nor the interest. I don't know if you realize, but Debu is going to go to class ten next year. And he still has no idea what he wants to do in life. So, I only have to decide.'

'I see. And what have you decided?' Mr Dutta asked.

'First, he has to get into a good engineering college. Engineering is always a good option in case IAS doesn't work out. He has to get into a good college like Shibpur or Jadavpur or BITS Pilani. IIT is too tough. No one from Shillong has cleared the entrance test in the last ten years.'

'But Ma—' Debu began.

'Let me finish first,' his mother cut him off. 'After getting your engineering degree, you will enroll in Rau's IAS Study Circle in Delhi. Then you will sit for the Civil Services exam with mathematics and physics as your main papers. Those are the scoring subjects.'

'How do you know so much about these things?' Mr Dutta asked with a bemused look.

'Because I read *Competition Success Review* each month instead of wasting my time smoking cigarettes,' Mrs Dutta retorted. 'Also, I have decided one more thing—next week onwards, Debu will start evening tuitions with Professor Bose. Everyone says that he is the best Mathematics teacher in Shillong.'

Debu leaped to his feet and let out a wail. 'But Ma, I play cricket in the evenings. This is not fair.'

'Do you think you are Sunil Gavaskar to make your living

from cricket?' Mrs Dutta snapped. 'You have your whole life to play cricket. It can wait. The most important thing right now is to get a good education and then a good job. Otherwise you will end up on the streets and no one will marry you.'

Two years ago, Debu's mother had seen a Hindi film called *Arjun*, starring one of her favourites—an impressively hirsute actor named Sunny Deol. Mr Deol had essayed the role of an educated young man who had been forced to become a politician's hired goon because he couldn't get a job. For all her reading of *Competition Success Review*, Debu's mother was strongly influenced by Hindi films. She believed that they were an accurate portrayal of the real world. One particular line from the film had deeply affected her:

Bekaar aadmi kisi ko bhi bojh lagne lagta hai.

This penetrating commentary on unemployment made by Mr Deol had stayed with Mrs Dutta long after the film was over. It had left her with a gnawing anxiety that, like Sunny Deol, her son too would end up 'bekaar' unless he managed to get into a premier engineering college.

Debu was aware of his mother's hopes and ambitions. But he did not share them. The air and water of Shillong were not conducive to ambition. Like the town, its residents were laidback, cool and relaxed. Ambitions were for the people in the plains—people who had chosen to run the rat-race from manager to Managing Director; clerk to CEO.

Like his father, Debu had little love for the plains. Calcutta, Bombay, Delhi—they were all the same. He had visited them during the annual family holidays and had no desire to go there. The heat, the dirt and worst of all—the people! Loud and pushy and as complicated as the coils of a jalebi, as his father used to say. He much preferred the cool hills of Shillong and its simple, uncomplicated life. He felt he would be perfectly happy with any ordinary job as long it was in

Shillong—schoolteacher, policeman, fireman, and maybe even a detective. Anything would be fine.

But in his heart of hearts, he knew that these were just dreams. He knew that his mother was right. There were very few jobs in Shillong—even ordinary ones. He knew that one day he would have to leave the hills and travel to the plains in search of employment. He would have to undertake the same journey that his grandfather had made nearly half a century ago, but in the opposite direction.

But all that was in the future. Right now, the important thing was to wriggle out of this tuition business. He gazed at his father in mute appeal.

Mr Dutta took the hint. He turned to his wife with a placating smile. 'Debu has just turned fourteen. Let him enjoy these last one or two years of childhood. Besides, don't you think it's far too early for him to start preparing for engineering and IAS exams and whatnot?'

'Early? What early? In fact, he may already be too late,' replied Mrs Dutta. 'The boys in Bombay, Delhi and Calcutta have started their preparations long ago. Haven't you seen the advertisements of Brilliant Tutorials, YG program?'

'YG what?'

'YG program! Young Genius program! Haven't you heard of it?'

'Umm...no. What is it?'

'I don't know which world you live in! It's a correspondence course to prepare for engineering entrance exams. Do you even know from which class other students start taking these courses?'

'Well...I suppose it must be—'

'Don't suppose! How can you suppose when it's a matter of your only son's future? It's class six. Debu will have to compete with students who have started doing Brilliant Tutorials two years ago. You think it will be so easy?'

'No, I think it will be extremely difficult,' Mr Dutta agreed meekly.

'Exactly! Which is why Debu has to start his tuitions with Professor Bose from next week itself. Is that understood Debu?'

'But Ma! That's not fair!' Debu wailed.

'Not one more word from you!' Mrs Dutta said. 'My decision is final.'

Mr Dutta and Debu exchanged helpless glances with each other. It was difficult to say who looked gloomier.

CLINT EASTWOOD LYNGDOH

A FEW DAYS later, one Sunday afternoon, Debu and his father went to meet Professor Bose at his house in Laitumkhrah. The Professor was a bachelor and lived in a crumbling cottage with his aged mother and a tabby cat. For a teacher of mathematics, he had a colourful reputation. Rumour had it that Professor Bose had once been in love with a Khasi woman. He had wanted to marry her but his mother was dead against it. Like a good Bengali boy, Professor Bose fell in line with her wishes. But bereft of love, he became a bitter man, seeking refuge in the twin sanctuaries of liquor and mathematics to heal his broken heart. Over time, he transformed himself into an amalgam of Devdas and Descartes—a perpetually intoxicated mathematical genius, composed, in equal parts, of alcohol and algebra.

The Professor's love life was a matter of speculation on which different people had different opinions. Many believed that the story of the star-crossed lovers was one hundred and ten per cent true. A few even claimed to know where his lost love stayed—somewhere in the hills near Polo Ground, they said. The Professor would go to her house every night after his mother had retired to her bed, spend the night there and return home at the crack of dawn. He had been seen staggering drunkenly on deserted streets, making his way to a midnight rendezvous with his secret lover, as he mumbled equations under his whisky-laden breath. Others dismissed these stories as malicious gossip spread by the Professor's enemies—the other mathematics tutors of Shillong who were jealous of his genius and the tuition fees that he commanded.

But on one point everyone agreed—Professor Bose had a fiery temper and a scathing tongue which he unleashed upon any student unable to satisfy his high academic standards.

Debu had heard these rumours from his friends and was as
nervous as a pig in a sausage factory when he and Mr Dutta
presented themselves to the Professor.

'Dutta and son?' Professor Bose said. 'Mission tuition?'

He was a tiny gnome of a man in his early fifties, with
thick bushy eyebrows that hunched over his blood-shot eyes,
and a white stubble over his chin that made him look older
than he was. He held a tumbler of whisky and soda in one
hand, and a filter-less Charminar cigarette in the other.

Mr Dutta nodded. 'Yes, Professor Bose. This is my son
Debojit.'

'Debojit, hmm?' the Professor's eyebrows shot up.
'Vanquisher of the Devas. But defeated in turn by the Asuras
of Algebra, eh?'

Mr Dutta gave a weak smile. 'Actually, Debu is quite
good at mathematics but we thought for competitive exams,
he needs—'

Professor Bose raised a hand and cut him off. 'Let the boy
speak. Which school? What class?'

Debu gulped. 'Errr...St Edward's sir. Class nine sir.'

'Oh. That Bagchi fellow teaches you mathematics, right?
What do you think of him?'

'He's okay, sir.'

'Okay? Rubbish! I know all about him. He's an ignoramus.
Wants to teach mathematics but doesn't even know what
componendo dividendo is,' he fixed his gaze on Debu. 'Do
you know what componendo dividendo is?'

'No, sir,' Debu admitted.

Professor Bose gave a smug smile. 'You see? How would
you? When your teachers themselves don't know anything.
Shoe-shine boys! Rote learning. That's all they are good for.
What else can you expect from these Gauhati University types?
There is only one place for learning mathematics in India—
Calcutta University. Everywhere else you get only jokers.'

As a young man, Professor Bose had studied mathematics

at St Xavier's College, Calcutta, under the tutelage of a Belgian missionary named Father Goreaux. The padré was a brilliant mathematician and had even co-authored a scientific paper with no less than the great Einstein himself. Professor Bose considered himself to be a protégé of Father Goreaux, and was of the firm belief that when it came to mathematics, no one in the entire Northeastern region could hold a candle to him.

'I will have to teach you from the basics,' he continued. 'If you can keep up with me, you may be able to do well in the competitive exams. I'll try you out for one month and see whether you are good enough for me. Three days a week. Every Monday, Wednesday, Friday—from four to five in the evenings.'

So Debu started spending three precious evenings every week in Professor Bose's classes. In the beginning, he felt as if he had been thrown into a medieval torture chamber. The Professor would pose a knotty problem and sip on his whisky as he watched Debu wrack his brains. If he got it right, the Professor would grudgingly grunt his approval and proceed to set an even trickier problem. The flow of whisky pegs and maths problems would continue until the point when Debu would finally fail to solve one, upon which the Professor would snigger gleefully and make withering observations about his feeble intellect and hopeless future.

But luckily, Debu possessed a natural aptitude for mathematics. As the days went by, he began to get better and better at jumping through the hoops that the Professor would set in his path. This helped him avoid the worst of his barbs, to the point where he no longer felt his stomach lurch in fear whenever he entered the Professor's lair.

Apart from Debu, there were only a handful of students who managed to keep up with Professor Bose's unreasonable demands. Clint Eastwood Lyngdoh wasn't one of them. In later years, Debu would often wonder how Clint's inability to solve a simple problem in solid geometry had caused their

lives to intersect, changing them in ways they could never
have imagined, on that cloudy afternoon in Shillong when
they first met.

* * *

By Professor Bose's standards, the problem was unusually
simple. It went as follows: 'Calculate the surface area of a
sphere that has been made by melting a solid cube of length
x cm.'

A tall, lean boy sat in the far corner of Professor Bose's
tuition room, repeating the question over and over again, in a
slow drawl that sounded like a chant. He wore a blue blazer
and grey trousers, the uniform of St Anton's School—the
traditional rival of Debu's own school. But he looked too old
to be in school. He had long sideburns, a tuft of beard on
the chin and he carried himself with a casual elegance that
had no trace of the usual gawkiness which was the curse of
teenage boys. Must be at least eighteen, thought Debu, as he
sneaked a quick glance at him.

The boy caught his eye. 'Hey,' he said.

Debu looked away and buried his nose in his maths
textbook.

'I'm Clint. Clint Eastwood Lyngdoh,' said the boy. 'What's
your name?'

Debu did not reply. After the incident at Jacob's Ladder,
he had become wary, even scared, of Khasis. He felt uneasy
in their presence—there was a slight quickening of his pulse,
a fear of looking them in the eye and an urgent desire to
get away. Even in school, he had started avoiding his Khasi
classmates, many of whom he had known for years. It was as
if an invisible barrier had suddenly sprung up between them.

'Hey. I'm talking to you,' Clint's voice sounded from across
the room. 'What's your name?'

Debu's mouth turned dry. 'Debojit,' he said with an effort.

'Debjit, hna. How are you in maths?'

'Okay,' Debu replied shortly.

'Good. I need your help. Come over here.'

Debu pretended he hadn't heard.

'What's the matter?' Clint asked. 'Come here, man. Help me with this problem. Otherwise Bose will screw my happiness.'

'I'm only in class nine,' Debu said. 'I don't know how to do college-level maths.'

'I'm also in class nine,' Clint said. 'Plugged maths last three years in a row. Didn't get promoted. I'm in St Anton's School. You?'

'St Edward's,' replied Debu. 'And I can't help you. I'm sorry.' He felt small even as he said it. He had heard Clint reading out the problem and he knew how to solve it. But he had no desire to help him.

'Please man, just tell me how to do the damned sum,' Clint said. 'I'll be in deep shit otherwise.'

Just at that moment, Professor Bose tottered back into the room and confronted Clint. 'So has our resident blockhead been able to solve the kindergarten problem that I had entrusted him with? Or have I been unduly optimistic?'

'No sir,' Clint mumbled. 'I did it. I mean I am doing it. I mean I know how to do it, but I haven't done it yet. I need a little more time.'

'More time?' the Professor asked.

'Just five more minutes.'

'Five more minutes? I already gave you five minutes. That's double the time required for even the meanest intelligence to solve such a trivial problem. And you still want more time?'

'Yes, sir. Please, sir.'

Professor Bose wordlessly examined the contents of his glass as he considered Clint's appeal. 'Alright,' he said presently. 'I have come to a decision,' he drained the whisky and set his glass on the table with a clatter. 'Clearly, there is no point in continuing this mutually inflicted torture. So—I am giving you one last chance. If you can solve that problem in the next two minutes, I will allow you to continue my classes. If you cannot, then I am afraid that we must part ways. Agreed?'

Clint nodded his head slowly. 'Okay, sir,' he said. 'As you say.'

'Excellent,' said the Professor. 'All right. Off you go then. Your time starts now.'

'Sir—one small request, if you don't mind?' Clint said.

'Yes?'

'I feel a little nervous if you are around when I do sums. So, would you mind, I mean...' Clint's voice trailed off.

The Professor looked as if he had just encountered a particularly ugly equation. 'I'll be back in two minutes,' he snapped and stomped out of the room.

'Okay, Debjit. Will you help me now? Please?' Clint said.

Debu was quiet.

'Can't afford to plug maths again this year. Dad says he's gonna kick me out of the house if I can't pass this time.'

Debu thought for a moment. 'Alright, fine,' he said finally with a shrug of his shoulders. 'I'll take a look at it. And the name's Debojit. Not Debjit.'

'Okay, Mr Deb-ohhh-jeet. Super,' a big happy grin lit up Clint's face. 'I hope you know how to do it. Only two minutes left.'

'Listen, it's quite simple,' said Debu. 'Just equate the volumes of the cube and the sphere.'

'No, you equate the goddamned volumes, whatever the hell that might mean. You think I'd ask you if I could do it myself?'

'Okay. Write—x cubed is equal to—'

'No, you write. I'll copy.'

'But it's not right to copy.'

'Oh, man! Who do you think you are? Saint Debojit? Write! There's hardly a minute left.'

'Alright. Only this one time then,' Debu said. He scribbled down the solution as fast as he could, while Clint copied it into his notebook with equal speed. He had just made a neat box around the final answer when Professor Bose staggered back into the room. He snatched Clint's notebook and scrutinized the answer. 'Not bad, not bad at all,' he said with an approving nod. 'Quite remarkable, in fact. It would seem that our resident cowboy is capable of doing more than just rounding up the cattle at dusk. Heh, heh. This calls for celebrations. Cheers!' he said and raised his whisky glass to Clint.

* * *

Pleased by Clint's unexpected performance, Professor Bose let them go early that day. Debu and Clint walked out together. A few yards away from the Professor's house stood a chestnut tree in full bloom, its leaves packed together so tightly, that from a distance, it looked like a giant green cloud of fur spread out against the deep blue of a crystal-clear Shillong sky. Clint stopped by the tree. It was bristling with fruit. Picking up a bamboo stick lying on the road, he knocked down a few chestnuts and offered them to Debu.

'No, no—I don't want them,' Debu said, warily eyeing the thorny fruits nestling in the palms of Clint's hands, like a prickle of tiny porcupines.

Clint gave him a hearty slap on the back. 'Keep them man. You saved my ass today,' he said. 'My father would have screwed me if Bose had chucked me out today. Thanks for helping out. I won't forget it.'

'That's okay,' said Debu.

'How come you are so good at maths?'

'I don't think I'm all that good. Just okay.'

'Stop being modest. You are good. Get it? Take it from me.'

'Well—I guess I quite enjoy doing maths.'

'You're crazy'

'No, I'm not. maths is cool. You don't have to mug up stuff like in history and geography. You only have to understand a few basic rules and work out the rest. It's easy.'

'You're talking just like Audrey. She says the same thing. Says maths is great fun—like a puzzle, a game,' Clint rolled his eyes. 'You guys are really weird, you know.'

Debu's ears pricked up. 'Who's Audrey?'

'Good friend of mine. Studies in LC, Loretta Convent. Same class as us. You guys would get along great.'

'Yeah? What makes you say that?' Debu asked, in what he hoped was a casual tone.

'Because you guys are just the same. She's also a crack in maths and science. Says she loves that shit. God knows what you guys see in it. It's so boring.'

'It's not. Maybe Audrey and I should try and teach you together sometime,' Debu said hopefully.

'Naaah,' Clint slapped Debu on the back. 'Who wants to waste time doing maths when Audrey is around? You're good enough for me. You'll do my sums for me from today onwards, won't you?'

'If I do your sums, how will you ever understand maths?'

'You think I give a damn about maths? I just hate that shit. It's completely useless. You think I'll ever have to melt bloody cubes into spheres when I grow up?'

'But you will have to get a job, right? And if you don't pass your maths exams, how will you get one?'

'Who wants a job? I'm going to become a painter.'

'Really? You paint?'

'Yeah. Want to see? I did this one yesterday,' he took out a sheet of foolscap paper from his school bag and held it up for Debu to see.

It was a watercolour painting of an old Khasi woman selling sour berries by the roadside. She was sitting beneath a pine tree, a basket of berries clutched in her gnarled fingers. Behind her, in the distance, was a low hill wreathed in fog. Every element of the painting had been coaxed out in gentle fluid lines which flowed into each other, as if the woman and her surroundings had somehow become one—the strands of her white hair floated out in the breeze to become the white mist on the green hills beyond, which in turn flowed back to merge with the chequered green patchwork of her tartan shawl, and the folds of her ochre jainsem had spread around her feet to become red earth.

Debu had never seen anything like it. He stared silently at it for a while, soaking in the sense of peace that seemed to radiate from the painting. 'So beautiful,' he said at last. 'So beautiful.'

'Thanks, man,' said Clint. 'Here—you take it,' he pressed the painting into Debu's hand.

Debu pushed it away. 'No, no I can't. It's too good for me. You must have put in a lot of work for it.'

'Keep it. I have lots more. This is my way of thanking you for saving my ass today.'

'Alright, if you insist. Thanks a lot, Clint. You know something? You're right. You shouldn't waste your time doing maths when you have a gift like this.'

'Exactly. After I somehow pass these stupid Board exams, that's all I'm gonna do—paint. And travel, see the world—that's going to be my life. I also want to start my own art gallery. I've even looked up a place near Dhankheti. You want to join me? I can make you my partner. You can take care of all the accounting and stuff like that.'

'No thanks. I have other plans.'

'Let me guess. Plan A—doctor. Plan B—engineer. Or is it the other way around?'

'Yeah, something like that.'

Clint clucked his tongue. 'That's all you Bangalis can do. Study, study, study and then go work for somebody else until you are old. But that's not what I'm gonna do. I'm going to live my life like I want to—my way, my terms,' he drew out a pack of cigarettes from his pocket. 'Cigarette?'

'No thanks. I don't smoke. Hey listen—I'd better get going.'

'Relax man. I won't bite you. You helped me today. You are my friend. Okay?'

Debu nodded uncertainly. Clint sat down on the footpath. 'Want some whisky? I have a bottle in my bag.'

'What! No way!' Debu said.

He was beginning to feel a little tense. In Shillong, everyone knew everyone, and it wouldn't do to be seen hanging around a guy who was smoking and drinking on the roadside.

Clint rolled his eyes. 'Should have guessed,' he fished out a quarter bottle of whisky from his bag and took a swig. 'So, got any girlfriends?'

'Umm...not really,' Debu said. He was in a mild state of panic by now. 'I should really get going.'

Clint grabbed his hand and sat him down beside him. 'Relax man. You're as frisky as a rabbit in heat. What the hell are you doing with your life, man? No smoking, no drinking, no girls. You're fourteen! This is the time to live it up.'

Debu ran a tongue over his dry lips. 'Yeah, well. My parents are a little strict.'

'Poor kid,' said Clint. 'Hey, I have an idea,' he jumped to his feet. 'First let's go to Kalsang and have some chow. Then we can go to Police Bazar and hang out for some time, have some fun. What do you say?'

Debu had heard of Kalsang. It was a cheap, shabby Chinese restaurant in Don Bosco Square that had acquired something of a name for serving some of the best food in town. It was frequented by a large number of college students, and was a particular favourite of clandestine couples and canoodling lovers. Its mildly risqué reputation and the presence of pork on its menu had led Debu's mother to regard it as one of the inner circles of hell.

Debu had once made the mistake of asking her if he could go there.

'Kalsang! That dirty Chinese restaurant in Laitumkhrah?' his mother had snapped, aghast by her son's predilections.

'Which bhadralok goes to such places? If you must eat hotel food, then why don't you have jalebis at Delhi Mishtan Bhandar?'

'But I don't like sweets,' Debu had replied.

'Then go to Regal restaurant. They make excellent masala dosa. Or have chhola-batura at Chirag's,' his mother said. 'And don't even think of going to these Kalsang-type places. Good people don't go there.'

But denial only inflames desire, and it so was with Debu as well. His mother's warning only made him even more determined that one day soon, he would go to Kalsang and find out for himself what was so great about it. Now that an unexpected opportunity had presented itself, he found himself sorely tempted.

But even as he was about to say yes, a sensible, prudent voice inside his head cleared its throat. You are being very rash, the voiced whispered to him. Look at the time. It's nearly five in the evening. If you go to Kalsang now, then it will be night by the time you return home. And you know what your mother will do to you then, don't you? You will be grounded. You're sure you want that? Do you want to give up your hard-earned freedom for a plate of chowmein at a seedy restaurant? That too with a stranger who seems to drink like a fish?

Disagreeable as its counsel was, Debu could not ignore the voice. If only they had a telephone at home, he thought despondently, then he might have called home and made some excuse for being late. But like most people in Shillong, they did not have a telephone. His father had applied for one almost two years ago, but it still hadn't come. On the other hand, he was feeling pretty hungry, and the thought of a quick bite at Kalsang was making his mouth water.

To go or not to go—that was the question. He shifted uncomfortably from one foot to the other, unable to make up his mind.

'Coming or not?' Clint asked. 'We're wasting time here.'

It was with a heavy heart that Debu made his final decision. 'No. You go ahead. I'll come some other day,' he said reluctantly and began to hoist his school bag upon his shoulders.

'Okay,' Clint shrugged. 'Your loss, not mine. I thought I'd get you to meet some good friends of mine. Audrey said she might come.'

Debu froze. 'Really?' he asked.

'Yeah. I think you guys should hit it off. You're her type.'

'What type?'

'You know—the goody-goody sorts. Books, studies, maths. How come you don't know her?' Clint shot him a quizzical look.

'Umm...' Debu mumbled.

'You seriously haven't heard of Audrey Pariat? Loretta Convent? Class nine? She's famous.'

Debu shook his head. His curiosity was bubbling over but he willed himself to keep quiet. 'Why's she famous?' he asked after a while, in as indifferent a tone as he could muster.

'Why la?' Clint's eyebrows shot up. 'Class topper, inter-school champion in debate, elocution, quizzing—you name it, she's won it. Pretty good looking too. What man—the coolest chick in town and you haven't even heard of her! I thought all you Edward's guys were crazy about her.'

'No—sorry I haven't,' he confessed.

'You living under a rock or something, Debu?'

Debu spread out his palms apologetically for his ignorance of Shillong's social circles. 'Guess I have. How come you know her?' he asked.

'Oh, we met a couple of years ago at some stupid inter-school meet. Got talking. Figured out that we liked each other's company. She's a great friend. Stood by me when I was going through some bad shit.'

'Oh, what happened?'

'Just some stuff at home. I had just lost my—' Clint stopped and took a swig of whisky. 'Anyway, I don't want to talk about that stuff now. You want to come with me to Kalsang or not?' Clint packed the whisky bottle into his bag and got up to leave. 'Well?'

'I would have loved to, I really would...but—'

'No problem. Bye then. I'll convey your regards to Audrey,' Clint said and set off.

Debu watched gloomily as Clint strode down the road. Even as his tall silhouette receded into the distance, Debu stood rooted in his place, torn between the fear of his mother and the prospect of spending an evening at Kalsang with the coolest chick in town. Clint was almost out of sight, when the torment of a million decisions and indecisions became too much to bear and he let out a loud cry.

'Hey Clint! Wait for me,' he shouted. 'I'm coming with you.'

Clint halted and turned to face Debu. There was a pleased smile on his face. Debu sprinted down the road to catch up with him. His heart was beating fast. He did not know whether it was from the effort of running or because of the excitement—but there came upon him a feeling that he was about to embark upon a great adventure.

THE EVENING OF FORBIDDEN
PLEASURES

IT WAS THAT still, silent time between late afternoon and dusk when Shillong stretched out like a drowsy cat, savouring the last lazy moments of its siesta. The children were yet to return home from school and the grownups were still at work—an army of babus huddled inside their offices and shops, wading through stacks of dog-eared files...human calculators muttering under their breath as they ran their ink-stained fingers down unending columns of numbers, adding them up and jotting down the totals with a flourish of their well-worn Wing Sung fountain pens.

Not a vehicle was in sight, nor a single person, as Debu and Clint walked down a narrow, crooked lane that meandered through Laitumkhrah like a strand of forbidden pork chowmein, an unwinding skein of thread leading them into the minotaur's lair at Kalsang. They were in a residential area, some distance away from the bustle of Laitumkhrah market. On either side of the lane stood rows of pretty cottages, their white-washed walls of wattle and daub punctuated by a broad lattice of timber beams painted black. Slanted red tin roofs peeked out from behind the hedgerows, a yellow-green border that diffidently separated the inside from the outside. Most of the houses had a well-tended garden in the front yard, with blooming gladioli, the glistening, waxy leaves of camellia bushes, and clumps of azaleas and monkey-faced pansies lining the cobbled stone pathways up to the front patio. By the wooden gates of one house stood an orange tree, its boughs weighed down by clusters of ripening fruit. A plump tabby cat sat at the foot of the tree, lazily grooming her mottled ash and white coat as she soaked up the mellow warmth of the evening sun.

It was a serene Shillong evening just like any other, watching with amusement the excitement bubbling inside Debu's heart as every step brought him closer to the secret pleasures of Kalsang. A short walk later they had arrived at their destination—a large, slightly run-down cottage that had been converted into a restaurant. Clint and Debu stepped inside, the wooden floor planks creaking in protest under the tread of their Naughty Boy shoes.

Clint scanned the room for a suitable table as Debu took in the sight greeting him. It was just as he had imagined—waiters gliding about bearing bowls of sizzling hot momos and soup, the exotic aroma of unfamiliar herbs and meats inside the dishes curling into the cool Shillong air like fumes of incense. A row of dimly lit private cabins stood on either side of the hallway. Curtains had been drawn across the openings to shield the occupants from the public gaze. Only their legs were visible—pairs of stockinged, high-heeled feet, brushing against their boot-clad companions, offering tantalizing glimpses of the secret trysts unfolding within. From behind the drawn curtains drifted the delicious tinkling of feminine giggles, along with a whiff of perfume entangled in the fragrance of pork chowmein. Debu felt like he had been transported into the world of the Arabian Nights. Pleasure and peril lurked in every corner.

Through an unspoken agreement, Debu and Clint decided that it would look odd for two boys to be holed up inside a private cabin. They sat at an open table with a view of the street. Clint lit up a Capstan cigarette.

Ah, Kalsang's! thought Debu, as he sank into his chair and soaked in the charged atmosphere. This was so much more glamorous than having masala dosas and chhola baturas in the sanitized confines of Regal and Chirag's. A waiter approached them and asked for orders.

'We'll have the usual. Okay?' Clint asked Debu.

'Umm...yeah. Sure. Fine. The usual,' Debu said. He had no idea what the usual was.

'Waiter. Two plates,' Clint said. The waiter nodded knowingly and left the two boys by themselves.

'Umm—I don't have any money,' said Debu. 'I mean I do. But just enough for the bus fare.'

Clint waved away his concerns. 'No probs. I have enough dough,' he said, taking a deep drag on his Capstan. 'It's cold. Want some whisky?'

'No, thanks.'

'Okay, I'll have a shot then. Tell you what? Why don't you do my maths homework for me while the food comes?'

Debu was in no mood for maths. But he felt it would be impolite to refuse his benefactor's homework. Besides, Clint would probably not force whisky on him if he was doing maths. Tearing himself away from the pleasures of Kalsang, Debu battled the sins of trigonometry as Clint sipped on his whisky and smoked.

An English song was playing on the rickety tape recorder kept by the cash counter. Clint closed his eyes and swayed to the music. Debu hadn't heard the song before, but he found himself instantly drawn to it. It was unlike anything he had ever heard before...

We don't need no education
We don't need no thought control
No dark sarcasm in the classroom
Teachers leave them kids alone.

'Nice song,' said Debu. 'Who's sung it?'

Clint's jaw dropped. He removed the cigarette from his lips and exhaled an incredulous gust of smoke into Debu's face. 'You kidding me or what? You don't know who that is?'

Debu's face turned pink. 'No, sorry. I don't,' he admitted. 'I only listen to Hindi film songs on the radio. And once in a while my mother makes me listen to Rabindra Sangeet,' he said. 'Which I really hate,' he added as an afterthought, hoping it would make Clint think less poorly of him.

'Who's Rabindra Sangeet?' Clint asked blankly.

'Not who. What. It's...anyway never mind. Who's singing this song?'

'Man! Don't you know anything except what's inside your school books? That's Pink Floyd man! Greatest band in the world. Ever. The Wall! Greatest album ever.'

'Oh,' Debu said, feeling really dumb about not having even heard of the greatest band in the world. Ever.

'Just listen. It'll blow your mind.'

And it did. Debu had never experienced anything like it before. He didn't know that music could sound like that. It touched a place inside him that Hindi film songs with their ishqs and zulfeins and chandnis had never reached. He soon found himself singing out loud along with Clint and head banging to the refrain:

Hey! Teachers! Leave them kids alone
All in all, it's just another brick in the wall
All in all, you're just another brick in the wall

He felt as if the music was seeping into the marrow of his bones and flowing into his bloodstream. It was an epiphany, a revelation. He felt like Buddha under the peepal tree.

'This is too good. Simply amazing,' he said after the last bar of music had faded.

'Yeah, sounds even better with whisky,' Clint said. 'Want a shot?'

Go on, sissy! Have your first drink! It's good. Trust me, hissed a nasal voice inside his head.

No cruel boy! You will bring shame upon the family name, a second voice pleaded, much feebler than the first.

Don't listen to him. He's such a boring old fart. I'm your friend and I'm telling you. This stuff is good. Go on, drink up. Believe me, you won't regret it. Go on now—live life a little! said the first voice in a honeyed whisper.

Nahiin, nahiiin!! Kabhi nahiin! screeched the second.

'What are you thinking so much about?' Clint said. 'Want that whisky?'

With a great effort and willpower, Debu said, 'No, thanks. Don't think I will.'

'Suit yourself,' Clint shrugged. 'Actually, better that way. More for me.' He winked and raised the bottle to his lips.

Debu watched him with fascination. 'You drink everyday?'

'You crazy or what? You think I'm an alcoholic?'

'I didn't say that.'

'Yeah, but I bet that's what you thought. It's okay. You Bangalis think we Khasis are all drunkards, right?'

'No! When did I say that? I didn't mean to—'

'I know what you meant. Anyway, it's no big deal. Everyone drinks in Shillong. It's cold. A nip of whisky makes you feel good and warm. That's all there is to it. Go to Eee Cee Restaurant in the evening and you'll see them—Khasis, Bangalis, Nepalis, Biharis—all of them drinking away to glory.'

'Yes, I know,' Debu lied. His mother had taken him to Eee Cee Restaurant a few times to treat him to the occasional pastry. He knew there was a bar in the basement, although he had never been inside it. But Clint was probably right. Every once in a while, his own father would come back home with a happier-than-usual smile, a slight slur in his voice and the whiff of alcohol on his breath. On such occasions, he would avoid all conversations with Mrs Dutta and head straight to the bedroom, quickly tucking himself into bed and claiming that he had a headache.

'The only difference is that we are open about it,' said Clint, as if he had read Debu's thoughts. 'But you guys hide when you drink—as if it's some big crime or something.'

'Will you please stop now?' Debu exclaimed. 'You're being too touchy about a simple question.'

'Yeah. Well—maybe I am. It's just that I don't like being asked so many questions.'

'I only asked because you are the youngest person I've ever seen drinking.'

'Hey, I'm not young. I'm seventeen and a half—an old man compared to you.'

'When did you start?'

'Oh, a couple of years ago.'

'Just about my age then. Not an old man. Why?'

Clint frowned. 'You ask too many questions, man. Why don't you finish off my trignometry homework while I have my drink in peace?'

'Okay,' Debu agreed, not wanting to start another quarrel. He opened Clint's textbook and turned to the chapter on trigonometry.

But just then the waiter arrived with two steaming plates of chowmein and trigonometry became a tangential concern. The aroma made Debu's mouth water. He quickly pitched a heaped forkful of noodles into it. His eyes closed in bliss. Just like the Pink Floyd song, it was completely different from anything he had ever experienced before. It was rich, delicate and filled with subtle new flavours and textures that made his taste buds explode in pleasure.

'Umm...delicious!' Debu mumbled as he chewed on a particularly succulent morsel, 'never ate such...good chow in my life.'

'Yeah,' said Clint. 'This place makes the best pork chow in town.'

Debu's fork fell clattering on the plate. Inside his stomach, the noodles turned into a pack of writhing snakes. 'P...p... pork?' he stammered. 'What the...why didn't you tell me?'

Clint was busy eating. 'You never asked,' he replied shortly.

Debu felt like throwing up. He was about to make a dash for the bathroom when Audrey Pariat walked into Kalsang and his life.

THE ARABIAN NIGHTS

THE PUKISH FEELING in Debu's stomach disappeared. A flutter took its place. The most wonderful girl in the world had just walked in. He had experienced similar feelings in the past but this time it felt different. There was something about this girl that made her very special.

He could not say what though. She was attired in the standard grey skirt, grey blazer and red tie uniform of Loretta Convent. She looked like any other school girl. And yet, there were tiny details that lifted her above the pale of the ordinary—the hazel eyes sparkling with intelligence, the lock of hair falling across her forehead, the tiny mole delicately poised just above her lip...he stopped himself, suddenly conscious that he was staring at her. Reluctantly dragging his gaze away from her, he tried to concentrate on the job of twisting a strand of chowmein on his fork. By now, he had quite forgotten that it contained pork.

Luckily, she did not seem to have noticed him gawking at her. She sat down next to Clint and immediately launched into an animated conversation with him. She seemed to be talking about eagles. It was a strange topic to discuss, thought Debu, because as far as he knew there were no eagles in Shillong. Must be a bird lover, he concluded, as he sneaked another quick glance at her. This time she noticed him.

'Hi there, I'm Audrey,' she sized him up with a quick glance. 'And you are?' The cool insouciance of her hazel eyes reduced him to a sticky strand of chowmein.

'H...hhi...Um...D...D...Debu,' he managed to mumble.

Audrey let out a little giggle, 'Dabboo? That's our dhobi's name. You from Bihar too?'

Debu cheeks turned crimson. 'Not Dabboo. Debu—short for Debojit. And I'm Bihari not Bengali...I mean the other way round.'

'Okay. Whatever. Nice meeting you Dabboo,' she said.
'Hey, can I have that chow if you don't mind? I'm starving.'
'Sure,' said Debu and pushed his plate across the table.
He wondered whether he should have reiterated that his real
name was Debu, but her attention was on the food and he felt
it would be impolite to intrude on her meal. He watched as
she lifted delicate forkfuls of noodles to her lips and chatted
away with Clint. Their conversation revolved around a range
of unfamiliar subjects—J.J. Cale, Rolling Stones, Led Zeppelin
and once again, those eagles.

Presently, he realized that 'the eagles' were their favourite
English music band, and his tension ratcheted up. He fervently
hoped that they wouldn't ask him to join the conversation.
He didn't want his ignorance of such matters exposed in his
very first meeting with Audrey. To his relief, they ignored him
and continued talking amongst themselves. She spoke with a
confidence and an energy that was infectious. Debu thought
she was quite simply the most fascinating girl he had ever
met in his life.

Not that he had met too many girls before. St Edward's
was an all-boys' school and female presence there was as
rare as a sunny week in Cherrapunjee. Though there was
one notable exception to this rule—the Annual Sports Day.
On this hallowed occasion, St Edward's School played host
to the young ladies from the neighbouring Loretta Convent
and Pine Hill School. Other boys' schools of Shillong were
also invited to participate, but they weren't of much interest
to most Edwardians.

The Annual Sports Day was a red-letter day for the sporty
types. They would compete fiercely for a place on the podium,
hoping to make a good impression on the Loretta and Pine
Hill girls watching them from the stands. Such hopes usually
came to nothing, but that didn't stop them from trying year
after year.

For the athletically challenged like Debu, the situation was gloomier. The sports day did not include cricket and football, the only games he was half decent at, and was restricted to a variety of races and jumps—none of which he was fit enough to participate in. Relegated to the class drill, he was deported to a distant corner of the field where he gamely twirled batons or flung his limbs about in abrupt jerky movements like a malfunctioning robot—far from the admiring gaze of any crazed female fans. He felt like a desert traveler who could see the hazy outlines of an oasis on the horizon, but knew that it was only a mirage.

The situation on the home front wasn't much better either. Of late, he had started noticing that the girls of his neighbourhood in Upper Jail Road behaved in a highly affected manner whenever he was around. They moved about in tightly-knit packs and would start whispering and giggling amongst themselves whenever their paths crossed. This would cause his cheeks and ears to turn red, which would only lead to more fervent whispering and giggling. He did not know the reason for this. He could only guess that there was some defect in him which was the cause of their amusement. When separated from the pack, they would purposefully avoid eye contact or look through him as if he didn't exist. As far as Debu was concerned, girls were exotic, unreachable fairy-like beings who would never have anything to do with mere mortals like him.

But Audrey seemed to be different. She had none of the typical feminine airs that made him feel so awkward. She didn't stare at him and then nervously turn her face away to hide her giggles like the others. She treated him as if he was perfectly normal. Over time, Debu's nervousness began to subside and with every passing minute, he felt more and more at ease in her company. She even seemed to be interested in him—a completely novel experience as far he was concerned.

'So what's your favourite band?' she asked him.

The old tension reared its head again. 'Umm…Pink Floyd,' he replied.

'Yeah, right!' Clint chuckled. 'He just heard Pink Floyd for the first time today.'

Debu's face turned red. 'Shut up, Clint,' he muttered.

'Hey, just relax, Debu,' said Audrey. 'Stop being mean to him, Clint. What's the big deal if he doesn't listen to Pink Floyd? Everyone's got their own tastes.'

'Hey, I was just teasing him, okay? He's a good guy,' Clint slapped Debu on the back. 'Helps me with my maths. He's damn good at it.'

'Yeah?' Audrey gazed into Debu's eyes. He felt a sudden rush of blood and hoped his face was not turning red again. He hated the way he started blushing at the most inappropriate moments.

'What's your favourite topic in maths?'

Debu perked up, greatly relieved to find himself in familiar territory. 'Geometry,' he replied confidently.

'Same here. I love pretty much everything in maths. But geometry's my favourite too,' said Audrey.

'Really? How come?'

She frowned. 'What do you mean, how come? You think girls can't like maths, is it?'

'No, no, that's not what I meant,' Debu hastened to explain, even as he cursed himself for his uncanny ability to shove his foot into his mouth as soon as he opened it.

Luckily Clint stepped in: 'I really don't know how the hell you guys like maths. It's so boring.'

'It's not!' Audrey said. 'It's really interesting. It's just like detective work, like solving a murder mystery. You're given the clues and you work through them logically, step by step, until you solve the mystery.'

'Exactly!' Debu said excitedly. 'Just like Sherlock Holmes.'

'Or Miss Marple,' Audrey countered.

'Holmes is better,' Debu said.

Audrey shrugged her slim shoulders. 'Well, to each to his own. Holmes has more adventure. But Christie's plots are better. I love solving those complicated murders she writes.'

'Yeah. Same here,' Debu said. There was a goofy smile on his face. He felt a connection with her that he had never felt with anyone before. Suddenly, the world seemed to have become a better, brighter place. The geraniums wilting in the pots by the window sill perked up their crimson heads, the black tabby that had been scrounging around for scraps grinned happily at him like the Cheshire cat, and even the harsh cawing of a raven flying past seemed like a nightingale's warbling.

A peevish, half-amused voice shook him out of his reverie. 'Man! What crap you guys talk about,' said Clint. 'maths, Miss Marple and whatnot. You two should try and get a life outside your books.'

'And you should try reading a little more,' Audrey countered. 'That way you might finally get to know that there's more to life than pork chow and rock bands.'

'Books are boring,' said Clint. 'Anyway, I gotta go now. Anyone wants a last shot of whisky?'

'I don't mind a small one. It's chilly outside,' Audrey said. 'Debu, you want to join us in a toast?'

'Ummm...' Debu mumbled, taken aback by her question. He did not know what to do. On the one hand, he would look like a proper, blue-blooded sissy if he didn't have a drink, especially when she was having one—in spite of being a girl and all that. On the other hand, how could he? It was a sin to drink alcohol. Good boys didn't do such things. Besides, his mother would surely skin him alive if she came to know of it. She only had to catch a whiff of alcohol on his breath, and he would be finished. But this was no ordinary drink. It was a momentous occasion. None other than Audrey Pariat—the coolest, hottest chick of Shillong—had personally requested him to join her for a toast. How could he say no?

Clint was watching him with amusement. 'He's the goody-goody types,' he informed Audrey. 'Doesn't drink.'

That settled the matter. 'Bullshit! You don't know anything about me!' exclaimed Debu. 'I drink, okay? I drink all the time!' Clint rolled his eyes. 'Okay. Cool. Whatever you say brother,' he said. 'So what are we waiting for?' He carefully poured out the whisky into three glasses and added a little water. 'Cheers,' he said and raised his glass.

'Cheers,' said Audrey and Debu. They clinked their glasses and downed their drinks.

A rancid liquid filled Debu's mouth and toxic fumes exploded inside his nostrils. He would have gagged at once, had it not been for the thought that he simply could not vomit in front of Audrey. No matter what happened, he just could not appear like a complete idiot before her. With a supreme act of willpower, he forced himself to swallow the vile liquid. A strangled gasp escaped his lips as a river of fire gushed down his throat and settled into a pool of lava bubbling ominously in the pit of his stomach.

'Oooof,' he whimpered as he bent over and clutched his belly. His eyes were watering and, through the blur, he thought he could see the Cheshire cat watching him with a slowly widening grin.

'You okay, Debu?' he heard Audrey say. Her voice was faint and muffled, as if she was speaking from a great distance. But even through the haze of alcohol, he was thrilled to note her apparent concern.

'Yeah, yeah, I'm fine,' he somehow managed to gasp.

'Okay. Then finish the rest of your drink and let's split,' said Clint. 'Cheers!' he said and raised his glass.

'Cheers,' said Audrey. She raised her glass and was about to knock it down when she paused. 'What's the matter, Debu? Not joining us for the toast?'

'Yes, yes. Cheers!' Debu croaked. Praying furiously that he wouldn't throw up, Debu somehow managed to gulp down the remaining whisky and sank into his chair. It seemed to be swaying below him. He held on to it tightly with clammy hands, hoping it wouldn't melt away from under him. The pool of lava was spreading outwards from his stomach. It felt as if an army of red ants was crawling all over inside him. Beads of sweat popped up on his forehead. He felt his tie tightening around his neck like a hangman's noose. He tugged it loose before it strangled him to death.

He felt a gentle touch on his hand. Audrey was looking anxiously at him. 'Are you okay, Debu?' she asked.

'Yeah, I'm okay,' Debu squeaked in a high-pitched voice. He had a feeling that the syllables were sliding unsteadily past each other like riders in a slow cycle race. But apart from that, he was okay. More than okay, actually. He was feeling good, pretty damn good.

'Yeah, I'm fine. Absholutely fine,' he slurred. He was totally relaxed now, limp with contentment, at peace with the world. Audrey's face swayed and shimmered before him, the lines blurring gently into the background, like in a watercolour painting. He was damn sure he had never seen anyone more beautiful in his whole life.

'Hey, Debu. I'm planning to have a birthday party at my place soon,' said Audrey. 'Wanna come?'

Debu sat bolt upright. Of course, I'll come, he was about to say but instead a loud burp came out. 'Sorry,' he mumbled, pressing his palm against his mouth. 'What were you saying?'

'I said, I'd like to call you home one of these days for my birthday party. Think you can come?'

'Party? Your birthday party?' Debu gave a big, happy smile. 'Of course, I'll come. No question about it. Definitely, positively,' he thumped the table with a new-found confidence. There was a niggling thought at the back of his head about what his mother would say. But bolstered by the whisky, he swatted it aside like a pesky mosquito.

'Great! Clint knows my place,' said Audrey. 'He'll bring

you. Make sure you come. I'll let you know the exact date soon. Most probably on a Saturday evening.'

Debu nodded vigorously in agreement. 'Sure,' he said.

'It's getting late. We should leave now,' Audrey said.

'You guys go ahead,' said Clint. 'I'll pay the bill and come. Need to buy some kwai too.'

'Okay, we'll wait for you near the bus stop,' said Audrey. 'Coming, Debu?'

'Yeah, coming,' said Debu, the whisky stretching out his lips into a goofy grin.

Audrey and Debu headed out to Don Bosco Square. Debu had been there many times before, but it had never seemed as beautiful to him as it did that evening. A soft, mist-like haze had shrouded the statue of Don Bosco—it seemed to be floating on clouds that had descended from the hills beyond.

Audrey pointed at the statue and asked, 'Do you know who he is the patron saint of?'

Debu shrugged. 'What does patron saint mean?' he asked.

'Christian saints like Don Bosco are supposed to be like guardian angels of certain people or certain things—their friends and protectors. That sort of thing. They are supposed to watch over their people, keep them away from harm and so on,' Audrey replied. 'Like Saint Francis is supposed to be the patron saint of animals and nature, and Saint Anthony is the patron saint of lost objects and lost souls,' she gave a wry smile. 'People like Clint, I guess.'

'Clint—a lost soul? Really?' Debu asked. 'He seems pretty cool to me. A real smooth guy, you know.'

'Yeah, I guess he comes across that way. But appearances can be deceptive. Clint's got...issues.'

'What sort of issues?'

'Well...I guess you could say...family issues.'

'Oh, that's nothing. I got family issues too. Big ones,' said Debu, hoping she would be impressed by the size of his family issues.

'Yeah? Like what?'

'You know—like my mother. She's pretty dominating. Doesn't let me have a moment's peace.'

'I know what you mean. Mothers can be like that sometimes.'

'Yeah. Mothers. I bet Clint's got the same problem?'

There was a pause before Audrey replied. 'He doesn't have a mother,' Audrey said.

'Oh, I'm sorry,' said Debu. 'I didn't know.'

'Yeah, well. She died a few years ago. When he was around twelve or so.'

'That's really sad.'

'Yeah. I know. And twelve, thirteen—what a horrible age to lose one's mother. As it is, there are so many crazy changes happening inside you—hormones and all that."

Debu blushed and examined his shoes as Audrey went on. 'Clint doesn't talk much about her these days but I know they were very close. He told me once how badly he was hit by her death. That's when he started losing interest in studies. Plugged a couple of exams and then...just sort of switched off. It's sad—he's a pretty smart guy, you know. He would have done just fine in studies, if he wanted to. Or if there was someone around to guide him.'

'No brothers, sisters?' asked Debu, who had often felt the loneliness of being a single child.

'He's got an elder brother who lives in Sohra. Has his own business there I'm told.'

'And his dad?'

'I think Clint and his dad...sort of drifted apart after his mother died. Hardly spends much time with him. He's always busy with his business and...politics and stuff. I guess that's why Clint's become a little wild in his ways. It's been pretty lonely for him these last few years.'

'Oh,' Debu said, suddenly grateful that both his parents were alive and they spent enough time with him...although once in while he wished they wouldn't. 'What's his dad's name by the way?'

Audrey smiled. 'John. John Wayne Lyngdoh. Quite a filmy family, the Lyngdohs—shooting at each other like cowboys.'

'What do you mean?'

'I don't think Clint and his dad get along very well. They're fighting all the time.'

'Fighting? Why?'

Audrey turned away from Debu. 'I don't think Clint likes the...the...business...that his father's in. He's just not cut out for that world. He's a different sort of guy, you know. Painting, music, friends—that's what makes him happy. He wants to become a painter.'

'I know. He told me.'

'He told his father too. But Mr Lyngdoh just laughed at the idea. He wants Clint to start working in the business, and eventually take it over from him. But Clint doesn't want to. He would hate that life. They have quarrels over it—all the time, he tells me. And now that Clint's growing older, it's becoming worse. That's why he tries to stay out of the house as long as he can—hanging around in the streets, killing time in restaurants, drinking, smoking.'

'You seem to know a lot about him. How did you guys meet?' Debu asked.

'Oh, we bumped into each other at an inter-school art competition a few years ago,' Audrey replied. 'He won, of course, and I was like, third from the bottom or something. But I just loved his painting. I thought it was brilliant. I went over to congratulate him after the prize distribution ceremony. We got talking and realized that we liked each other's company. Bumped into each other a few more times and soon we became pretty good friends. It was a few months after his mother's death. He was quite vulnerable at the time. I think my being around helped him through those days. He was a lost soul, like I said. Still is, I think sometimes?"

'Who's a lost soul?' Clint drawled from behind them.

'No one...' Debu muttered feebly, caught unawares.

'We were just talking about Saint Anthony,' Audrey came to his rescue. 'The patron saint of lost souls—isn't that so Debu?'

'Yes, yes that's right,' Debu agreed in relief.

'Alright, enough chit-chat. It's late. We should call it a day,' Clint said.

'Yeah,' Debu said reluctantly, watching the fiery orange clouds as they drifted over the far hills beyond the statue of Don Bosco. 'Who's Don Bosco the patron saint of?'

'Youths, juvenile delinquents and magicians,' Audrey replied.

'You mean us,' Debu and Clint said together.

'Exactly,' said Audrey and burst out laughing.

Clint clasped his palms together in prayer and looked up at the statue. 'O, Don Bosco,' he declaimed. 'Bless us, your devoted devotees. Remember to protect us and help us, especially when the shit hits the fan. Amen,' he said and made the sign of the cross with his fingers. 'Say amen, you lazy dogs.'

Audrey and Debu sank to their knees. 'Amen,' they said solemnly and crossed themselves.

They lingered there, passing the time over rambling conversations and shared sips of whisky, until the shadows of the evening began to lengthen and the inevitable moment of parting arrived.

* * *

Clint and Audrey shared a taxi home while Debu boarded the bus to Police Bazar. As it lurched forward, the confidence that had been bubbling inside him until then evaporated. He felt an urgent need to get off the bus and throw up somewhere by the roadside. But in Shillong everyone knew everyone else. He could not afford to be seen drunk in public. He somehow managed to hold in the contents of his stomach until he reached home.

As he had anticipated, Mrs Dutta was waiting for him, her lips pressed grimly into a thin line, straight and sharp like the edge of a knife. He carefully avoided all eye contact with her and, before she could speak, rushed to the bathroom with as much gravitas as he could muster. Once inside the blessed sanctuary of the bathroom, he hunched over the wash basin and retched. Out came the pork chowmein and the whisky, gushing forth in a fountain of blissful relief.

His mother was knocking on the door.

'I have a stomach upset. Need some time,' he croaked.

'Come out when you are done. We need to talk,' she said in a wintry voice that spelt trouble with a capital T.

Debu cleaned the basin as best as he could and swilled himself down, hoping to remove any incriminating odours. After the retch and the wash, he felt a little better, but certainly not strong enough to face his mother. He put out the lights and crawled into bed, covering himself from head to toe with a blanket. A few minutes later, his mother entered the room calling for him. He shut his eyes tightly and pretended to be asleep.

Mrs Dutta sat down by his side, a troubled expression on her face. She touched his forehead to check if he had a fever and placed her palm over his nose to see if he was breathing. Having satisfied herself that he was still alive, she gently stroked his head a few times before leaving the room.

Debu heaved a sigh of relief. The danger had passed—at least for the moment. He knew that there would be hell to pay the next morning, but he would cross that bridge when he came to it. Right now, he was unable to think of anything except the surreal evening that had just gone by. A contented smile appeared on his lips and soon, he was fast sleep.

That night he dreamt of Audrey Pariat. She was standing on the wooden bridge that arched across Ward's Lake, singing *We don't need no education*, as the pallu of her red chiffon sari fluttered in the breeze.

So ended the first of the Thousand and One Nights of Debojit Dutta. And even the stench of thrown-up whisky drifting in from the open bathroom could not dilute the perfumed promise of the thousand more that he believed were yet to come—beginning with the birthday party of Audrey Pariat.

GULMAAL

'Sad, sad. Very sad. I did not expect this from you, Debu. Chhee, chhee. Is this how we have brought you up?' said Debu's mother, her head shaking from side to side.

'Sorry Ma,' Debu said forlornly. He had said sorry eleven times in the last twenty minutes, since his mother's inquisition had begun. It had commenced in the evening, as soon as Debu returned home from school. Unfortunately, his father was away at work, and Debu was left to fend for himself as his mother bombarded him with her questions.

It did not take Mrs Dutta long to figure out what had happened. Even before interrogating him she had an inkling of what her son had been up to. She had smelt the whisky on him the moment he had entered the house the previous evening. A quick inspection of the bathroom in the morning had revealed tell-tale traces of chowmein. A few sharp questions from her were all it took before Debu realized that he wouldn't be able to lie his way out of this one. Lying would have probably made matters worse. Besides, he had a splitting headache and the more he tried to make things up, the more it hurt.

So, he told her the truth—although it wasn't the whole truth-and-nothing-but-the-truth. He told her about his meeting with Clint, their visit to Kalsang, the whisky drinking (which Clint had forced on him, Debu explained, and it was just one tiny sip anyway), the chowmein (he was famished and it was only chicken not pork, he lied). The one thing that he didn't tell her about was Audrey. That, he suspected, would be like setting a lit matchstick to a keg of gunpowder.

At the end of much frantic explaining, he offered several more sorrys and steeled himself for his mother's explosion. But to his surprise, her reaction was uncharacteristically subdued. She did not scold or scream or threaten him with house arrest, as he had expected her to. But when she spoke, there was a disappointment in her voice that hurt him more than her harshest rebuke.

'You are growing up, Debu,' she said. 'You are going out into the world by yourself. You will meet many people, be tempted by many things. Today it is liquor, tomorrow it will be drugs. If you can't distinguish right from wrong, then no one can help you. It's your life after all. You will have to live by the choices that you make.'

'I said no, I'm sorry Ma. I won't do it again,' Debu said.

'So you say. But I'm not so sure of it. You will meet this Clint boy again, won't you?'

'Yes, I guess so.'

'That's the problem. A man is known by the company he keeps. And very often, he becomes the company that he keeps.'

'I don't know what you have against Clint. What's so bad about him? You don't even know anything about him.'

'He drinks. He makes you drink. Besides, he is a Khasi. Isn't that enough? I am warning you, if you mix with him, you will become like him. You will become like them.'

'And what is so wrong with them? Sometimes I don't understand you, Ma. What have you got against the Khasis? Like Clint, for example. He has a drink or two, yes but otherwise he seems to be a really nice guy. Even Baba says the Khasis are good people.'

'You father is too simple, too innocent. He thinks he is still living in the Shillong of his childhood. He does not want to see the changes that are taking place under his very nose. He refuses to believe that the Khasis have changed, that they are not the people that he once knew. But I know what they are like. They think that we are their enemies. They resent us because they think we are better than them.'

Mrs Dutta's attitude towards tribals, especially the Khasis, was not uncommon amongst the Bengalis of Shillong. It stemmed from a misplaced sense of superiority caused by the belief that inside the veins of every Bengali flowed the blood of Rabindranath, Netaji, Satyajit Ray and Chuni Goswami. Another theory traced the roots of this superiority complex to a rash but flattering declaration made by Gopal Krishna Gokhale over one hundred years ago: 'What Bengal thinks today, India thinks tomorrow.'

Like the recipe for steamed hilsa in mustard sauce, Gokhale's pronouncement had been faithfully transmitted across the generations through shruti-vidya, and had resulted in the permanently inflated ego of the Bengali bhadralok and bhadramohila.

'Yes, they resent us because we are better than them,' Mrs Dutta repeated.

'Who says we are better? And in what way?'

'I say so! Isn't it obvious? Go to any government office and see how many Khasi officers there are. Most of them are Bengalis. Go to Calcutta and see what a modern city looks like—trams, buses, buildings, roads, lights. And what is there in Shillong? Only forests and hills and pine trees. What good are those to anyone? Wherever they look, they see how advanced we are, and how backward they are. And that is why they are so jealous of us.'

Debu thought that if the chaos of Calcutta represented an advanced civilization then Shillong was much better off being backward. But he held his tongue as his mother went on.

'They are scared that we will take away all the jobs from them. That their women will marry non-tribals and they will lose their lands and properties to non-tribals.'

'What has marriage got to do with property?' Debu asked.

'Don't you know the strange rules? According to their customs, the youngest daughter inherits the property. If a Khasi girl marries a non-tribal then along with the girl, the property will also go out.'

Debu couldn't help wondering if Audrey was also the youngest daughter. He hardly knew anything about her family.

He made a mental note to ask her the next time they met. Not that it mattered, but it would at least help him make some small talk.

'But I sometimes really want to ask them,' Mrs Dutta continued. 'What are you so scared of? We are just a handful of us here, less than a drop in the ocean. You are the kings here. You even got a separate state all for yourselves—to run as you please. And still you aren't happy!'

Seven years after Meghalaya had been awarded full statehood, Shillong was to erupt in an outpouring of violence that would scar the town beyond all recognition. The bloodshed and hatred that followed would resurrect the traumatic memories of Partition in the minds of many Bengalis. But they were to give it a misleadingly innocuous name—gulmaal.

* * *

'It is they who started the gulmaal,' said Debu's mother. 'It is they who ruined our beautiful Shillong. It's about time that you knew what they did. There used to be a time when Shillong was the best place in the world. Green, beautiful, peaceful. It was like heaven. But the gulmaal destroyed everything. Everything.' A shadow fell over her face. 'People say that it all started in autumn of 1979, during the Kali Puja.'

'I don't remember anything,' said Debu.

'You were too young, only five or six. We didn't tell you because you would have been scared by the terrible things that happened. But now you are old enough to know.'

Debu's curiosity was aroused. 'What terrible things?' he asked.

'Many terrible things. I think it all started at a place not very far from your school,' his mother sighed. 'At the Ram Villa Puja Pandal. You were in KG then. Luckily, your school was closed for the Diwali holidays, or god only knows what could have happened. Anyway, on 2nd October, Thursday

evening, the Kali Puja had just ended at the pandal. They say
that the idol of the goddess was being taken out for visarjan—
the immersion in Umshyrpi stream in Polo Grounds—when
all of a sudden, two young Khasi men, or maybe they were
just boys, barged into the pandal. They pushed the idol and
it toppled over. The idol of Ma Kali fell to the ground. She
lay there—sprawled in the dust, her face upturned. Some
people say...

She stopped. Debu got up and poured her a glass of water.
She ignored it.

'Some people say,' she resumed after a while, 'that they
walked over Ma Kali, walked over her face. I can't believe
that anyone could do such a thing...but that's what they said.
People who were there when it happened. The two boys just
walked over her face, they said, our mother's face...'

She was finding it difficult to speak. Debu didn't know what
to do. His mother had always been so strong, so in control.
He felt helpless seeing her so distraught.

'It's all right, Ma,' he said, gently patting her hand. 'Even
if it happened, they were just some stupid boys. That's all.'

She took a sip of water and made a visible effort to collect
herself. 'Yes. I suppose so. Just some stupid boys,' she said.
'Sorry—I got carried away.'

'What happened after that?'

'For a while, our people were too shocked to react. Then
a fight broke out between them. But in the confusion, the
culprits managed to escape.'

'Didn't the police do anything?'

'The police?' his mother spat. 'They were all Khasis.
Wouldn't lift a finger against their own kind. Of course, a
complaint was made. Two men were even arrested. But they
were out on bail a day later. And that was that. Some people
thought it was a one-off incident. But it wasn't. The real
horrors were about to begin. Because we had dared to file a
police complaint against them, the Khasis decided to teach

us a lesson. Shops belonging to Bengalis were forcibly shut down. Landlords evicted Bengali tenants. Houses owned by Bengalis were set on fire. Overnight, hundreds of families became homeless. A mass exodus followed. Terrified non-tribals fled from places like Jaiaw, Mawprem and Mawlai, flocking to the only safe locality in town—Jail Road, which had always been a Bengali-majority area.'

'Lucky that we live here,' said Debu.

'You have no idea how lucky! For Bengalis, Jail Road was the one safe haven in Shillong. Overnight, the Jail Road Boys' High School was converted into a makeshift refugee camp. Seven–eight families were crammed together into a single classroom. The classrooms in which children should have been studying became kitchens, bedrooms, bathrooms. They became their homes. Months passed by. The camp became unfit for humans but the government just sat twiddling its thumbs.'

'I think I remember some things,' said Debu. 'It was full of people and I remember the smell. You couldn't go near it—it was so bad. I thought that the school had been turned into some sort of hotel. I even remember asking Baba what was happening.'

'And he must have told you whatever we thought fit. You may have forgotten about those times. But we adults are not that lucky. There are so many things that happened then which we can't forget, no matter how hard we try,' his mother paused. 'Like what happened to the Purkayasthas.'

'Who?'

'Shibani and Sanjeeb Purkayastha—a young couple who used to stay in Mawlai, a Khasi-dominated area. They were quite well known in Shillong. Shibani was a good singer and Sanjeeb used to play the tabla. They used to perform in the Durga Puja music programs. When the gulmaal started, the Purkayasthas were evicted from their home. They decided to leave Shillong for Calcutta, to stay with their relatives. So they boarded the bus to Gauhati from where they planned to take the train to Calcutta. The bus left Shillong and was speeding down the highway, when it came to an abrupt halt. A group of armed men had blocked the road. All the non-tribals were forced to get off the bus and marched off into a nearby forest. And then, people say, an interrogation began. One by one, each non-tribal was asked the following question—"Are you Assamese?"'

'Why Assamese?'

'Because during those days, the Assamese were also agitating against the influx of foreigners into their state. The Khasis considered them comrades-in-arms and refrained from harming them. But Bengali or Assamese—all non-tribals look the same. So there was no way of knowing from someone's looks whether he was Bengali or Assamese. The Purkayasthas must have realized that they had a chance of escape.

'"We are Assamese," the Purkayasthas said, hoping against hope that their ploy would work.

'But the attackers had come prepared.

'"Assamese? Really?" one of them asked. "Then count from one to ten in Assamese. Softly—whisper the numbers into my ear."

'"Ek, dui, teen, char, paanch..." the Purkayasthas began to whisper.

'"Stop. That's enough, dkhar," the man said. He took out a knife and slit their throats. Shibani and Sanjeeb died on the spot.

* * *

The room had gone very quiet. All that could be heard was the faint murmur of the drizzle outside. The distinctive Shillong drizzle was heralded by tiny droplets of rain sparkling in the light of the sun, like diamond dust, but swiftly swelling into fat blobs the size of sour berries that would splash against the earth with soft thuds.

Debu shifted uncomfortably in his chair.

'How did they guess that they were not Assamese?' he asked.

'Because they did not know that the Assamese word for three was "teeni" not "teen".'

'Like in Bengali?' Debu said.

'Like it is in Bengali,' said his mother. 'Their death warrants had been signed by their mother tongue.'

A shiver ran down Debu's spine. He hadn't known any of these people, but they were no different from him or his parents. It was only a matter of chance that it had been the Purkayasthas and not his parents, or even he himself, who had been killed. Were their lives so fragile, so uncertain as to hang from the thread of a single misplaced vowel?

'News of this incident spread like wildfire,' his mother was saying. 'Other people who were also thinking of leaving Shillong were now terrified of travelling on the highway. Trapped inside the city limits, surrounded by hostile neighbours and strangers, they lived in constant fear of their lives. Each day brought a new horror.'

'I had no idea,' Debu mumbled.

'You were too young to be told,' his mother replied with a sad smile. 'But you are not a child anymore. You have to go out into the world on your own. That's why it's important for you to know these things. You must be careful. You must be on the lookout for danger. Bad things have happened here before. And in spite of what your father says, they can happen again. Now do you understand why I'm so scared for you every time you leave home?'

'Yes, Ma,' said Debu. Then a terrible fear suddenly gripped him. 'But what about Baba? He goes to the shop in Iewheh every day. What if they—'

'You think it doesn't worry me sick? But what can be done?'

'Can't he just shift the shop somewhere else?'

'How can you shift a business just like that one fine day? The shop has been there for over forty years, ever since your grandfather started it. Your father has been running it for the last twenty years. He knows everyone in the area, has a loyal clientele. How can he suddenly move?'

'But what if something—'

'Enough. You are too young to think of all that. Your father and I will manage somehow. But what about you? Do you think you can stay in a place like this? Do you think they will let you? That's why I'm so anxious for you to study hard and concentrate on your career. That's why you must leave this place. Do you understand now?'

'Yes, Ma,' Debu nodded his head.

'And about this boy, Clint,' she continued. 'You have to stay clear of him. He's drinking, encouraging you to drink, taking you out to Chinese restaurants and whatnot. These are very serious matters. You told me the truth today, so I am letting you go. But this is the first and last time—you understand?'

Debu nodded obediently.

'If I hear of anything like this happening ever again, then no one will be worse than me. Clearly, this Clint is a most dangerous boy, a bad influence. He is sure to misguide you. I will have to complain to Professor Bose about him.'

'Please don't do that Ma,' Debu said. 'Then he'll know that I told you and he might...he might not like it.'

Mrs Dutta paused to think. 'That's true. Who knows if he does something to you, if I complain? There is a risk, yes,' she looked worried. 'Debu, you have to promise me something today.'

'What?'

'Promise me that you will cut off all contact with this Clint boy. You will not meet him or talk to him ever again.'

Debu hesitated. He really liked Clint (and Audrey). He had loved the time they had spent together and he couldn't wait to meet them again. He didn't think Clint was dangerous, and he certainly couldn't imagine being ruined by him—as his mother had warned. Besides, he could not help thinking that they were meant to be friends. He couldn't exactly say why, but it just felt that way.

At the same time, what his mother had said weighed heavily on him.

'What are you thinking so much about?' his mother asked. 'Promise me that you will stay clear of this Clint character.'

He couldn't think anymore. It was too complicated. 'Okay, Ma,' he said. 'I'll do what you say. I won't talk to Clint anymore.'

For the first time that evening, Mrs Dutta looked happy. 'Very good,' she said and gave him an affectionate pat on the head. 'Go to your room now and finish your studies. And remember what I told you today. It's for your own good.'

* * *

Debu went to his room and sat down at his desk. He opened up his history textbook and began to read the chapter on the Indus Valley Civilization. The history exam was only one day away and he had reason to be worried. It was a subject in which he had been weak. This time, he was in a particularly bad shape. Too much had happened in the last twenty-four hours for him to be able to concentrate on his studies. He listlessly flipped through the pages as his mind kept wandering back to the events of the previous evening, and all the things that his mother had just told him. He didn't give a hang about history, when his present had suddenly become so much more interesting.

Through sheer willpower, he somehow trudged through the pointless plains of the Indus Valley and plodded down the never-ending banks of the Ganges littered with the soporific deeds of the Aryans, Mauryans and the Guptas. He sleepwalked past them, pressing forward until he finally arrived at the edge of the Deccan Plateau, where the Chalukyas and the Rashtrakutas awaited him. Loathe to make their acquaintance, he decided to take a break. He looked up at the clock. It was almost eight in the night.

An uneasy feeling took hold of him. Why hasn't Baba returned home yet, he thought. Why was he so late? Had something happened to him?

'Ma,' he called out. 'Has Baba come home?'

'No,' she said. 'Why?'

'Just asking. Did he say that he would be late tonight?'

'No. Why so many questions? Don't you have your exams? Concentrate on your studies.'

Debu returned to his room and switched on the radio, hoping the music would help calm him down. The silken voice of Mohammad Rafi drifted over the airwaves as Debu turned to the exploits of Dantidurga, the founder of the Rashtrakuta dynasty. But neither the Rashtrakutas nor Rafi could hold his attention for long. The music was drowned by the ticking of the clock and his gaze kept shifting to its arms circling along the dial. As the minutes ticked by, the tension built up inside him like a slowly wound up spring.

Finally, at half past eight, he could he could no longer bear it. He tossed aside his books and went out into the garden. He paced up and down, ears pricked for the sound of footsteps. Dark thoughts scurried inside his head like rats trapped inside a maze—what if they had beaten up Baba, what if they had thrown him into the Umshyrpi stream, what if...?

The front door creaked open and Mrs Dutta stepped out into the garden. 'What are you doing here?' she asked. 'I thought I told you to study.'

'Sorry Ma, just taking a break. I'll get back in a minute,' said Debu. He was about to return to his room when an important point occurred to him. 'Acchha, Ma, does Baba know how to swim?' he asked.

Mrs Dutta threw up her hands in exasperation. 'What is the meaning of these stupid questions? Why are you wasting your precious time like this? I just don't know when this boy will grow up!'

Debu slouched back to his tryst with history. With great

difficulty, he managed to read half a page more before giving up the struggle. The minutes dragged on like hours. At last, when the hands of the clock were about to close in on nine, he heard the tread of footsteps on the gravel path. He shot outside and heaved a deep sigh of relief when he saw Mr Dutta walking in.

He felt like rushing to his father, hugging him, and burying himself in the warm, tobacco-scented comfort of his embrace. But it would be totally uncool for a self-respecting teenager to demonstrate any signs of affection for his parents. So he held himself back and gave his father a casual nod instead.

'Hi,' he said.

'Hi, how was your day?' his father asked.

'Okay. So late today?'

'I had work,' Mr Dutta peered at Debu. 'You look worried. Anything wrong?'

'Nothing,' said Debu.

'Exams coming up? Is that why?' his father asked kindly.

'Umm...yeah,' Debu muttered.

On that night, a secret dread took hold of Debu—that there would come a day when his father would leave home and never return. It was a fear that never quite left him as long as his father was alive.

THE HISTORY EXAM

THE ATMOSPHERE IN Class 9C of St Edward's School was unusually sombre. The history examination was underway. But Debu wasn't making much progress. He read the first question once again.

'Discuss how Akbar's policy of matrimonial alliances brought about political stability and peace in India. [5 marks]'

Unfortunately, during his revision, Debu had polished off Akbar in ten minutes. He hadn't the faintest idea of the ladies that the great Mughal had married and why. In any case, it seemed a rather silly question. How could marriage have anything to do with peace and stability?

He moved on to the next question. It demanded to know who the Lion of Punjab was and why he had been so named. There was no point in even trying. He had encountered all sorts of places during his cramming sessions but Punjab wasn't one of them.

History was a real pain, he said to himself. He hated it even more than geography. On second thoughts, nothing could be worse than geography, with its endless obsession with alluvial soils and laterite soils and red soils. Actually, geography and history were equally bad, he concluded. Although, the stuff that his father was talking about the other day on Partition and Bangladesh and all—that was also history in a way. But it was so much more interesting than the stuff they taught in school.

'Fifteen minutes left,' the invigilator announced.

Debu was jerked out of his reverie. He had hardly written anything so far. He was headed for trouble, big trouble, he thought, as he quickly moved on to the next question.

'Describe three salient features of the Great Bath of Mohenjo-Daro. [3 marks]'

He wracked his brains trying to remember what he had learnt about the Great Bath of Mohenjo-Daro. Three salient features, eh? It was big...had lots of water and it was...clean? Hell, I don't remember a thing, he swore under his breath, I'm going to fail this test—pucca.

He looked around. Everyone else seemed to be doing fine. Across the aisle next to him, sat Banman Blah, writing as if there was no tomorrow. Banman was pretty good in social studies and usually topped the class. An unworthy thought now occurred to Debu. It was risky. He had never done it before. But desperate times called for desperate measures. He sneaked a look at the invigilator, Mr Chakraborty. He was seated comfortably at his desk in the front of the class, reading the newspaper. Debu decided to take his chance.

'Hey, Banman,' he hissed. But Banman was hunched over his desk, furiously writing away.

'Banman,' he called again.

This time Banman looked up. 'What?' he hissed back.

Show me your paper, Debu gesticulated silently. Banman's eyes widened in surprise. Debu wasn't the copying types. At first Banman thought he must have misunderstood. But Debu was continuing to gesture for help. It looked like he was in trouble. Banman felt sorry for him. He and Debu had known each other from nursery. How could he refuse to help? After a brief hesitation, he pushed his answer sheet at the edge of his desk and angled himself away from it to give Debu a clear view.

Debu gave Banman a quick thumbs-up to express his gratitude. He shot a quick glance at Mr Chakraborty to check if the coast was clear and quickly got down to business. Craning his neck at Banman's paper, he started scribbling down whatever he could see.

The Great Bath, he copied, measures 11.9 meters by 7.1 meters, and has a maximum depth of 2.4 meters. It is girded by two wide staircases, on the north and the south which... how boring it was to even copy out this stuff, Debu was thinking, when he noticed a shadow falling over his answer sheet. He looked up to see Mr Chakraborty looming above him, a grim look on his face.

Mr Chakraborty snatched Debu's answer script and whacked him on the head with it. 'So this is what you have learnt after nine years of school? How to do cheating-baazi?'

'No, sir. I wasn't cheating. I was...thinking,' Debu explained.

'Thinking? I'll give you something to think about, you rascal!' Mr Chakraborty said. He grabbed Debu by the scruff of the neck and dragged him all the way to the front of the classroom. 'You think you can fool me. I have been watching you all this time.'

'Please sir, sorry sir. I'll never do it again,' Debu pleaded.

'I am sure you won't,' Mr Chakraborty said. He fished out a malacca cane from the teacher's desk and pointed it at Debu. 'Now please, bend down.'

By now the class had forgotten all about the exam. They were tittering in anticipation. Canings were good, clean fun and there hadn't been one in a while. Moreover, it was Mr Goody Two-Shoes Debojit Dutta who was about to be caned.

'Give him one solid whack, sir,' someone yelled from the back. 'Hey Debu, hope you wore some proper undies today,' another one called out.

Mr Chakraborty spun around to face the unruly class. 'Chup! You think this is a fish market! If I hear one more word, I'll cane the whole lot of you.' After the class had calmed down a little, he said, 'Debojit, bend down. Go on—touch your toes! Quickly now, I don't have all day.'

Amidst much cheering and hooting, Debu reluctantly bent down and presented his upturned bottom to Mr Chakraborty. The cane landed on it and Debu gasped in pain as a line of fire suddenly blazed up across his buttocks. The procedure was repeated two more times, by the end of which Debu felt as if a volcano had exploded in his nether regions.

Mr Chakraborty looked satisfied with the results. With a grim smile, he replaced the cane in the desk and said, 'Now please go to the Principal's office and wait for me there. I will come after the exam is over.'

'No sir, please don't do that sir,' Debu begged, in a strangled voice. 'First time, sir! I won't do it again.'

'You are in class nine, Debojit,' said Mr Chakraborty. 'You should know by now that in this school, cheating is taken very seriously.'

'But sir—'

Chakraborty held up his hand and cut him off. 'No buts. Please leave the class immediately and wait for me in the Principal's office. I will be there soon.'

'Please sir, give me one more chance, sir,' Debu pleaded.

'Out,' replied Mr Chakraborty, pointing his finger at the door.

Debu slowly hobbled out of the classroom and made his way to the Principal's office, his mind crunching with the dread of what lay in store for him.

* * *

It had been over ten minutes since Debu was kicked out of class. He was standing in the corridor just outside the Principal's office, waiting for Mr Chakraborty to arrive. By now the pain in his buttocks had subsided a little, but the fear of what would happen to him had grown manifold. The Principal was known to be a strict disciplinarian. Debu was sure that he would be hauled over the coals, perhaps even thrown out of school. At the very least, his parents would be informed of his cheating. And then the fireworks would really begin. Even if there was a half-chance that his father might take a lenient view of things, he was sure his mother would go berserk. And he didn't want to be around when that happened.

Such dark and deep thoughts were swirling inside his head

when he heard a cheerful voice calling out to him. 'Hey Debu,' it said. 'What's up?'

It was Clint. He was striding down the corridor with a big grin on his face. 'Hey man, good to see you here. Don't have to waste my time to search you out now. Come—let's go. We have work to do.'

'What...what work?' Debu stammered. For the life of him, he couldn't figure out what Clint was doing in his school, that too in the St Anton's school uniform. 'What are *you* doing here?'

'Came to meet you. Thought I'd catch you at lunch break.'

'Meet me? But...what for?'

'I need some help with maths, man. Urgent. Bose gave me all these stupid sums for homework and I haven't done a single one so far. I have an extra class with him tomorrow and he's already warned my father about throwing me out.'

'Don't be crazy. I can't help you.'

'Why not?'

'Can't you see? School is on. Besides, I'm in trouble. Big trouble.'

'What happened?'

'Got caught cheating in the history exam.'

Clint burst out into laughter. 'Oh, boy! I don't believe this! You were cheating? Goody-goody fellow like you?'

'Shut up! I'm not a goody-goody.'

'Oh yeah? So, what's the worst thing you've done in your life?'

'Lots of things...like—' Debu froze. At the far end of the corridor had appeared the figure of Mr Chakraborty. He was marching rapidly towards them. 'Oh no! He's coming! You'd better get out of here fast.'

'Who's coming?'

'The history teacher. The guy who caught me cheating.'

'That baldy there?' Clint asked.

'Yes. And stop pointing your finger at him,' Debu hissed.

'You'll only make things worse. Just go, will you! Oh, hell! What'll happen to me now?'

Clint was peering down the corridor. 'Hey, isn't that Chakraborty? He's got a cute daughter, right?'

'I have no idea about his daughter. But yes—his name is Chakraborty. Now will you please—'

'Relax man. I know him. He stays in our locality.'

'You know him?'

'Yeah. Cool—it's all fine. You don't have to worry about him. He won't do a thing to you.'

'What do you mean he won't do anything? He's damn strict. The whole school is shit scared of him.'

'Just trust me, okay? Nothing will happen. Just watch.' He turned and waved at the history teacher who was now only few paces away from them. 'Hello, Mr Chakraborty, how are you doing today?' he smiled.

Debu groaned. He wished he was miles away from Clint, from Chakraborty, from school, from everything. 'What are you doing!' he whispered at Clint. 'You're definitely going to get me expelled now.'

'Keep quiet and let me handle it,' Clint drawled.

Mr Chakraborty appeared to be flabbergasted by Clint's presence. He stared at him and mumbled, 'Mr Lyngdoh? You here?' he said as he took out a frayed handkerchief and mopped his forehead.

'Yes, Mr Chakraborty. I have come to take my friend Debojit home,' Clint replied.

'Your friend?' Chakraborty said uncertainly, his gaze flitting back and forth between the two boys.

Debu didn't know what to say but Clint seemed to be in total command of the situation. 'Yeah, I told you no, Mr Chakraborty,' he drawled. 'Debojit here is my good friend. I've come here to take him home.'

'Why?' asked Chakraborty.

'There's a problem at his house. He needs to go there now.'

'What sort of problem?' Debu and Chakraborty asked together.

'Can't be mentioned in public,' Clint replied with a prim expression on his face. 'It's a family matter. Now if you don't mind. We have to leave right now. Come Debu,' he grasped Debu's hand and began to walk away.

'Wait, wait. Not so fast, Mr Lyngdoh,' Chakraborty blocked his path. 'This is a school. We have some procedures. A written application signed by his father must be submitted to the school office, permission must be taken.'

Clint fixed his gaze on Mr Chakraborty. The squat, bandy-legged Chakraborty was considerably shorter than him and had to crane his neck upwards to make eye contact. With a deliberate slowness, Clint crossed his arms over his chest and asked, 'Mr Chakraborty, are you suggesting that I am lying?'

Chakraborty again mopped his brow with his handkerchief. 'No, of course not, but rules are rules. The letter...' his voice tapered off.

'Let me make myself absolutely clear Mr Chakraborty,' Clint said, speaking very slowly, as if he was talking to a particularly dull-witted child. 'I have already told you that there is a Situation at his home. How do you expect his parents to write a letter under such circumstances? That is why I have come here personally with the message.'

'I see, I see,' Mr Chakraborty mumbled. He turned to Debu. 'Debojit, Mr Lyngdoh is your friend? You will go home with him?'

Debu was completely lost. Too much was happening too fast—what was Clint was trying to do, what was this situation at home, why was Chakraborty so nervous, why was he so deferential towards Clint...there were just too many things that he couldn't wrap his head around. He felt like a deer caught in the headlights. His mouth opened and closed in quick succession but not a sound came out of it.

In the end, all he could say was, 'Ummm.'

Clint gave him an approving nod. 'Excellent. You see, Debojit has agreed,' he said to Chakraborty. 'He wants to come with me. Very good. So, we can leave now.'

Chakraborty gave a resigned shrug. 'Okay, Mr Lyngdoh... since it's an emergency, I will allow it this one time. But a letter signed by his father must be submitted to the school office by tomorrow morning.'

Clint patted Chakraborty on his back. 'Excellent. Thank you for your cooperation, Mr Chakraborty. We'll be off now.'

He grabbed Debu's hand and led him down the corridor. A few steps later he stopped, as if something had occurred to him. 'Mr Chakraborty?' he said. 'Just one more thing.'

'Yes?' said Chakraborty.

'In case Debojit misses any exams, you will give him the necessary re-tests, right? Since it's because of a family emergency. Like, I think he's missing his history exam today.'

Chakraborty grimaced. 'A re-test? I am sorry but that won't be possible,' he snapped. 'He was caught cheating. There is no question of giving him a re-test.'

'But you have to understand, Mr Chakraborty,' Clint said with a philosophical smile. 'This poor boy has been under a lot of stress recently. Because of this family emergency. Pressure makes people do strange things. You should let him go this time. He won't do it again—my guarantee.'

'I'll think about it,' said Chakraborty in a strangled voice.

'Very good. I'm sure there won't be any problem for Debojit,' Clint said. 'Live and let live. It's the best policy, isn't it, Mr Chakraborty?'

Chakraborty nodded slowly. His legs were trembling. He leaned against the wall for support and watched Debu and Clint make their way out of school. When they were out of earshot, a suppressed curse escaped his lips.

'Phungir bai! I'll show you.'

* * *

Debu felt that he was climbing out of a nightmare. He found himself obediently following Clint as they walked across the school grounds and down the winding path of Lady Veronica Lane, which led onto the main road. The journey from the Great Bath to the Great Escape had barely taken fifteen minutes, but to Debu, it seemed like a lifetime. He couldn't believe that he was loitering on the streets in broad daylight instead of writing his exam.

Like a flock of vultures, the fears wheeled inside his head—would he be thrown out of school? Out of home? Would he become like one of those kids in dusty rags who worked in the roadside tea shops? And then the biggest fear of all—was there really an emergency at home?

Debu grabbed Clint and brought him to a halt. 'What's happened at home?' he demanded.

'Nothing,' Clint shrugged his shoulders. 'It's just something I made up on the spot. Now let's see—we have the whole afternoon free. First, we'll go to a good restaurant in Laitumkhrah, maybe Kalsang, and then—'

'Shut up! Just shut up for a moment, will you!' Debu yelled. 'What the hell do you think you are up to?'

'Now what? If you want to have lunch in Police Bazar instead—'

'Stop talking! I have something to say!' Debu grabbed Clint's collar and shook him hard. 'What the hell do you think you were up to?'

Clint looked genuinely puzzled. 'I was only trying to rescue you.'

'Rescue me? Who the hell told you to rescue me? Barging into my school, talking to my teachers like that,' Debu sat down in the middle of the road and let out a loud wail. 'Oh god, oh my god! I'm sure to get expelled. And it's all because of you,' he buried his face in his hands and rocked back and forth, moaning loudly. 'Oh god, oh god, what will happen now.'

'Okay, okay, cool it. People are looking. And if this is what I get for rescuing you, I wish I hadn't bothered,' Clint said in a hurt tone.

'I wish you hadn't either. You should just have stayed away from me,' Debu whimpered. 'I should have stayed away from you. Just like my mother said.'

'What did you just say?' Clint frowned.

Debu bit his tongue. 'Nothing,' he mumbled. In spite of his fears, he was beginning to feel a little ashamed of himself for yelling at Clint. After all, in his own way, he had only tried to do whatever he thought was best for Debu. 'I'm sorry I shouted at you. Guess I was tense,' he said after he felt a little calmer.

'Cool, no probs,' Clint said.

'But I'm really scared of what will happen to me now. Chakraborty won't let me off so easily.'

'Relax, man. I told you, Chakraborty won't touch a hair on your head.'

'Why not? And by the way, why is he so scared of you in the first place?'

There was a split-second pause before Clint replied. 'He's not scared. He respects me, respects my family.'

'Why should he respect you?'

'Well, my dad is a big-shot,' he said.

'What sort of big-shot?'

'He's a businessman,' Clint said. 'Runs a big business. He's an important guy in Mawpar, okay? Everyone respects him. I'll take you home one day. You'll see for yourself.'

'Okay...but what if Chakraborty—'

'Oh stop worrying so much, will you,' Clint cut him short. 'Nothing's gonna happen to you. I'll make sure of that. You are my friend. And I look after my friends. Now let's go for lunch. After that, you finish my maths sums for me. Then we'll go to Police Bazar or to Ward's Lake or—'

'Hang on. Just hang on for one bloody minute,' Debu interrupted. 'I can't do this stuff every day.'

'Why not?'

'Because...because...I can't always do whatever you tell me to do,' Debu protested. 'I can't hang around in Police Bazar in the middle of a school day.'

Clint shrugged his shoulders. 'Why? What's the problem? You can't go back to school anyway now.'

'Because—oh, forget it! You wouldn't understand,' Debu threw up his hands. 'I have to go home.'

'Going home!' Clint exclaimed. 'You crazy or what? It's only one o'clock now. What will you tell your parents when they ask why you came back home so early?'

This was a valid point, one that had not occurred to Debu until now.

'Tell you what,' said Clint. 'Just hang out with me until evening and go back at the regular time. That way, no one will know anything. And I really need your help with my maths. So, let's go for lunch now. We'll try a different place today. How about Abba's? You finish off my maths quickly like last time and after that we can go to Kelvin cinema and watch a movie. There's a new one that came just yesterday. We should be done with everything by four o'clock. Perfect time for you to get back home, right? What do you say?'

Debu's resolve wavered. Clint's plan was sounding better and better with every passing minute.

'You think maybe...Audrey might be interested in joining us?' he asked in as level a voice as he could muster.

'Naah,' said Clint. 'She's in school now, right?'

'Oh yes, of course,' said Debu, trying not to show his disappointment.

'In any case, even if she wasn't, we couldn't have taken her with us.'

'Why not?'

'You stupid or what?' Clint said. 'You think we could have asked her to come watch *Heavenly Bodies* with us?'

Debu drew a sharp breath. 'H...heavenly Bodies?' he stammered.

'Yep. And it's not about stars and planets—that much I can tell you,' Clint winked at him. 'I hear it's good. Very good.'

'Oh,' was all that Debu could say.

'In fact, my friends tell me that it's the best they've ever seen,' Clint went on.

'The best,' Debu repeated dumbly, his heart now hammering against his ribs.

'Even better,' Clint gave a sly grin.

The last vestiges of doubt sailed out of Debu's mind—an assortment of imagined heavenly bodies taking their place.

'What are we waiting for? Let's go,' he said. He hoisted his school bag upon his back and marched briskly down the road towards the bus stop, Clint following close behind.

THE WRITING ON THE WALL

CLINT WASN'T EXAGGERATING. As far as Debu was concerned, *Heavenly Bodies* turned out to be an out-of-the-world experience. Debu hadn't seen anything quite like it before. The grainy quality of the film and the absence of a storyline did nothing to diminish his viewing pleasure. When they came out of the hall, his face was hot and flushed with excitement, and a delicious tingling sensation suffused his entire being. On returning home, he quickly retired to the privacy of his bathroom, spending a few short but intensely satisfying moments reliving the best bits of the film.

Later that night, he felt a deep gratitude towards Clint for having introduced him to more novelties in the last fourteen days than he had experienced in the last fourteen years. As he turned in for the night, all thoughts of the Chalukyas, Chakrabortys, history exams and other worldly worries were far from his mind. He fell asleep in a state of happy exhaustion.

But if the previous afternoon had been like Paradise Gained, the morning after was like a Ramsay Brothers' horror film. It began pleasantly enough. When he awoke, Debu was still basking in the warm remembrance of things past. It was only after he reached school that he realized the half-yearly exams were still going on. Heart sinking rapidly, he entered the classroom to the raucous cheers and hoots of his classmates. Debu had always been the quintessential good boy—studious, obedient and a bit of a teacher's pet. His sudden fall from grace was a source of much amusement.

'All ready for the physics test Debu?' a back-bencher called out to him.

'Don't get caught cheating today again!' said another.

'Hope you remembered to pad your bum with newspapers,' a third sniggered.

Debu sat down at his desk with whatever dignity he could muster and waited for the test to begin. Moments later, Mr Chakraborty walked into the classroom and Debu nearly blanked out from shock. Where was Mr Fudge, the physics teacher?

Chakraborty seemed to have read his thoughts. 'Mr Fudge is unwell today,' he announced. Debu could feel the man's accusing eyes drilling through him. 'I will be invigilating the test instead of him'. He began to distribute the question papers. 'Start writing. You have one hour's time.'

Debu glanced at the question paper. Physics was one of his better subjects and he had a faint hope that he would wing his way through it. But as he browsed through the questions, he realized that he couldn't make head or tail of most of them. He scribbled down whatever little he could manage and doodled idly until, much to his relief, Mr Chakraborty finally announced that time was up.

Debu slouched to the front of the classroom and turned in his answer sheet. The test had been an unmitigated disaster. He had no doubts that he would fail. He was about to slink away quietly when Mr Chakraborty tapped him on the shoulder.

'You wait,' said Chakraborty. 'I have to talk to you.'

The rest of the boys filed out, tittering and winking at Debu.

After the class was empty, Chakraborty cleared his throat theatrically and said, 'Your friend Clint came to my house last night. Do you know what he said to me?'

'No, sir,' Debu replied truthfully.

'He begged me, I repeat, begged me, not to punish you for cheating,' Chakraborty said.

Debu nodded uncertainly. 'Yes sir,' he said.

'Do you know what I told him?'

'No sir.'

'I said okay,' Chakraborty shrugged casually.

'Okay, sir?'

'Yes. Okay. That's what I said to him. Okay,' Chakraborty spread out his hands in a magnanimous gesture.

'Okay sir...' said Debu, confused about where this conversation was heading.

'You may well ask why I said that. And I'll tell you. It's because he is just a foolish, young boy who doesn't know any better. Am I correct?'

'Yes sir.'

'But given what actually happened yesterday, I should be complaining to the Principal and to your parents, and maybe even to the police. Right?'

'Right.'

'I should fail you in the history exam. Right?'

'Right.'

'But I won't do any of those things.'

'You won't?'

'No. Do you know why?'

'Errr...why?' asked Debu, thoroughly mystified by now.

'Because I know you are a good boy and a good student. I don't want you to get into trouble,' said Chakraborty with a smile that stopped short of his eyes.

'Oh,' said Debu. He knew that he should be feeling grateful but somehow he wasn't. He felt uneasy, as if something bad was about to happen.

'But don't think that I am not taking action against you because I am scared of your friend. Shibdas Chakraborty is not afraid of anyone,' he banged his fist on the table, sending a puff of chalk dust flying into the sunbeam slanting across the classroom. 'I am not afraid of anyone,' he declared. 'Do you understand me?'

'Yes sir. Thank you very much sir,' Debu said.

'I am letting it go only because you are a good boy. You are very lucky,' Chakraborty continued. 'But next time you may not be so lucky. And let me tell you something else today, Mr Debojit Dutta. Not that it matters to me. I am saying it only for your own good. Because I am your teacher and I am worried about your future.'

'Yes sir?'

'This Clint—how well do you know him?'

'I met him in tuition classes a few weeks ago, sir.'

'So you don't really know him very well?'

'No sir.'

'Then you should know that this Clint fellow is not a good boy. In fact, he is a very bad boy.'

'Really sir?'

Chakraborty drew close to Debu. 'Yes, really. He is a ruffian, a goonda.'

'How do you know sir?'

'I know. You friend Clint extorts money from shopkeepers which he spends on drinking and gambling. Go to his house in Mawpar and find out for yourself if you don't believe me. And there is something else that you should know about him.'

'What sir?'

'He is friends with the USF. And I am sure you know what type of people they are.'

* * *

The USF or the United Students Federation was a prominent students' association of Shillong. It was anything but student-like. Over the last few years, it had become politically active and increasingly strident in demanding the elimination of foreigners from the state of Meghalaya.

It is said that the USF drew its inspiration from an ancient legend which said that the Khasis were the first humans on earth. Their provenance went back to the very beginnings of time—when there were only sixteen families of humans. These were mortals, but they walked with the gods themselves as friends, and moved freely between heaven and earth by means of a divine umbilical cord. Then one day, sin entered the world and the umbilical cord snapped. Of the sixteen original families, nine continued to live in the sinless world, while the remaining seven remained on earth. They were called the Hynniewtrep—the children of the seven huts—the ancestors of the Khasis.

The USF tried to strengthen the belief that the Hynniewtrep were a special people, different from the plains-people, the Indians. Several among its ranks believed that it was time to permanently sever the Hynniewtrep's umbilical cord from India, and this desire for autonomy soon found expression in what was to become its most famous slogan: KHASI BY BLOOD. INDIAN BY ACCIDENT.

The slogan quickly caught on. It was painted across many prominent public spaces in town, including famously, the boundary wall of the Meghalaya Legislative Assembly. The graffiti stayed there for years, in the shadow of the Indian National flag which fluttered on above—a clear visual marker of the indifference and high-handedness of the Indian state towards the Northeast.

The feeling that the Central Government in New Delhi did not give a fig about the Northeast was widespread and went beyond the ranks of the USF. There was an overall sense of hurt and neglect that had been festering for many years. It had been caused by several incidents—ranging from Nehru's willingness to give up the Northeast to China after the 1962 war, to the Central Government's apathy in stopping the influx of illegal immigrants from Bangladesh.

The original Hynniewtrep ethos, which had shaped the USF and its political ideologies, was based on a profound love and respect for man and nature—Mei Ramew, mother earth, and Mei Mariang. It exhorted man to live a righteous life which was founded on a love of man and God. It emphasized the fundamental unity between man and man, and man and nature.

But the USF's concerns were far more prosaic. They wanted reservation for the Khasis in government jobs, school and college seats, complete reservation of all MLA seats for tribals, curbs on non-tribal men marrying their women, restrictions on buying and selling of property by non-tribals and, of course, the most important demand of all—the elimination of all foreigners from the state of Meghalaya, in particular, the Bangladeshis.

* * *

Like most Bengalis, Mr Chakraborty did not make any bones about his fear and dislike of the USF.

'What is a good boy like you doing, mixing around with people like Clint Lyngdoh?' said Chakraborty. 'Don't you know what they are doing to us? How can you call yourself a Bengali? Don't you have any shame?'

'I don't think I did anything wrong, sir. At least not on purpose,' Debu said sullenly. He had had enough lectures for one day. Besides, who was Chakraborty to poke his nose into his life?

'Didn't do anything wrong?' Chakraborty bared his kwai-stained teeth in a snarl. 'Your goonda friend from USF didn't threaten me?'

'Clint didn't threaten you, sir. And stop calling him a goonda. He is not. He has nothing to do with the USF,' Debu said. 'I know him better than you do.'

'Really?' Chakraborty smirked. 'Do you know that he grew up in the same locality in which I have lived all my life? I have known him since he was this high,' he pointed to his knees. 'I know him, his father, his whole family. They are all well-known goons! If you don't believe me, then go to Mawpar and find out for yourself. Go and talk to the shopkeepers from whom he extorts money. Go to the bars where he and his USF friends spend their time drinking and gambling. Then come and talk to me.'

Debu kept quiet. He was finding it hard to believe Chakraborty but the teacher's conviction had shaken him. What if Clint really was like that? Chakraborty was accurate about two things—that Clint always seemed to have plenty of money, and that he liked to drink.

'I know that what you do outside school hours and who you meet is none of my business,' Chakraborty continued. 'But as your teacher, it is my duty to warn you one last time. If you continue to mix with this boy, then your future will be ruined. You will end up in jail. You mark my words, Debojit Dutta. Clint Lyngdoh will destroy you.'

***

That evening, as Debu walked back home from school, his mind was in turmoil. He felt like confronting Clint directly. But he did not know where Clint stayed or his phone number. His questions would have to wait until they met again in Professor Bose's class.

Despite all he had heard, he just could not think of Clint as a goon. He couldn't imagine him extorting money from shopkeepers. Why should he, when his father was a big-shot businessman? Yes, it was true that he was fond of drinking, but then he was a painter and it was common knowledge that artistic people had a weakness for liquor. There was nothing so terrible in that.

The more he thought about it, the more he was convinced that Chakraborty had been bullshitting. What he said didn't make any sense. If Clint was from the USF, then why would he have bothered to become friends with him—the enemy? Wasn't it Clint who had initiated their friendship? Wasn't it Clint who had gone out of his way to introduce him to the pleasures of life—his first drink, his first chow at Kalsang, his first experience of bunking school to watch a movie (*Heavenly Bodies*, no less), his first proper evening with a girl...?

Clint had been the saki who had poured out to him the heady brew of freedom. Now that Debu had had a taste, how could he give it up? Chakraborty and his mother could say whatever they wanted, but he and Clint would be friends for life.

THE WORLD BEYOND THE HILLS

A FEW WEEKS after the exams ended, a momentous event took place in the Dutta household. On a late autumn afternoon, a Nepali porter arrived bearing a large carton on his bent back. Behind him was Mr Ranajit Deb Nath, the sole proprietor of Excellent Electronics Enterprises. He was followed by an assortment of curious neighbours who had got a whiff of something exciting happening at the Duttas'. The porter carefully set down the carton in the living room as the three Duttas and their neighbours gathered around in hushed anticipation.

Like a magician performing his star act, Mr Deb Nath opened the carton box and unveiled the secret package. 'Mr Dutta, you are now the proud owner of an EC TV!' announced Mr Deb Nath.

There was much *oooh-ing* and *aaah-ing* as everyone pressed forward to get a good look at the newly arrived technological marvel. They clucked around it excitedly, praising its looks and features, as if it were a newborn baby. Mr and Mrs Dutta tried to look modest, although they were secretly feeling rather proud. For it was a truth universally acknowledged, that to be the owner of an EC TV in Shillong, in the eighties, was a fairly big deal. It was the Rolls Royce of television sets in Eastern India and there were only a handful of families on Upper Jail Road that possessed one.

The decision to buy an EC TV had been taken about a year ago after Mrs Dutta insisted that a television would be good for the family. It would open their minds, she said, and Debu, in particular, would benefit from exposure to Indian culture, something that they were deprived of staying in a place like Shillong. Mr Dutta immediately balked at the cost but Mrs Dutta was insistent, and his protestations soon petered out, as they usually did. Mr Dutta now turned to his eldest sister for advice. Phool Pishima, as she was called, lived in Calcutta and was the undisputed matriarch of the extended Dutta clan. She was considered an authority on everything, including TVs.

'If something is worth doing, then it is worth doing well,' Phool Pishima declared magisterially. 'And if a TV is worth buying, then EC TV is the only TV worth buying.'

Mr Dutta made a few noises about KELTRON TV being almost as good and much cheaper to boot, but such vulgar arrivistes were promptly dismissed by Phool Pishima. If her own brother was buying a television, then it had better be an EC TV, she said, and the matter was settled. So it was a year ago that Mr Dutta had placed an order for a new EC TV set with Excellent Electronics Enterprises. Demand for EC TVs was far greater than their supply and there was a one-year waiting period before the set could be finally shipped from Calcutta to Shillong.

It had arrived at last and everyone agreed that it had been worth the wait. Debu was fascinated—his gaze lingered over the gleaming curved blue screen, the shiny round dials, the red light twinkling on the booster and the polished wooden shutters that could be drawn across the screen. It looked like something straight out of the gizmo collection of Ming the Merciless, the villain of his favourite science fiction comic, *Flash Gordon*.

With the solemnness of a priest making an offering to the gods, Mr Deb Nath turned one of the dials. With a hiss and splutter the TV came to life and a wash of white and grey bubbles surfaced on the screen. Concerned murmurs broke out amidst the gathering.

'These black and white blobs all over the screen? What are they?' asked one neighbour.

'Must be snow. Could be Shimla. Or Kashmir,' another replied.

'Isn't modern technology simply wonderful? Sitting here in Shillong, we can see snow in Kashmir,' a third gushed.

'That's not snow!' said Mr Deb Nath testily. 'There is no image because there is no signal. I need to fix the antenna first so that it can catch the signal from the TV tower. Only then will you be able to see anything properly.'

Everyone watched with keen interest as Mr Nath proceeded to set up the antenna. He first fixed the fish-bone like metallic frame of the antenna onto a long bamboo pole. Then he placed a ladder against the roof and climbed on to it. The Nepali porter joined Mr Deb Nath and, between the two of them, they finally managed to hoist the bamboo pole on to the roof. The onlookers below broke out into loud cheers, as if they had just witnessed Hillary and Tenzing raising the flag at the summit of Mount Everest.

The antenna swayed uncertainly in the wind, sniffing for the elusive signal emanating from the Doordarshan Kendra downtown. Catching a clear TV signal in Shillong was no mean feat—the hills came in the way. Mr Deb Nath and his Nepali sherpa wrestled with the bamboo pole while everyone else assembled in front of the TV—providing feedback on their efforts.

'I'm turning the antenna to the left now,' Mr Deb Nath called out from the roof as he rotated the pole. 'Is the picture any better?'

'No. It's become worse,' the TV watchers replied.

'Okay, I'm turning it to the right,' Mr Deb Nath said. 'Is it clear now?'

'No, even worse. We can't make out a thing. Full snow,' came the reply.

And so, in a sort of reverse enactment of 'Uncle Podger Hangs a Picture', Mr Deb Nath struggled to fix the antenna in the right position, as the gathering cheered him on. Two hours later, a distinctly grimier and sweatier Mr Nath descended to the ground.

'I am sorry,' he said to Debu's father. 'There is a real problem getting a good signal in this area. I will have to fix a more powerful booster to your TV. But for the moment this is the best we can do,' he said as he pointed sorrowfully to the television screen.

'It's alright Ranajit-babu,' said Mr Dutta. 'You tried your best. Besides, it's not too bad, is it? We can at least see something. It's a start.'

This was true. Several blurry human shapes could now be seen on the screen. The fact that they were all upside down and swaying rhythmically to the background music was another matter. But for Debu and his neighbours, who were seeing television for the first time in their lives, it was thrilling.

'Are those people hanging from the ceiling?' someone asked.

'No, No! It's a shipwreck!' another said. 'Isn't it obvious? The ship has overturned and the passengers are trapped inside. That's why they are upside down.'

'Can't be! Looks like they are dancing. Have you ever heard of anyone dancing when they are drowning?'

'That too disco-dancing!'

'Who knows maybe they *are* drowning? See, see, they seem to be in uniform. It could be some navy ship that is sinking.'

Mr Deb Nath, fuming silently all this while, could not take it anymore. He had had it up to his eyeballs with these yokels who had never seen a TV in their lives. 'Are you all blind?' he exclaimed. 'Those are soldiers! And they are marching, not dancing! It's perfectly clear.'

When they looked more carefully, it was indeed clear that a troop of soldiers were marching. It was a repeat telecast of the previous year's Republic Day parade in Delhi. No one had seen such a sight before and they watched with great excitement as the blurred, inverted soldiers of the Indian Army disco-danced to the beats of 'Kadam Kadam Badhaye Ja'.

But Mr Deb Nath's professional pride had been hurt. How could people watch the Indian Army upside down—that too on his television set? He rolled up his sleeves and, after another hour of antenna wrestling, he finally managed to get the image upright.

This led to loud cheering and the neighbours congratulating themselves and Mr Dutta that 'their' TV was finally working. As far as they were concerned, the TV belonged to all of them. Later that evening, as they bade farewell, they assured the Duttas that they would come again the following day to watch television together.

* * *

In those early days of TV in Shillong, Doordarshan was king—and the neighbours who flocked to Debu's house every evening quickly became its loyal devotees. Mrs Dutta would place a mat before this temple of entertainment, upon which the visiting pilgrims would genuflect to receive DD's blessings. The evening telecast usually started with Krishi Darshan, an educational program for farmers, which was as exciting as watching weeds grow. But the program had its takers, and a few people even trickled in early so that they could occupy the best seats. The traffic would increase sharply when it was time for Chitrahaar, a compilation of Hindi film songs. By the time India's first soap opera, Hum Log, came on air, it would be a full house.

Like Debu and his neighbours, the rest of Shillong was swiftly succumbing to the charms of the idiot box. Time that once used to trickle at a leisurely pace in the hills suddenly became a precious commodity. People discovered that they no longer had time for rambling addas with friends or making impromptu visits to relatives. Personal routines were adjusted around the broadcast schedule of Hum Log and conversations often revolved around why Dr Ashwini still hadn't proposed to young Badki.

Those who owned a TV rushed to their houses as early as possible to catch their favourite shows. Those who didn't, rushed to their neighbours'. In the beginning, this communal experience was quite enjoyable. It was fun watching TV together, fiddling with the booster and adjusting the antenna to improve the reception. It was like being in a joint family for a few hours. The tea and biscuits, served by the host, tasted all the sweeter for the shared pleasures and pains.

But as the days passed, the novelty of community TV began to fade, and the milk and honey of human kindness began to dry up. TV owners started pretending that they were not home when the door-bell rang. Sometimes when a particularly tenacious neighbour dropped by, they would yell from inside that no was at home, hoping that he or she would finally get the message.

Debu was very grateful that they had their own TV and he didn't have to go to a neighbour's place to watch the programs that he liked. For he liked pretty much everything, including the Hindi serials which the boys in his school thought were so uncool. There were only two exceptions—Krishi Darshan and The News, which was read out every night by a granite-faced lady called Salma Sultana. His favourites were the English serials like The Lucy Show and Star Trek. They were his first glimpse of the 'foreign', his first encounter with strange new worlds and new civilizations that lay beyond the hills of Shillong. But just as television was exposing Debu to the culture of alien civilizations, another cultural influence was about to infiltrate into the Dutta household.

It went by the name of Shyamal Lahiri.

GLAXO BABY

STRANGELY ENOUGH, IT was Debu's father who brought Shyamal Lahiri into their lives, and not his culture-obsessed mother.

'There is a new medical representative from Glaxo who has been posted here. His name is Shyamal Lahiri,' Mr Dutta said one night as they sat at the dining table. 'I have invited him home tomorrow evening. He's a bachelor and I thought it would be nice for him to have a home-cooked meal with us.'

'And just who do you think will do the cooking?' Mrs Dutta snapped. 'As it is, I have so much work and now this—'

'Ah! Listen to me first,' Mr Dutta said. 'He is a very cultured young man. He is from Calcutta. But he studied in Shantinketan. Very cultured. Knows Tagore by heart.'

Mrs Dutta's face lit up. 'Ohhh, Shantiniketan! Calcutta! Then he must be very sophisticated. Yes, yes, then we must definitely invite him home. Where does one get the chance to meet such cultured people in Shillong? Debu can learn so many things from him.'

Debu groaned. Of late, his mother's determination to improve his cultural education had reached unhealthy levels. She was always pestering him to watch boring classical music programs on TV, and now this new threat loomed on the horizon. But he knew there was no way of avoiding it, and he steeled himself for another unwanted dose of culture.

The following evening saw the arrival of Mr Shyamal Lahiri, the medical representative from Shantiniketan, Calcutta and Glaxo (in that order of importance). He was in his mid-twenties—a short, roly-poly, teddy bear of a man with a waddle of a walk. Debu immediately coined a name for him—Glaxo Baby—after the cherubic infant from the advertisements of Glaxo baby food. Like a true Calcuttan, Glaxo Baby believed

that it was his bounden duty to initiate his fellow men into the
world of Tagore—especially his unfortunate Bengali brethren
languishing in the wilderness of the Northeast. Not one to
waste any time, he launched into his mission as soon as the
preliminary pleasantries were over.

'So, shall I sing a song?' Glaxo Baby asked.
The Duttas were delighted. This was a good start. 'Oh
yes!' they said enthusiastically. Debu's shoulders slumped. Mrs
Dutta gave him a sharp poke to make him sit up straight, as
Glaxo Baby cleared his throat and sent out a few exploratory
notes. A grave expression slipped over his face, his eyes closed
and he began to sing in a deep, quavering voice.

Marana re tuhu momo shyam samaan
Megha-barana tujha, megha-jatajuta

The song appeared to be a mixture of Sanskrit and Hindi.
Debu couldn't make head or tail of it. His parents however
seemed to be engrossed in it. They shut their eyes and swayed
to the cadence of the recital. And the more they swayed, the
more emotional Glaxo Baby's singing became.

Raktakamalakar rakta-adharaputa
Tapbimochana karuna-kora tava
Mrityu amrita kare daan

With every passing minute, it was becoming less intelligible
to Debu. But his parents seemed to be having something akin
to a mystical experience. They kept uttering ecstatic *ah-aahs*
and *bah-baahs*, which was odd, since their Hindi was even
worse than his. It was a long song and Glaxo Baby had a way
of repeating the same line over and over again in extended,
palpitating notes that went on and on. By the time Mr Lahiri
reached the final stanza, Debu's eyes had begun to droop.

Bhanu bhane ayi Radha chiya chiya
Chanchala chitta tohari

Jivan ballava marana adhik suno
Ab tuhu dekh bicharai

Glaxo Baby threw his hands into the air and ended the song with a triumphant flourish. Mr and Mrs Dutta were gazing at him with an adoration that other people normally reserved for rock stars, when their admiring silence was broken by a gentle snore.

Glaxo Baby's nose wrinkled up as if it had detected a dead rat in the vicinity. 'Bhanu Singh's Padabali—one of Tagore's greatest works. But not great enough for your son, it would seem...heh heh heh,' he sniggered.

Two crimson spots burned angrily on Mrs Dutta's cheeks. She gave Debu a sharp knock on the head and pulled him up by the ear. 'Go inside and wash your face right now. You just wait, I'll show you afterwards,' she hissed through gritted teeth.

'Please don't mind him too much, Mr Lahiri,' Mr Dutta hastened to explain as Debu slouched out of the room. 'He must be tired after a long day at school.'

'Besides where does he get exposure to such things?' Mrs Dutta simpered. 'Bhanu Singh and all is completely new for him. But I am hopeful that if he meets more people like you, he will slowly get to learn more about our rich Bengali culture.'

'I certainly hope so,' Mr Lahiri sounded slightly mollified. 'We live in dark times. If the young don't preserve our culture, then who will?'

* * *

After a while, dinner was served. Mrs Dutta reserved her sweetest smiles and the best cuts of fish for Mr Lahiri, while Debu received her glares and a bony tail piece.

'So how are you finding Shillong, Mr Lahiri?' Mr Dutta asked.

'What should I say?' Mr Lahiri shrugged as he delicately plucked a bone out from his fish. 'The weather is good. The air is fresh. The trees are green. But...'

Debu knew what was coming next.

'But there is no Development,' said Mr Lahiri.

The dreaded 'D-word'—Debu had heard it many times before. Almost anyone who visited them from Calcutta, or anywhere else in the plains, believed that they could condense the entire Northeast region into two words— NO DEVELOPMENT. There was a second D-word which occasionally followed the first. And sure enough, Glaxo Baby uttered it next.

'After all, what can you expect from a place where people eat DOG meat?' Mr Lahiri said as he sucked contentedly on the fish bone.

In all likelihood, Mr Lahiri's question was the fallout of an infamous newspaper article that had been written in 1976 by a famous Bengali novelist from Calcutta. This ill-researched article on the dog-eating habits of a certain Naga tribe had created a sensation when it was first published in Calcutta. It went on to cause lasting damage to the culinary reputation of the people of the Northeast, Naga or not.

Since then, almost every Shillong-ite has, at least once in their lifetime, been asked the famous 'D' question. 'You're from Shillong? So, you eat dog meat, hna?'

The 'D' question was often followed by the 'C' question. And Mr Lahiri did not disappoint. 'So when do you plan to move to Calcutta?' he said.

No damsel in distress could have been more grateful than Mrs Dutta. Mr Lahiri was turning out to be her knight in shining armour—her own Sir Lancelot Lahiri. 'Exactly Lahiri-babu,' she said. 'You have taken the words out of my mouth. This is exactly what I keep telling my mister. That we should move to Calcutta while there is still time. But he just does not listen to me.'

'Please,' Mr Dutta raised his hand. 'We have discussed this topic often enough. There is no need to bore Mr Lahiri with it. Let him eat in peace.'

Glaxo Baby spread his hands in a magnanimous gesture. 'No, no. It's absolutely fine. And I agree with your missus. I seriously think you should shift to Calcutta if you can, Mr Dutta. After all, what future is there in this place?'

'And what future is there in Calcutta?' Mr Dutta retorted. 'With so much of politics and strikes and lockouts all the time?'

The next 'C' word was on its way.

'But what about Culture?' Mr Lahiri said. 'Surely, that is the most important thing. And you cannot deny that Calcutta is the cultural capital of India, maybe even the world.

'Besides, for a Bengali, all roads finally lead to Calcutta, don't they, Mr Dutta?'

OH, CALCUTTA!

THE RELATIONSHIP THAT the Bengalis of Shillong had with the city of Calcutta could be described in two words: it's complicated.

At one level, Calcutta was regarded as the mother ship to which they were all moored by an invisible umbilical cord. Like the space shuttles of Star Trek returning to the USS Enterprise after their solitary forays into space, the Shillong Bengalis believed that one day, they too would inevitably have to seek refuge in the bowels of Calcutta. This was the dominant feeling, even among those who had never laid their eyes upon the place. Calcutta was to the Shillong Bengali what Israel was to the Jews—an imagined sanctuary from the various 'Bongal Khedao' (Banish the Bengalis) movements that were flaring up across the Northeast. It was a shelter from the gathering storms that threatened to burst upon them at any moment. Where else can we go, who else would accept us, where else would we be safe?—they would ask each other from time to time.

Yet, people like Mr Dutta, who had lived in the mist-covered hills of Shillong all their lives, dreaded the day when they would be forced to leave their cozy wattle and daub cottages in the mist-covered hills of Shillong, and flee to some ghastly little flat in the chaos of Calcutta. To older generations, the prospect of an exodus from the Scotland of the East to the City of Dreadful Night brought back bitter memories of Partition, and their exile from Bangladesh. It troubled them to think that, once again, they could become strangers in a strange land—eternal refugees—cursed forever to be called dkhars in a hundred different tongues.

The same unspoken fears lurked inside Mr Dutta's heart. A true-blooded Shillong Bengali who had had his fair share of exposure to the Calcutta Bengali, he had come to accept that they were as different as chalk from cheese. To begin with, there was the minefield of language. Like most Shillong Bengalis, Mr Dutta spoke Sylheti, a dialect of Bengali that was almost incomprehensible to his Calcuttan relatives. The differences were sometimes so great that it was possible that the same sentence spoken in Sylheti Bengali would not have a single syllable in common with Calcuttan Bengali (or Calcatian, as it was sarcastically called by the Sylhetis). For example, the sentence 'He is very dirty' would be spoken in Calcatian as, 'O na, bheeshon nongra'; while in Sylheti, it would become far more evocative: 'Hota akta phyarot.'

Sylheti and Calcatian were like two edges of the same knife. It was a knife that cut deep and left lasting scars on the psyche of the Shillong Sylheti. The probable cause could be traced to one of the three all-time favourite words of the modern-day Bengali. These, in order of importance, were: Struggle, Culture and Acidity (the last being a common affliction usually referred to as 'ambol' in Calcatian and 'gyaash' in Sylheti).

In matters of Struggle and Acidity, both communities were equal in their suffering. But when it came to Culture, the average Sylheti believed that he was far behind his Calcuttan brethren. Mr Dutta, in particular, had often felt like a gauche schoolboy while conversing with his urbane brother-in-law, the formidable Phool Pishima's husband—Shushobhan-da.

Just as Phool Pishima was the gadget goddess of the family, Shushobhan-da, who had recently retired from the Calcutta Municipal Corporation, was its cultural czar. He was a tall, reedy man with a long, thin moustache, which he superciliously stroked as he bestowed upon Mr Dutta his pontifications on the galaxy of stars sparkling in the firmament of Bengali culture—who, of course, were all Calcuttans. Tagore, undoubtedly, was the dazzling centre of this universe, but around him revolved many other luminaries such as Bibhutibhushan Bandyopadhyay, Sunil Gangopadhyay,

Shakti Chattopadhyay, Salil Choudhury, Ritwick Ghatak and of course, the redoubtable Satyajit Ray. Their creations were undeniably of great significance and had gone on to receive much national and global acclaim. But the problem was that they were all Calcuttan. In comparison, there were hardly any works of literature, cinema or music in Sylheti that came even remotely close. And into the ears of the Mr Duttas of this world, there whispered a chorus of insidious voices:

Sylheti is not Bengali. In fact, it isn't even a proper language.
It's just pidgin.
You live with the tribals and you speak like them too.
The Calcuttans make fun of you. And why shouldn't they?
You Sylhetis are so funny!

The voices convinced them that as a language, Sylheti was inferior to Calcatian. From this they internalized the notion that Sylhetis were inferior to Calcuttans—they would never be as clever or as cultured as them. And yet, in the face of increasing tribal hostility towards the Sylhetis, there was no one else that they could think of as their kin, apart from their Calcutta cousins and brothers-in-law: no safe haven apart from Kolikata, the City of Kali.

Kali Kalkattewali! The fierce goddess who wore a garland of skulls as she danced upon her supine husband and delivered her devotees from evil and injustice. To the likes of Mr Dutta, Ma Kali was the essence of Kolikata—the loving yet terrifying mother, dark with mystery yet luminous with hope. It was only in the folds of her arms, they believed, that they would finally be safe. But Ma Kali's blessings were not free, they had to be earned the hard way. For she was a goddess who demanded sacrifice, sometimes even human sacrifice.

And deep down, Mr Dutta and countless other Sylhetis knew that a day would come when they would have to make that sacrifice and submit themselves to her dark forces—they would have to endure the heat, the humidity, the traffic, the load shedding, the open wound of the never-ending Metro construction along Central Avenue and the spectre of unemployment. But above all, they would have to endure the derision of those hordes of snooty, smarmy and ridiculous Calcuttans who spent much of their lives moaning about acidity or marching in rallies to the cries of 'Cholbe na! Cholbe na!'

And as the hostilities against non-tribals kept increasing, like the Prince of Denmark, Mr Dutta was forced to confront the increasingly pressing dilemma of his life—to become a second-class Bengali in the terrifying chaos of Kolikata or to survive as a third-class Indian in the beautiful hills of Shillong.

* * *

For Debu however, there was no such dilemma. The Duttas would usually visit Phool Pishima's house in Ballygunge for a few days during the annual winter vacations. Debu had seen enough of Calcutta and Calcuttans to realize that it wasn't for him. Shushobhan-da alone would have been enough but the advent of Shyamal Lahiri in his life firmly cemented his views.

In Debu's eyes, Lahiri was the archetype of the typical Calcuttan—full of hot air and himself. Much to his horror, the man had now become a regular fixture at home. He would arrive in the evenings soon after work and help himself to generous portions of tea and snacks that Mrs Dutta would dotingly prepare for him. He would then proceed to recite unbearably long and complicated poems, which Mrs Dutta would insist Debu listen to. But the worst was yet to come.

One evening, after a particularly rousing performance by Mr Lahiri, Mrs Dutta said to Debu, 'I have decided that you will learn Rabindra Sangeet from Mr Lahiri. He has very kindly agreed to take classes two days a week.'

'What! No way!' Debu yelped.

'Don't talk to me like that!' Mrs Dutta smacked him on the head. 'You don't know how lucky you are. If only we had got such opportunities when we were your age, then we would have reached somewhere else by now.'

'Then why don't you take classes with him instead of me?'

'Aiiee, chup!'

'What chup! As it is I have to go for maths tuitions three days a week and then this! When will I get the time to play? When will I get any time for myself?'

Mrs Dutta changed tack. 'I understand that you don't have much free time, Debu,' she said in a gentler tone. 'But you also have to understand that this is not the age for playing games. This is the age to work hard and learn as much as you can. You cannot learn music when you are older. This is the time. And we are so lucky to have Lahiri-babu right here in Shillong. He has been trained in Shantiniketan, no less. He has agreed to teach you from the goodness of his heart. He is even willing to come home.'

'Of course. For the free tea and snacks,' Debu muttered.

His mother either didn't hear him or pretended not to. 'You just have to sit and learn from him,' she continued, 'and even that much you don't want to do. Our parents never gave us even one per cent of what we are giving to you.'

'But I don't want to learn Rabindra Sangeet. It's slow! It's boring. I hate it! I hate it!'

The mildest utterance against Tagore in a Bengali household was asking for trouble. There was a sharp sound like the bursting of a fire-cracker as One Tight Slap landed on Debu's cheek.

'I don't want to hear a single word more,' said Debu's mother in a glacial voice that could have frozen the Hooghly on a midsummer's afternoon. 'Your lessons will start from Monday. Tomorrow we will go and buy a harmonium for you. Mr Lahiri has said that it is necessary to practice scales using a harmonium.'

'H...harmonium?' Debu spluttered as he rubbed his cheek. 'No Ma, please!'

'*Now* what's the problem?' his mother snapped.

'I can't play the harmonium, Ma! If it was a guitar, it would have been fine. But not a harmonium. Please! It's so sissy, so old-fashioned. If my friends come to know about it, then they'll tease me to death!'

'Don't be stupid. All great singers play the harmonium when they sing—Hemanta, Manna—'

'Exactly,' Debu cut her short. 'Old men wearing dhotis—those are the only people who play the harmonium.'

'Enough! I can't listen to this nonsense anymore.'

Debu made one last, desperate attempt. 'Can I play the guitar instead? Please Ma!'

'Don't be ridiculous! Rabindra Sangeet and guitar! What rubbish! I don't want any more arguments. My decision is final. We will go to Melody House tomorrow evening to buy your harmonium. And that is that.'

* * *

The following afternoon, Mrs Dutta and Debu arrived at Melody House in search of a suitable harmonium. Melody House was a small store near Dream Land Cinema at the edge of Police Bazar. It was a favourite destination for the countless young would-be musicians of Shillong. A few youths in leather jackets were lounging near the entrance, discussing someone called Iron Maiden. Throwing them a suspicious look, Mrs Dutta marched in, Debu in tow.

'I want to buy a scale-changing harmonium for my son,' she said to the salesman at the counter. 'Can you show us a few? Not too expensive please.'

A harmonium was plonked in front of Mrs Dutta. 'Aiiiee, Debu!' she called out. 'Come here. Try and play it.'

Head hung low and face turned away to avoid being spotted, Debu dragged himself to the counter. He was pressing a few random keys when he felt a sharp rap on his head.

'No, you silly boy!' Mrs Dutta said. 'That's not how you

play a harmonium. You have to pump the bellows while pressing the keys. Otherwise no sound will come out. Go on now. Do it in rhythm—pump in, pump out, pump in, pump out,' she instructed.

Debu pumped in and pumped out without any enthusiasm. 'What's the matter? Why isn't the sound coming properly? Are the bellows too tight?' asked Mrs Dutta.

'No, they're fine,' Debu muttered and pumped harder. 'Can we please go home now?'

'Of course not. We have come here to buy a scale-changing harmonium, not a sack of potatoes,' said Mrs Dutta. 'These things don't come cheap. Everything has to be properly tested and checked thoroughly before spending your father's hard-earned money. As it is, he made so much fuss over the expense. Anyway—try playing once again. You have to press the keys and pump the bellows at the same time. Pump, pump, press, press. Pump, pump, press, press—yes, like that.'

The leather-jacketed youths were staring curiously at them. Or at least Debu thought they were. He silently gritted his teeth and pressed on, when he heard a familiar voice behind him.

'Hiiii, Debu! What's up?'

It was Audrey. Debu took a moment to recognize her as the schoolgirl whom he had first met. The ponytail had gone and instead, her long, lustrous hair flowed out freely from beneath a leather cap worn at a rakish angle. The severe gray uniform of Loretta Convent had been replaced by a pair of ripped blue jeans and a black T-shirt that said, 'Peace, Love, Rock & Roll.'

Debu thought she looked utterly charming. But clearly, his mother did not. A frown slipped over her face as she inspected Audrey from head to toe. Her lips moved silently as she read the words on the T-shirt and her frown deepened.

Oblivious to Mrs Dutta's scrutiny, Audrey gave Debu a friendly slap on the back. 'Heyyy, so good to see you. Didn't expect to find you in this place. I didn't know you played music.'

'Ummm...I don't really. My mother wants to buy a harmonium,' Debu said. 'For herself,' he added quickly in a low voice.

'Your mother plays the harmonium? Wow! That is so cool. Hello ma'am,' she said turning to Mrs Dutta.

'Hello,' Mrs Dutta replied stiffly. 'I don't play. It's for Debu. He's learning to sing.'

Audrey's eyes widened in surprise. 'Really, Debu? You never told me that you sang. You are full of surprises,' she patted him playfully on his arm.

'Yeah well,' Debu said with a weak smile. He was flattered by her interest in his musical abilities, but in light of his mother's frosty demeanour, he didn't think it wise for their conversation to go on much longer. 'So, yeah, nice meeting you here, but we should leave now. Shall we go?' he said, turning to his mother.

'We will in a minute,' said Mrs Dutta. 'But won't you first introduce me to this new friend of yours? I don't think you have told me about her before.'

'Really, Debu? You didn't tell your parents about me?' Audrey said mischievously. 'Hello aunty. I'm Audrey. Debu's friend. We got introduced through Clint. Guess you know him?'

'Clint Lyngdoh?' said Mrs Dutta. "Isn't he the same boy that you went to Kalsang with, Debu?'

'Yes, exactly,' Audrey replied before Debu could speak. 'In fact, that's where Debu and I met—at Kalsang.'

'Oh I see,' Mrs Dutta said grimly. 'I understand now. All right, Debu, I think we are done here. We should leave now.'

She instructed the salesman to pack up the harmonium. 'Come Debu,' she said and marched towards the exit.

'Bye Debu, bye aunty,' Audrey said. 'See you soon.'

They were about to step out onto the street when Audrey called out, 'Hey Debu, just a minute.'

She ran up to them and said, 'I'm finally having my birthday party the week after next, on Saturday. I'll send you the details through Clint. He'll tell you everything—when, where, how to get there. You'll come right, Debu?'

'Ummm...I...mean,' stammered Debu. His gaze shifted from Audrey to his mother. Her eyes had turned into a pair of icepicks and her lips into the familiar, forbidding knife's edge. 'Come on, Debu. Don't say no. It's my birthday,' Audrey insisted. 'You have to come Debu. It'll be great fun, I promise. Lots of singing and dancing—'

'Yes, yes,' Debu muttered as he flapped his hands up and down, desperately gesticulating her to stop talking.

'And remember to bring your harmonium,' she continued relentlessly. 'That way we can get to hear your singing.'

'Okay, okay,' squeaked Debu in desperation, catching a glimpse of his mother's thunderous face. And then, much to his relief, a taxi pulled up beside them. 'Got to go now. Bye,' he said and bolted inside the taxi. Mrs Dutta followed, the harmonium was loaded into the boot and, at last, they were ready to leave.

'Bye aunty. Byeee Debu, see you soon,' waved Audrey as the taxi rattled down the narrow lane in front of Dream Land Cinema, heading for Jail Road.

* * *

A dense silence prevailed throughout the journey, growing heavier and more oppressive with every passing minute. The storm burst as soon as they reached home.

'Girls! Parties!' Mrs Dutta exclaimed. 'So this is what you have been up to! Now I understand. This is why you were so adamant about your father not dropping you to school and back? This is why we are spending all our hard-earned money to give you the best possible education? So that you can party with your Khasi girlfriend?'

'She is not my girlfriend. I can explain everything,' Debu said.

After many apologies and a few liberties with the truth, Mrs Dutta became a little calmer.

'I have heard what you said,' she said. 'I don't know what
to believe anymore. I don't know what it is that you and Clint
and this Audrey girl are upto but—'

'We are upto nothing Ma,' Debu interrupted.

'Don't talk when I am talking. Like I said, I don't know
what you are up to. I only hope that you don't come to any
harm. You are getting older now, Debu.' A gentler, sadder
expression came over her. 'There will be so many things that
will tempt you, excite you—parties, drinks, drugs, girls. Do
you think I don't understand? It is that age—that beautiful
but dangerous age when you are half-child and half-man. You
are growing up, and everyone makes mistakes while growing
up. As your mother, I can only pray that you don't have to
pay a heavy price for your mistakes. I can only hope that you
don't do something wrong.'

'You don't have to worry so much about me, Ma. I am
not doing anything wrong,' said Debu.

'I certainly hope not,' she said briskly. She was back to her
old self. 'From now on, I will be watching you very closely.
One false move and you will be grounded. And don't even
think of going to any parties. You understand?'

'Yes, Ma,' Debu nodded obediently.

But already, his mind was on Audrey Pariat's birthday
party. There was no way that he would miss it.

BISCUITS FOR BEGGARS

DEBU'S MOTHER WAS as good as her word. She watched his every move and, Torquemada-like, she questioned everything. They didn't have normal conversations anymore, only a series of interrogations from morning to night:

Where are you going?
Who are you meeting?
Why do you have to meet him?
Or is it a her?
Why can't he come here to meet you?
When will you come back?
Why do you need so much time?

Worse was on its way.

A few days after the encounter with Audrey, Debu received his test results. They were dismal—the worst he had ever done in nine years of school. Usually among the top three in his class, this time he was among the last two. He had scraped the bottom of the barrel in almost all subjects except physics, in which he had failed. The only saving grace was that he had passed history with 35 marks, the cut-off—no doubt the result of Clint's little pep talk with Chakraborty. Debu was grateful for the small mercies.

As expected, his mother's jaw dropped when she saw his report card. It took her a while before she could speak.

'This! This! This!' she spluttered finally, stabbing her finger at the report card.

Debu nodded his head mournfully.

'This result! In class nine?' she said. 'Board Exam? What will happen?'

'I'll do better next time, Ma,' Debu said. 'I promise.'

'How will you do better? Drinking, partying, going out with girls?'

Debu kept quiet. There was no point in trying to defend himself. That would make her even more angry, which could lead to the immediate suspension of the few remaining human rights he still had—like the right to independent movement. She might even decide to personally drop and pick him up from school. Besides, there was the all-important matter of attending Audrey's birthday party. Unless he managed to get his mother to drop her guard, all his plans would come to naught.

Debu decided that the wisest course of action was to be on his best behaviour, hunkering down until the storm had passed. During the next few days, he tried to do everything to get back into his mother's good books. Like the three wise monkeys of folklore, he closed his eyes, ears, mouth and mind to all the good things of life. He watched no TV, heard no radio and opened his mouth only to memorize his lessons aloud. He did not even utter a word of protest when his cricket sessions were sacrificed at the altar of Mr Lahiri's Rabindra Sangeet lessons. Every other evening, Mr Lahiri would arrive home and squat on the sofa, sipping on his tea while Debu sat on the carpet below, gamely pumping the bellows of his new harmonium and singing lustily, if not quite tunefully. But try as he might, Debu found it difficult to not feel sleepy under Mr Lahiri's tutelage. He soon discovered that he could grab quick catnaps during Mr Lahiri's demonstrations—closing his eyes and swaying to the beat, looking like he was lost in the music.

Like everything else, Mrs Dutta was keeping a strict watch on her son's musical progress.

'How is he doing?' she would ask Mr Lahiri at the end of every class.

'Not bad,' Mr Lahiri would say, as he helped himself to the last of the complimentary biscuits. 'He lacks sur. But his taal gyaan is excellent. Whenever I sing, he sways to the rhythm.'

* * *

In this stifling atmosphere, Professor Bose's tuitions were like a breath of fresh air—for here he could meet Clint. There was of course, the occasional twinge of worry, ever since Chakraborty's warning that Clint was connected in some way with the USF. But he brushed it aside, for Clint's very presence could lift Debu's mood in a way that none of his other friends could. Perhaps it was because he was so different from everyone else—a free spirit seemingly unburdened by the pressures crushing everyone else around him. Studies, exams, careers, curfews, parents—nothing seemed to bother him.

'I wish I could be more like you,' Debu said to him one day during a break in their tuition class. Professor Bose had stepped out for his drink.

'What do you mean?' asked Clint.

'I mean you are so cool. I've never seen you worried or upset about anything.'

Clint shrugged and lit up a cigarette. 'Yeah, I take things easy. Don't sweat the small stuff—that's my motto.'

'In my house there's no small stuff. Everything's a big deal.'

'You having trouble at home?'

'Yeah. My mother is really pissed with me.'

A wry smile appeared on Clint's lips. 'Really? What for?'

'Oh, the usual things. Mostly studies,' Debu said. He didn't want to talk about the Audrey episode at Melody House—in case Clint thought that he came from a really uncool family.

'I thought you were the topper types?' said Clint.

'I got screwed in the tests. And my mother went ballistic,' Debu explained.

There was a pause before Clint replied. 'Yeah, mothers can sometimes be like that,' he extended the cigarette to Debu. 'Here, want a quick drag before Bose comes back?'

Debu took a hesitant puff. He didn't like smoking but he figured it that might not be bad idea to practice it once in a while. It might help impress the girls, in case the opportunity came up at Audrey's upcoming party.

'What about you?' said Debu. 'Does your dad get mad at you when you screw up in your exams?'

'Yeah, I guess,' Clint replied.

'What do you mean—guess? Doesn't he tell you anything?' Debu asked.

'I've told you already. He just wants me to pass the damned Board Exams this year so that he can—' Clint came to an abrupt halt.

'He can what?'

'Nothing,' said Clint. His face had become blank, as if a mask had suddenly fallen over it.

Inside Debu's head, Chakraborty's voice whispered once again, his tongue flicking out the old forked warnings—goading him to believe that Clint was hiding something from him. 'Just shut up Debu and do some work, okay?' Clint snapped. 'You need to solve these stupid permutation-combination problems before Bose gets back.'

'You think I'm your personal slave or something?' Debu hissed back. 'You think I have nothing better to do than solve your stupid maths sums for you? You think you guys can just push us around just because—' Debu stopped himself.

'We guys? Meaning?' Clint asked, his eyes narrowing.

'Nothing,' Debu muttered. 'I don't like being pushed around—that's all. I answer all your bloody maths questions for you. But how come you don't answer anything I ask you. How come you never talk about your dad, your family?'

'There's nothing to talk about.'

'Your dad, what's he like?' Debu persisted.

'I've already told you, right? My dad's a businessman.'

'Yeah? What kind of business?'

'Timber.'

'But last time you told me limestone.'

'Yeah. We got a limestone business too. Listen, it's my dad's business, okay? Not mine. If you want to know so much about it, go and ask him,' Clint said irritably.

'Okay, last question. You got any brothers, sisters?' Debu asked. Audrey had already told him about a brother but today, he wanted to hear it from Clint.

'Yeah. Brothers in Arms. Dire Straits. Great album. You want to borrow it from me? I'll give it to you. Might stop you asking dumb questions.'

He had only wanted Clint to tell him the truth, to drown out Chakraborty's insidious whispers hissing inside his head. He wanted the old, simple days of their friendship back—days that hadn't been darkened by the shadow of fear and doubt. Debu was feeling betrayed by Clint's silences, his evasions, and maybe even his lies. And it made him more determined than ever to dig out the secrets that Clint was hiding from him.

'Clint, tell me—'

'What the fuck man!' Clint exclaimed. 'What's wrong with you today?'

'No, this is serious. I need to ask you this. I have to know.'

'All right, what is this terribly important thing that you have to know?'

Debu took a deep breath and said, 'Clint, are you with the USF?'

Clint went very still. He looked away from Debu, gazing at the smoke from the cigarette as it curled up into the air and hung between them like a grey fog. Ash lengthened at the end of the stick.

'What USF?' he said as he flicked his cigarette and took another drag.

'Oh come on,' said Debu. 'Don't pretend you don't know. I'm talking of the USF. The "Khasi by Blood, Indian by Accident" guys.'

'Yeah, what about them?'

'Are you on their side?'

'What does "being on their side" mean?'

'You agree with them? With what they say? What they do?'

Clint turned his gaze to the hills in the distance. 'Not everything. But a few things, maybe.'

'Really? So you think all Bengalis should be thrown out of Shillong?'

'I'm not saying that. And neither is the USF. They only want the illegal Bangladeshis, the foreigners to be thrown out.'

'So you think all those people who lost their lives and their homes in the '79 riots were illegal Bangladeshis?'

'Why are you raking up the past? What's the point? Many things happened then. Wrong things, bad things,' Clint's head sank to his chest. 'But whatever happened, happened eight years ago. It's over and done with. Why bring it up again now? We have to move on.'

'You think it's over and done with?' Debu returned. 'Do you know that only two months ago, three Khasi boys attacked me at Jacob's Ladder.'

'Really?'

'Yes, really. They threw stones at me, nearly broke my leg. If they had caught me then they might even have killed me.'

'Oh, come on. Stop exaggerating.'

'I'm not exaggerating. They were after me. They abused me, they called me names—Bangladeshi, foreigner, dkhar. Is that what your USF friends think of me, of my family—dkhars? Is that what *you* think of me?'

Clint rose to his feet and flicked the still glowing cigarette butt into Professor Bose's garden. 'Listen Debu, whatever happened in '79, whatever happened to you in Jacob's Ladder—it's wrong. It should never have happened. I'm sorry that it happened to you. But I had nothing to do with it. And you have no proof that the boys who attacked you at Jacob's Ladder were from the USF. That's just bullshit.'

Debu was feeling strange—on the one hand, it gave him a grim satisfaction to finally get under Clint's skin, that their usual guru-chela relationship had suddenly been reversed. But at the same time, there was a sense that he was crossing into forbidden territory.

'Don't try and avoid the question, Clint,' said Debu. 'I want to know what you think of the USF.'

'All right, Mr Debojit Dutta, since you are so interested, let me tell you what I think of them. I think that the USF is absolutely right in asking for more jobs and better opportunities for the tribals. It's our land after all, right? We have been here for centuries. It is our home.'

'But it is my home too!' Debu exclaimed. 'It is my home as much as it is yours. I was born here, my father was born here. And yet you people call us dkhars.'

'I never called you that and I don't think of you that way either. Of course, this is your home, as much as it is mine.'

'Oh yeah? Go tell that to your friends and see what they say. I can't understand how you can be friends with them and with me at the same time.'

'Because you are not like the others! Okay?'

'Not like who others?'

'Like the other Bengalis. You don't look down on me. You don't call me a dumb Khasi like they do.'

'Who does?'

Clint's face darkened. 'Who doesn't? Bose does it on my face. You've seen it for yourself. The other Bengali boys in my school do it behind my back all the time. They call me a dumb, good for nothing, lazy tribal. They think I don't know what they say about me. But I know. I know exactly what they think of me. It's the same with all you people. You're all the same.'

'And that makes it okay to kill such people, is it? People like me?'

Clint banged his fist on the table. 'Just shut up, will you Debu. Don't put words in my mouth. When did I ever say anything like that? Besides who the hell is killing anyone? Not me. It happened once in '79 and it shouldn't have happened like I keep saying.'

'But it could happen again.'

'Yes, it could. Unfortunately, you may be right. There are some bad guys among us, I know. I only—'

'You only what?'

'Oh, never mind! Can we stop this discussion now? I came here to do my frigging maths tuitions, not to talk bullshit politics with some dumb kid who doesn't understand anything anyway.'

'I'm not a kid. And you're too scared to discuss anything serious.'

'I'm not scared.'

'Yes you are.'

'Am not.'

'Are too.'

'Okay, man,' Clint raised his palms in surrender. 'I can't take this anymore. This conversation is just too bloody stupid. You and I are not going to solve anything by talking bull crap. So why don't we just solve what we can? Finish these goddamned maths problems for Bose and get the hell out of here. Okay?'

'Okay.'

'Great.'

'Yeah, great.'

They opened their books and turned to the problem that had been assigned to them by Professor Bose. It was from the chapter on Permutations and Combinations:

In how many unique ways can N biscuits be distributed among n beggars so that each beggar gets at least 1 biscuit? (Assume N > n)

It sounded a little bit like the problem that Shillong was facing, thought Debu. Too many beggars, too few biscuits. If some people weren't happy with their share of the spoils, then well...they might get pretty mad and start beating up the others, he concluded philosophically. A nudge from Clint interrupted his thoughts.

'Hey, I can't make head or tail of this stupid beggars and biscuits problem,' said Clint. 'You know how to do it?'

'No,' Debu replied curtly.

'Hey c'mon man. I know you can do it,' Clint said. 'Come on. Show it to me quickly before Bose comes back.'

Debu turned away. He did not feel like talking to Clint. Something had changed between them. There was an uneasiness that he could not quite put his finger on. Perhaps Clint was just using him, he thought. In any case, it was quite clear by now that there was something in what Chakraborty told him. If Clint had nothing to hide, he wouldn't have been so cagey. There was more to Clint than met the eye and it was probably wise to keep a distance from him.

'Hey, come on,' Clint said. 'Bose has been threatening to throw me out if I can't keep up.'

'Stop bugging me,' said Debu. 'Do it yourself for a change.'

'I would if I could. Hey, look I'm sorry. Okay?'

'Sorry for what?'

'For anything I said that may have hurt you. I don't really like everything that these USF guys are doing. But some of them are my friends. I've known them since I was a kid. And you have to be loyal to your friends, right?'

'Even when they do the wrong things?'

'Yeah. Sometimes even then. You gotta to stick to your friends no matter what. That's what friendship is all about, right?'

'Stop making it sound so grand. Friendship, my foot! I bet if I didn't do your maths for you, it would be ta-ta bye-bye to our friendship the next day.'

'And you stop pretending to be such a goody-goody. I bet if I didn't introduce you to Audrey, you wouldn't do my maths for me.'

Debu cheeks went red as a berry. 'Shut up,' he muttered.

'Oooh look, someone is very sensitive. You like her right?' Clint nudged him. 'Come on, admit it.'

'I don't.'

'You do too,' Clint gave him a knowing wink.

'I don't.'

Clint shrugged his shoulders. 'Okay, cool. Guess you don't want to see the card she sent for you then?'

'What card! Where? Give it to me!' Debu exclaimed.

'Calm down, calm down. I thought you just said you didn't like her.'

'I don't. I mean I do…but not in the way that you are saying.'

'And what way is that?' Clint gave him a crooked smile.

'Oh, quit joking. Where's my card?'

'Right here in my bag,' Clint drew a square blue envelope from his bag and waved it in front of Debu's nose. 'Here it is. But I guess I'll just return it to her.'

Debu tried to snatch the envelope but Clint whisked it out of reach.

'Just give it to me, okay? She sent it for me,' Debu said.

'I might,' Clint grinned. 'If you let me copy the answer first.'

Debu glared at him. He finished solving the problem in record time and said, 'Here, it's done. You can copy it. Now give me the card.'

'That's like a good boy. See? Give and take—that's what it's all about,' Clint handed over the envelope and started copying the answer in his notebook.

Debu opened the envelope. Inside it was a classy looking note paper that had an elegant floral design along the edges. Heart hammering against his ribs, Debu unfolded the paper and read the brief message that had been written on it in clear, flowing letters. It said:

Dear Dabboo,
I'm finally having my birthday party on 19th September, Saturday, and you are cordially invited. It's at my house and starts at 6 PM. Come with your harmonium. We all want to hear you sing. You have to come. No excuses!
Yours affly,
Audrey

PS: Here's my house address:
Audrey Pariat
C/O Neil Pariat
Rose Cottage,
Nongrim Hills,
Near Post Office
PPS: It would be best for you to come with Clint. He's been here before and I think it would also be safer if you came with him, given the way things are these days.

Debu read it several times, the grin on his face widening with each reading. The personal handwritten invitation itself was enough to send him over the moon, and her concern for his safety was the icing on the cake.

'If your mouth opens any wider, it'll hit the floor,' Clint drawled.

'Sorry,' said Debu and tried to collect himself. 'Any idea what does affly mean by the way?'

'I think it means affectionately. So, I'm guessing you've been invited to THE party,' said Clint.

'Yes,' said Debu.

'Cool. And I also take it that you will be coming?'

'Yes, yes. Of course, I'm coming,' Debu said. He had no idea how he would go to Nongrim Hills at six in the evening when he had strict instructions to be back home by five o'clock at the latest. All he knew was that wild horses couldn't stop him from going. 'She suggests I go with you. Is that okay with you?'

'It's okay with me. The question is whether it's okay with you?'

'What do you mean?'

'You sure you want to come with a big, bad USF fellow like me? That too to a place like Nongrim Hills. Aren't you scared you won't come back in one piece?'

'Hey, come on Clint. I didn't mean it that way okay? I'm sorry if I said anything that hurt you.'

'Yeah sure. Now that you need my help to go to Audrey's party, you're sorry huh?'

'No really. I know you're not like that. I didn't mean—'

'It's okay. I know you didn't. I was just pulling your leg. Anyway, you're just a kid. What does it matter what you say?'

'Hey, I'm not a kid—'

'Okay, okay never mind. Now, let's get back to the party. We are meeting here next Saturday anyway. We can leave for the party after tuitions. But it won't get over until eight, nine o'clock. I'll see if I can drop you up to Police Bazar, but it'll be late when you get back home. You'll be able to manage your parents, right?'

'Yep, sure,' Debu said with a confidence that he did not feel. But there was still a week to go and he was hopeful that he would find some way of managing the parent problem by then.

Meanwhile, there were other problems to be solved—of a more mathematical nature. But Debu was in inspired form and he disposed of them with ease. Pleased with Debu's elegant distribution of biscuits amongst beggars and other such exotica, Professor Bose left them early for the day.

*   *   *

There was a spring in Debu's step as he walked back home that evening. Audrey's letter nestled reassuringly in his breastpocket like a talisman against the slings and arrows of the outrageous music teachers and outraged mothers that had become the leitmotif of his life. He took out the letter, smoothened it carefully and read it once more. The part about bringing his harmonium and singing was a little worrying...but he brushed it off (surely, she was joking). What was important were the clear instructions at the end: *You have to come. No excuses!*

The coolest girl in Shillong had personally invited him to her party—with a handwritten letter, on a special, thick notepaper that had pink and purple flowers drawn on it. Well...printed at least, if not drawn. A very special invitation, for a very special party, to which, no doubt, only very special people had been invited. Debu beamed at the very thought. It was a red-letter day, a watershed event, a historic moment—one that called for a celebration. He rummaged through his pocket—it contained a five-rupee note that had seen happier days, and a few coins. He counted them. There were eleven rupees in all—not enough for a half plate of chowmein at Kalsang, he thought regretfully. However, eleven rupees would certainly buy him a samosa at Delhi Mishtan Bhandar in Police Bazar. Maybe even a piece of jalebi. His mouth watered at the thought of the jalebis frying inside the huge iron vat that stood at the entrance of the restaurant—tangled loops of flour and besan, bobbing up and down in a sea of boiling oil, turning swiftly from soft white to a crispy, golden brown.

He wished he could have taken the bus from Laitumkhrah to Police Bazar. But that would deplete his already meagre funds. Squaring his shoulders, he decided to walk it. Ever since the episode at Jacob's Ladder, he had started avoiding shortcuts and lonely by-lanes, sticking to the main roads even though this had considerably increased his journey time. He walked down Don Bosco Square, acknowledging the patron saint of juvenile delinquents with a nod of his head, then past the Cathedral Catholic Church that towered over the intersection of Dhankheti and Laitumkhrah. He walked in the shadows of its looming turrets, their magnificent stained-glass windows caught in the warm yellow light of a thousand slanting sunbeams.

A few minutes later he had crossed Dhankheti and was at the borders of Malki. He felt a little yaw in his stomach—for this was one of those places where bad things happened to good Bengali boys.

He half walked, half ran down the main street, not knowing whether to be relieved or worried that the streets looked unnaturally empty for that time of the day. Presently, he arrived at the edge of Malki Bazar, from where a short

walk would bring him to the relatively safe neighbourhood
of Lady Hydari Park. He walked past the bazar as fast as he
could, when a thunderous roar from behind chilled him to
the bone. He turned around fearfully in the direction of the
noise, fully expecting to see a furious mob charging at him,
when he realized that the roar had come from the Malki
football grounds—a flat expanse of green that stood several
feet below the main road.

A game was in progress and a goal had just been scored—
the cause of the uproar that had rattled him. The sidelines
of the football field were packed with men in tartan shawls,
jackets and caps cheering and hooting loudly. No wonder the
streets were empty, thought Debu in relief, as he hastened
away from Malki towards Lady Hydari Park. Before long,
he had passed by the park. He veered right to arrive at the
State Central Library—a sprawling, double-storied building
that housed a large, eclectic collection of books and the most
comfortable sofas that Debu had ever sat on.

He felt calmer now. State Central Library was in no man's
land, neutral territory that stood in between the badlands
of Malki and the non-tribal strongholds of Jail Road and
Police Bazar. A bottle-green battle tank from World War II
stood incongruously inside the library grounds, surveying the
surroundings like a peacekeeping mission from the United
Nations. In spite of its great age and dilapidated condition,
the turret of the tank could still be rotated by means of a
steering-wheel-like contraption that was located inside the
hull of the tank. Debu wondered for a moment, whether he
should climb inside the tank, as he often did in his younger
days, and rotate the turret in the opposite direction. He didn't
like the way the tank's gun was pointing towards Jail Road.

But time was short and he was feeling hungry. The war
games could wait. He pressed forward and stopped only
after he had arrived at Delhi Mishtan Bhandar, where the
fragrance of hot jalebis swam out into the street, attracting

hungry passersby like flies to a honey pot. The potbellied cashier gave Debu a dirty look when he placed his order for one jalebi and one samosa. The minimum order for jalebis was one plate, he informed Debu, and it cost twelve rupees. So much for celebrations, thought Debu, as he bought a samosa for six rupees and left. He stood on the roadside eating it, as he took in the sights and sounds of Police Bazar—people jostling at the newspaper stalls to buy a day-old copy of *The Telegraph* that had just arrived by airmail from Calcutta; street-side kwai and fruit-sellers in their spotlessly clean jainsems, expertly slicing through betel nuts with their razor-sharp knives; middle-aged clerks, mufflered and monkey-capped against the evening chill, hurrying back home, the tail of a fish peeking out of their jute shopping bags; pretty tribal girls, stylishly attired in matching scarves and jackets, their svelte figures singing in their body-hugging jeans, laughing and chattering as they strode confidently through the milling crowd; harried sari-clad Bengali women flapping in their hawaii chappals on their way to Bangalakshmi Stores for the month's provisions, while the men hung around chewing kwai and solving the problem of world hunger.

Debu finished his samosa and rounded off the celebrations with two rupees' worth of sour berries which he bought from an old lady. 'Khublei shibun, kong,' he thanked her, watching the laugh-lines deepen on her weather-beaten face, as she flashed him a toothless smile in return.

God's in his heaven, all's right with the world, he thought as he headed home.

* * *

His mother was standing at the front door. The moment she saw him she rushed forward to enfold him in a tight embrace. Debu's heart sank. It was extremely rare for his mother to display her affection with such fervour. He couldn't remember the last time she had given him even a pat on the back. Something terrible must have happened, he thought, as she ran her fingers through his hair, mumbling incoherently.

'What's happened, Ma?' Debu said after he had managed to free himself of her grasp.

'Thank god! Oh, thank god you are back home!' she said through muffled sobs. 'I was so worried for you, Debu.'

'What's happened, Ma?' Debu said. Had his worst fears come true? 'Is Baba...' he stopped, unable to say any more.

She read his unsaid thoughts. 'No, your father is safe. Thank god for that,' Mrs Dutta joined her palms in a namaskar and touched her forehead. 'It's Mr Lahiri. He was beaten up badly this evening. They attacked him in Sweeper's Colony in Iewheh.'

'Sweeper's Colony? That's not too far from Baba's shop. Where is he now?' Debu asked.

'Roberts Hospital,' Mrs Dutta replied. 'Some kind-hearted taxi driver found him lying unconscious on the road and took him to the hospital. Your father's visiting card was discovered in his wallet and they informed him. He came back home to tell me that he was going to the hospital and that he would be late getting back. Then he rushed off, without even eating anything. Mr Lahiri is in a critical condition, I believe.'

'He won't die, will he?' asked Debu. He was feeling awful. Even in their last class, he had dozed off right in front of Mr Lahiri. It was true that he was a really boring teacher, but he wasn't a bad sort. Debu wished now that he had been more respectful towards the man. He made a quick promise to take his singing lessons with absolute seriousness from now on, if nothing happened to Mr Lahiri.

'We can only pray that he will come out of this all right. Poor man, all alone here in Shillong,' there was a catch in his mother's voice. 'No friends, no family. And such a gentle soul he was too, wrapped up in his music and poetry,' his mother continued. 'Why did this have to happen to him of all people?'

LAND OF THE LOTOS EATERS

IT TURNED OUT that earlier that evening, a violent mob had attacked Sweeper's Colony—a slum in Iewheh that was home to a large number of destitute Sikh sweepers, sanitation workers and their families. For decades, these people had kept Shillong clean. But on that evening, they were victims of a vicious pogrom. As was Mr Lahiri. As luck would have it, he was doing his rounds of the medicine shops in Iewheh market when the attack on Sweeper's Colony had taken place. Mr Lahiri was caught in the turmoil.

'Who knows what would have happened if your father had been there?' Mrs Dutta said. 'I know he sometimes passes by Sweeper's Colony on his way to the shop. Thank god, nothing happened to him.'

'But why isn't he home yet?' asked Debu. 'It's almost ten o'clock.'

'He must be in the hospital still,' his mother said. 'These things take time.'

'What things?'

'Doctors, police, hospitalization procedures—there are so many things. I don't think Mr Lahiri knew too many people in Shillong apart from us. There may be no else besides your father to help out.'

'Can't we go to the hospital and see what's going on?'

'Don't be silly, Debu. Roberts Hospital is in Jaiaw. It's not safe to go there, especially not today. The city is on the boil after what happened at Sweeper's Colony.'

'But then, it's not safe for Baba to be there either. Why did you let him go?'

'I told him not to. But does he ever listen to me?' Mrs Dutta sighed. 'You know what he's like. Always rushing off to help people in trouble. He's always been like that,' she said with a resigned smile. 'Are you worried about him?'

Debu nodded. 'Yes, a little,' he said.

'Don't worry,' Mrs Dutta said. 'He knows Shillong like the back of his hand. Nothing will happen to him. Come—it's late, we should eat something.'

They sat down for dinner but neither had any appetite, picking desultorily at their plates. Their gaze kept returning to the clock as the minute hand advanced inexorably along the circular dial. Tick-tock, tick-tock, it went, shattering the dead silence of the night with the metronomic explosions of a machine-gun in slow motion.

Dinner ended, but there was still no sign of Mr Dutta. It was becoming unbearable to stay inside the house anymore. Debu and his mother went out into the garden and continued their vigil—ears primed for the slightest sound that might signal his return.

Mrs Dutta pulled Debu close to her and laid his head on her lap. She stroked his hair gently and said, 'Don't worry, he'll come back. He'll come back any moment now.' There was a tenderness in her voice that Debu had never heard before. He felt a prickling sensation in his eyes. He knew what was coming next: clamping his teeth over his lower lip and pressing down hard, he willed himself not to cry. But as the minutes ticked by, it became too much to bear and presently, a whimper broke out of him.

'Don't cry, don't cry,' his mother said gently. 'He'll come back, he'll come back home.'

He buried himself in her lap—once more a little boy afraid of the dark. Mother and son clung to each other as they waited under the stars.

* * *

It was nearly midnight when Mr Dutta returned home. He looked like an old man, his grey face scarred by a patchwork of lines cutting deep rivulets across it.

'You're back,' Mrs Dutta whispered, as if she couldn't

believe that it was indeed him. She took his hand in hers and pressed it against her face. He gave it a gentle squeeze. In all his fourteen years of existence, Debu had never seen his parents so much as even touch each other. This unprecedented display of affection embarrassed him, and he looked away in the other direction.

'Angry with me, Debu?' his father asked affectionately.

'Why wouldn't he be? Going off like that all by yourself to Jaiaw!' his mother said, back to her old waspishness. 'You don't know how worried we were. What if something had happened to you?'

'I had no choice. Someone had to go there,' he hobbled inside the house and sank into a chair, as if his legs would crumple under him.

'Are you okay?' Mrs Dutta asked. 'You look ill. Why didn't you see a doctor yourself while you were in the hospital?'

'I'm fine. Just a little tired,' said Mr Dutta.

'And Mr Lahiri?' Mrs Dutta asked.

Mr Dutta shook his head. 'By the time he was brought to the hospital he was already dead,' he said. A gasp escaped Mrs Dutta. 'He had no chance. His skull had cracked open. There was massive bleeding. The doctors are guessing that he was struck on the head with some heavy object—probably a shovel or a spade or something like that. He must have died on the spot.'

'Poor man, poor man,' Mrs Dutta said. 'And so young too. I can't imagine what his family must be going through. Have they been told?'

'Yes, the hospital made a trunk call to Mr Lahiri's uncle in Calcutta. It took a long time to get the line but they could finally manage to get through. I believe he has two old parents and a younger sister who's still in school. He was the breadwinner of the family. I don't know what they will do, now that he is...' Mr Dutta stopped and lit up a cigarette. 'He was a good man. What wrong had he done? He came all the way from Calcutta to make a living for himself and his family. He would have gone back in two years after completing his posting here. He was our guest. But we couldn't take care of him.'

'What about the police? Did they come? Did they say they will take action against…against these murderers?'

Mr Dutta gave a wry smile. 'Yes, a sub-inspector came and asked a few questions. But you know how it is. We can't expect the police to do anything,' he blew out a cloud of smoke. 'Why did he have to die? Why did those poor sweepers have to die? What harm had they ever done to anyone? What will happen to all their families now?'

'And what about us? Have you thought of what will happen to us?'

'I don't know. I don't know anymore. I never thought that things would go so far.'

'And I always told you that they would.'

'Yes, you were right.'

'Then you should listen to me from now on.'

'Yes, I suppose I will have to,' Mr Dutta's head sank to his chest and he slumped deep inside the chair, as if overcome by a great weariness. 'From now on, I will listen to whatever you say.'

* * *

But by the following morning, Mr Dutta had forgotten his promise. Debu woke up to the din of his parents quarrelling with each other at the top of their voices. He was used to his mother yelling, but it was disturbing to hear his mild-mannered father shouting back at her. He hardly ever raised his voice.

Debu went down to the dining room and sat quietly in the corner. His parents were too busy arguing to notice him. An eerie feeling passed through Debu as he watched his father. He seemed to have changed overnight. It was as if a switch had been flicked inside his head. Gone was the gentle, soft-spoken man that he had always known and, in his place, there was a loud, angry stranger.

'I am telling you we have no other choice left,' Mr Dutta thumped a fist on the dining table. 'We have to fight back. Otherwise we will be finished.'

'And I am telling you that it is foolish to even think of fighting them. We are too few, too weak. You are being even more stupid than usual,' Debu's mother was slicing potatoes as if she had a personal grudge against them. 'I can't understand what's wrong with you! All these years you kept on saying that nothing would happen to us. When the gulmaal happened in '79 you said that it was an aberration, that your precious Shillong was safe. You said that the Khasis were your friends... and now suddenly you want to fight them?'

'They are still my friends—some of them, at least. But the people who attacked Sweeper's Colony killed innocent people like Lahiri, they cannot be anyone's friends.'

'Worse things happened in '79. But that time you didn't say such things.'

'I was hopeful then. I sincerely thought that whatever had happened was a one-off incident. Maybe it was because I was younger. Or stupider. Or maybe because I didn't see anyone die with my own eyes. But Lahiri's death—I can't get over it,' Mr Dutta's face creased in anguish. He turned his gaze to the window and looked out.

'Do you know Lahiri was on the way to the pharmacy when he was attacked?' Mr Dutta said after a while, as if talking to himself. 'I had run out of stocks of Becosule capsules and a few other medicines. I told him to come to the shop in the evening to take fresh orders. Who knows, if I hadn't—'

'It's not your fault,' Mrs Dutta cut in. 'Stop blaming yourself. It's no one's fault except the people who killed him.'

'No, it's my fault as well. He was new to this place. I should have warned him to be more careful when moving around in a place like Iewheh. But I didn't do anything. I kept quiet. Who knows why? Maybe because I never faced a problem myself. Maybe because I was too proud of my Shillong to admit to a Calcuttan that things were bad here.'

'You are blaming yourself for no reason,' Mrs Dutta said. She poured him a cup of tea. 'Here, have this. You need it.'

Mr Dutta added a spoon of sugar to the cup and stirred it absently. 'This may be only the beginning. Things will start going from bad to worse now. I hear things, I see things that I didn't earlier. I can feel the hate stirring, rising. Like it did in '79. But this time, it will be different. Last time, it was spontaneous. This time it will be more organized, it will go on for longer, it will cut deeper.'

'What will we do now?' Mrs Dutta asked.

'I told you. We will have to fight back.'

'Again this talk of fighting? You *have* gone mad,' Mrs Dutta retorted. 'We are a tiny minority in this place. They outnumber us ten to one. How can we even think of fighting back?'

'I don't know how, but we will have to,' said Mr Dutta. 'It is a matter of our survival. All the non-tribals will have to unite as one—Bengalis, Nepalis, Biharis, Marwaris, Punjabis— everyone. We will have to organize ourselves better, work for the protection and safety of all non-tribals. We will approach the government, the police and demand our rights. We will form self-defense squads, we will patrol the streets at night to protect our families and our houses. All these days, we have been attacked. But now we will fight back.'

Mrs Dutta abandoned her potatoes and grabbed her husband's shoulders with both hands. 'Stop it, please!' she shook him vigorously, as if drying out a towel. 'What has got into you today? You are behaving extremely strangely. This is just loose talk! It's dangerous talk. Word gets around in this place. If they hear what you are saying, they'll be after you.'

'But it is the only way out. The non-tribals have never organized as one. United we stand, divided we fall. If they see that we are united, then they will be forced to listen to us.'

'Just listen to you talk! As if you are some big neta. I am telling you—no one will listen to you and your long speeches. Why should they? You are just a—'

Mr Dutta went very still. 'Go on,' he said. 'Why did you stop? I am just a—what?'

'Nothing,' Mrs Dutta returned to the kitchen and placed a frying pan on the gas stove. 'I can't stand here talking with you the whole day. I need to finish my cooking.'

'No, no, say what you wanted to say,' Mr Dutta steepled his fingers and fixed his gaze on her. She looked away. 'I am just a small-time shopkeeper, right? Isn't that what you were going to say?'

'And so what if I did. Is it wrong?'

'No, you are right of course. I am a small-time shopkeeper. And perhaps you think that I am good for nothing else,' he retrieved a pack of cigarettes from his pocket and lit one.

To Debu's surprise, Mrs Dutta did not tick off his father for smoking in the kitchen. Instead, her voice was unusually soft as she said, 'I knew you were a shopkeeper when I married you. And to tell you the truth, it did matter to me at that time. I was young and foolish then and my head was full of silly dreams. Yes, it's true—I would have preferred my husband to be working in a government office and not running a medicine shop. But we have been married for twenty years. And it doesn't matter anymore now. I have no complaints against you. You have been a good husband to me, a good father to Debu. We have never wanted for anything.'

'But you still think I can't do anything because I am a shopkeeper?'

'Not because you are a shopkeeper but because you are not rich, you are not powerful and you are not crooked. Whatever else you may be, you will never be a neta. That much I can tell you. You are too straight and simple and this loose talk of fighting—it frightens me.'

'But that is what I keep telling you. If we fight alone then there is reason to be scared. But not if we fight together. There are so many of us. If we raise our voices together, then we might be able to do something. We sat back and watched quietly during the riots of '79. We should not make the same mistake again.'

'These are all day-dreams. You know very well that Bengalis are cowards. No one lifted a finger in '79. No one will lift a finger now. They will just sit back and watch.'

'All right, then what do you think we should do?'

'We should just leave this place and go.'

'Go where?'

'Calcutta. Where else?'

'Calcutta! Calcutta! Don't you get tired of singing the same old song again and again? I've told you so many times why we can't just leave everything and go to Calcutta! My business, Debu's school, our lives here—what will happen to them? Let me make something absolutely clear to you once and for all today—this is my home. I was born here. I have been living here for fifty years. I will fight if I have to but I will not go anywhere. I will stay here.'

'No, you will rot here and die. And take us all with you. Including your only son,' Mrs Dutta said.

'I don't want to talk about this anymore. I'm going out,' Mr Dutta got up to his feet.

'So go. Who's stopping you? But take this with you,' she thrust an umbrella at him. 'It's raining outside.'

Mr Dutta snatched it out of her hand and stormed out of the house.

* * *

It was evening when Mr Dutta returned home. In his hand was a longish package wrapped in a newspaper. Without looking up from the magazine she was reading, Mrs Dutta said, 'Wipe your shoes before you come in. I don't want mud all over the house. And keep the umbrella outside in the verandah. It must be dripping.'

Mr Dutta stuck out his tongue and smacked his forehead. 'Oh no! I forgot to bring it.'

Mrs Dutta set down her magazine and gave him a look. 'One more umbrella lost? It's the third one this month!' 'No, no I must have left behind somewhere. I'll get it back tomorrow.' Her lips curled up in disbelief. 'A likely story,' she said. Her gaze shifted to the object in his hand. 'What's that?' 'That's what I had gone out to buy. Lucky I found it,' Mr Dutta removed the newspaper wrapping and held it out. 'Hey Debu, take a look at this.' He held up a short leather scabbard which was curved at the centre. Mr Dutta grasped the hardwood handle protruding from the scabbard and unsheathed the blade.

'What is it?' Debu asked, fascinated by the way it glinted in the light.

'A khukri. It's the traditional weapon of the Gurkhas, who as you know, are the bravest soldiers in the whole world.'

'Why do you need it?' asked Debu.

'Because he thinks he is the bravest Bengali in Shillong,' his mother said. 'Your father is trying to become like Subhash Bose. He's building his own army—a one-man army.'

'There's no need to be so sarcastic. I bought it so that I would have something to protect myself if I am attacked. I will keep it with me in the scooter.'

'So you think you can protect yourself with that knife when a mob attacks you?'

'It's better than nothing, right? What is wrong with you? I thought you would be pleased that I was being careful. But these days nothing I do seems to satisfy you.'

'Because you do nothing that I want. It's always what *you* want. It's always *your* way.'

'Because you only want the one thing which I cannot give. Calcutta! Calcutta! You sound like a stuck record.'

Debu walked out of the room and went to the garden. His parents were really getting on his nerves of late. All they did was quarrel and shout at each other. And it wasn't just them. Everyone seemed to be on edge these days—at school, on the roads, in the shops—like rubber bands stretched to the breaking point, ready to snap at the slightest touch.

It had stopped raining. A rainbow vaulted across the Umshyrpi stream and sank gently into the hills in the distance. He watched two dragonflies chase each other through the clean air, until they settled upon a clump of yellow and blue gladioli in full bloom. Their gossamer wings shimmered with the colours of the rainbow. A clear puddle of rainwater had collected at the foot of a gardenia bush. Debu tossed a pebble into it, the tiny plop drowned out by the angry voices of his parents inside.

He wondered if there were any dragonflies in Calcutta and whether rainbows danced upon their wings.

* * *

The khukri was only the start of Mr Dutta's newly-acquired obsession with self-defense. Over the next few days, several other safety measures were put in place. Debu and his mother were given plastic pouches containing chilli powder, which they were to carry with them whenever they went out. It was to be used only as a last resort. In case of an attack, Mr Dutta said, the first thing to do was to run. If that was not possible for some reason, then they were to pretend to be Assamese. Lessons were conducted for Debu and his mother so that they could speak basic Assamese and, most importantly, know how to count from one to ten. Having completed the essentials, Mr Dutta moved on to his next project—the construction of a makeshift armoury in the bedroom. One morning he came back home with a number of shovels and iron rods.

Mrs Dutta watched in astonishment as he placed them in a neat pile inside the bedroom and kneeled down in front of the bed. 'Are you going to put these shovels and spades under the bed now?' she exclaimed.

'Yes,' replied Mr Dutta.

'What for? To dig our own graves?'

'For our safety obviously. Haven't you heard the news? It's all over town.'

'What news?'

'The USF has called for a series of blackouts starting from tonight,' Mr Dutta replied.

Blackouts were the latest in USF's arsenal of protest. They had started issuing diktats that all houses in Shillong were to switch off all their lights from seven to ten at night in protest against the unabated influx of foreigners into Meghalaya. Any non-tribal house that wasn't pitch dark during the duration of the blackout ran the risk of being attacked. This usually involved stone-pelting, accompanied by loud threats to burn down any house that did not observe the blackout. But things soon started getting more dangerous.

A few days later, Mr Dutta returned home one evening and said, 'Things are going from bad to worse. Last night they were shooting arrows from Wahingdoh at the houses in Lower Jail Road because some people had lit candles inside.'

'Arrows? Really? That's so cool! Can I see one?' Debu said.

Mrs Dutta gave him a sharp rap on the head and said, 'You think this is a joke? Those are real arrows, not toys. They can kill people,' she turned to Mr Dutta. 'They are firing arrows at Lower Jail Road? For lighting candles? The danger has come so close to our home?'

'Yes, unfortunately,' Mr Dutta said. 'Things have become really bad. Even Upper Jail Road cannot take its safety for granted anymore.'

The locality of Jail Road sat along the sides of a small hillock. The Duttas stayed in the upper reaches of the hillock, which had been imaginatively named Upper Jail Road. It was a non-tribal ghetto, widely regarded as the only safe haven for Bengalis in Shillong. But Lower Jail Road, which was at the foot of the hillock, was a different matter. It sat cheek by jowl with Wahingdoh, one of the hotbeds of the anti-tribal movement and so, became a natural target for attacks on non-tribals. Until now, the laws of projectile motion and the higher altitude of Upper Jail Road had protected its residents from the slings and arrows of their outraged neighbours.

'Why else do you think I got these things?' Mr Dutta pointed at the shovels and spades under the bed. 'And I'm not the only one. Other people are doing the same. The Dutta Guptas, the Dhar Choudhurys—everyone. A group of twenty young men will be keeping a neighbourhood watch every night, starting today. I'm hoping we will be safe. But in case there is an attack on the house, we will have to fight back with these,' he picked up a shovel.

'Even Debu and me?' his mother asked.

'If there is an attack then men will go out first,' Mr Dutta replied. 'You and Debu will stay inside the house. But if they come right up to our doorstep then...' he left the words hanging as Mrs Dutta drew a sharp breath, hugging Debu to herself.

The blackout began at seven o'clock sharp that evening. The lights went out on Jail Road and darkness swooped upon Shillong like a black fog, pierced only by the radiance of glow-worms bobbing in the wildflower bushes, and the long tail of the Milky Way vaulting across the sky. Not a soul stirred out of their homes. Families sat huddled over secret coal fires glowing orange and red behind drawn curtains, listening to the radio as it played out its muted music.

It felt like a real adventure to Debu—a Holmesian vigil in the dark that could explode into action at any moment. But to his mild disappointment, the evening went off without incident. At ten o'clock, the lights were switched on and a sigh of relief went up all over the neighbourhood. The following night ended peacefully as well. But on the third night, just before the blackout was about to end, a commotion sounded in the distance. Mr Dutta leaped to his feet and snuffed out the only candle that was burning in the house.

'Stay away from the windows. I'll take a quick look outside and be back,' he said and grasped a shovel.

'I won't let you go,' Mrs Dutta seized his hand. 'Let the others go. There are so many others, so many men who are younger than you.'

'They must be out there already,' Mr Dutta replied. 'I can't hide inside the house like this when they could be in danger. I have to go.' He tried to free himself from his wife's grip when suddenly, there was the sound of shattering glass. A large rock had come flying in through the living room window, scattering shards of broken glass across Mrs Dutta's lovingly polished wooden floor. The clamour of voices outside grew louder and angrier as a mob clambered up the flight of steps leading from Lower to Upper Jail Road. Foreigners go back, Bengali dogs leave our country, shouted the voices.

'Get down, get down!' Mrs Dutta hissed as she pulled Debu and his father to the floor. They lay prostrate, three trembling bodies huddled into one, while a fusillade of rocks rained on the tin roof above like giant hailstones. And then, as suddenly as it had started, the commotion diminished and came to a stop. There was a deathly silence, broken only by the singing of the cicadas outside and the laboured breath of Debu and his parents.

Mr Dutta crawled to the window and lifted a tiny corner of the curtain. He peered outside and said, 'Looks like they've finally gone. I think we can get up now.' He helped Mrs Dutta and Debu up on their feet. 'This time we got away with some broken windows. We might not be so lucky next time. We have to be better prepared.'

Mrs Dutta sank into a chair and said, 'If even Upper Jail Road is not safe, then which place is? Where will we go now?'

'There is nowhere to go. We will have to stay here and wait for the storm to pass,' said Mr Dutta.

* * *

The following morning, several agitated Bengali men congregated in the small field adjoining the Jail Road Boys' High School. The rumours flew thick and fast.

'They were firing arrows from Wahingdoh again last night. Three of them landed inside my house.'

'Forget arrows! A bunch of Khasi men barged into my house and threatened to throw us out if we didn't leave in three days. I don't know what I will do now.'

'Arre, poor Deb Choudhury's son was returning home in the middle of the blackout. The mob caught him and beat him black and blue. The poor boy somehow managed to escape, otherwise he would surely have been beaten to death.'

'Twenty Nepali families were thrown out of their houses yesterday.'

'I hear the Bihari doodhwalas are leaving Shillong. Their cows were slaughtered last night.'

'Ghosh Babu's shop in Mawprem was burnt down.'

Their frenzied chatter was interrupted by a loud voice. A public announcement blared from a police loudspeaker:

In view of the deteriorating law and order situation prevailing in Shillong, an indefinite curfew has been imposed within the city limits. It will commence at 10 A.M. and will continue until further notice. Any person found in a public place during curfew hours will be arrested.

The assembled men glanced anxiously at their watches. There was only half an hour left for the curfew to come into force. Their chief concern now shifted from the mayhem of the previous night to the more mundane question of whether there were sufficient provisions at home. The shops would shut down any moment now and reopen only when the curfew was lifted. But who knew how long that would be—twelve hours, twenty-four hours? In the meantime, babies would need their milk, the sick their medicines and everyone their food. The men bade each other hurried goodbyes and headed for Jail Road Bazar, mentally jotting down their shopping lists.

Curfews were soon to become a way of life in Shillong, the days falling into a familiar pattern. First would come the announcement on the public loudspeakers, followed shortly after by the rumble of shutters being dragged down the shop fronts, and the crowds scuttling back to the safety of their homes. Next, the blare of police sirens issued the final warning for people to clear out. And finally, like a shroud falling over a hearse, a dense silence settled over the empty streets.

Inside countless homes would begin the fearful vigil for a loved one who was late in returning, sometimes ending in a gasp of relief at the tread of a familiar footstep, and sometimes not. Families would huddle around the radio, one ear on the latest news, the other pricked up for that much-awaited announcement on the loudspeakers:

Curfew will be lifted for one hour between 0900 and 1000 hours. People are advised to complete purchases of all essential commodities only during this time. Any person found in a public place during curfew hours will be arrested.

As soon as the announcement ended, streams of people scurried out of their homes like rats to the Pied Piper's summons. The business of life would be squeezed into that single hour between curfews, while all work ground to a standstill during the remaining twenty-three—no school to drag oneself to, no college to be bunked, no office to be reluctantly attended, no business to be managed, no salaries to be earned, no profits to be turned. Only books and board games, radio by day and TV by night, some gardening and much gossip, food, drink and sleep. With no work to be done, the chief use of time became time-pass.

In an endless repetitive cycle, each night turned into another slothful, selfsame day and Shillong slowly turned into the land of the Lotos Eaters—inert, indolent and purposeless.

CITY OF GHOSTS

IN THE BEGINNING, Debu had no problems with the curfews. They meant that there was no school, no studies—only cricket, TV and comics. It was great fun for a while. But as the curfews dragged on without respite, things started looking less rosy. For one, he could no longer go to Professor Bose's tuition classes, which meant there was no more hanging around with Clint and no more exciting adventures. More importantly, there was no news of Audrey's birthday party. It was supposed to have been held long ago. He must have missed it, he concluded glumly. At moments like this, he wished his friends had phones, or at least knew each other's postal addresses so that they could keep in touch through letters. But unfortunately, they didn't, and he was completely cut off from Clint and Audrey. Of course, there were other boys of his age in the neighbourhood and he played cricket with them every day. But he didn't really enjoy their company. He had always found them pretty boring, and after meeting Clint and Audrey, he found them even duller.

The other problem was the food. Debu felt hungry all the time, and the long hours of playing cricket only made it worse. Unfortunately, the menu at home had taken a distinct downturn. One evening, when they had sat down for dinner, he took one look at his plate and grimaced, 'Dal and rice again! Ma I can't eat the same thing every day.'

'Keep quiet and eat,' Mrs Dutta said, ladling some more dal over his rice.

'But Ma, I just can't eat this anymore,' Debu protested. 'I hate it. I want to eat mutton.'

'Don't talk like that or I'll give you one tight slap,' Mrs Dutta glared at him. 'This is all we have. Your father can't afford anything else these days.'

'Ah, don't be so hard on him,' Mr Dutta said. 'He's a growing boy. It's only natural for him to feel hungry at this age,' he turned to Debu with a wan smile. 'I'm sorry, Debu. But as you know, I can keep the pharmacy open only for an hour every day. Sales have fallen badly. Where will I get the money to buy fish and meat? As it is, the prices are sky high because of these stupid curfews. But let me see if I can buy some mutton for you this Sunday.'

'Forget the mutton,' Mrs Dutta said. 'Think of your son's future. Have you seen his face recently? It's burnt black from playing cricket all day long. No school, no studies, no nothing! He's roaming around like a monkey without a tail. God only knows what will happen to him.'

Several more dinners of dal and rice came and went before the worst of the violence subsided. Daytime curfew was finally lifted and Shillong limped back to a semblance of normalcy. And for Debu, disappointingly, it was back to school. But he needn't have worried. For the Great Shutdown was just around the corner.

One fine day, the USF issued a diktat to all the schools and colleges in Shillong ordering them to shut down until their political demands had been met. The chief demand was for the passing of laws that would ensure the detection and deportation of all foreigners from the state of Meghalaya. Members of the USF set up pickets in front of educational institutes—teachers and students were warned against entering the premises. Most of them did not dare to risk the wrath of the USF and meekly fell in line. The few enthu-cutlets who retained their thirst for knowledge were dealt with—roughly. The principal of a prominent college who tried to keep it open was beaten up. As usual, the police stood by without lifting a finger.

It was the beginning of a very long forced holiday for the entire student population of Shillong—back to the glory days of uninterrupted cricket, comics and TV. This made

Debu very happy. Mrs Dutta of course, had the opposite reaction.

'Ma Kali! How much more suffering is there in store for us?' she wailed. 'Indefinite shutdown! Now my poor son won't even be able to pass out of school, let alone get a job! Can't you do something about it!' she confronted her husband.

Mr Dutta spread his arms in helplessness. 'What can anyone do except wait and watch? Right now, the USF is too powerful. Many of the politicians are in their pockets. No one will dare oppose them.'

'But do you realize that Debu's Board Exams are only eighteen months away?' said Mrs Dutta. 'How will he pass out if school is shut down? How can you simply wait and watch?'

'Don't worry Ma, I'll manage somehow,' Debu said.

'Manage what? A marksheet full of rosogollas?' Mrs Dutta snapped. 'And that too if your Board Exams are held in the first place.'

'Will you stop scolding him for something that is not his fault? What can he do about it? He is just a boy. You should stop scaring him like this,' said Mr Dutta.

'I am so tired of both of you,' Mrs Dutta said. 'Sometimes it feels like I am talking to a pair of walls. Don't you realize how serious this is? Don't you understand that if the schools don't reopen soon they will declare it a zero year? And if that happens, Debu won't be allowed to sit for his Board Exams. He will lose a whole year, maybe two.'

'Yes, but the schools might also reopen anytime soon. How long can this go on?' Mr Dutta said.

Two months later, the schools had still not reopened. One Sunday morning, as he sat in the verandah reading the newspaper, Mrs Dutta confronted him again.

'Sometimes I wonder whether you care more about the stupid news or your son's future,' Mrs Dutta said.

'Hmmm,' Mr Dutta mumbled, his attention fixed firmly on the newspaper.

Mrs Dutta snatched it away from him and said, 'At least pretend to be interested when I talk to you. This is about Debu, your only son.'

Debu was in the garden, watching a plump caterpillar with orange and black spikes, nibbling away at the tender green leaves of a hibiscus plant. At the mention of his name, he perked up his ears.

'What about Debu?' Mr Dutta said wearily.

'Tomorrow will be the ninth week Debu won't be able to go to school,' Mrs Dutta said. 'What are you going to do about it?'

Mr Dutta shrugged. 'What do you want me to do? Start a school of my own?'

'Stop being sarcastic. Don't pretend you don't know what the solution is. We have already talked about it.'

Debu left the caterpillar to its own devices and joined his parents. 'What solution? What are you talking about?' asked Debu.

'What else but the solution to all our problems?' Mr Dutta replied with a brittle smile. 'Calcutta. Your mother thinks it's time to seriously start thinking of shifting to Calcutta.'

'But I thought you said that you couldn't leave your business and everything else and move to Calcutta?' Debu asked.

'That's correct. All of us can't go to Calcutta. It's not practical,' Mr Dutta said.

'Then what?' Debu asked.

'But you can,' replied Mr Dutta.

'Yes Debu. Your father and I are thinking of sending you to Calcutta to study there,' Mrs Dutta said.

Debu's bowels turned to water as the meaning of her words sank in. 'Send me to...and what about you and Baba?' he asked.

'We can't leave this place right now,' Mrs Dutta replied. 'Although that would be the best thing to do. But your father has to run his business here, otherwise we won't have any income. So unfortunately, we have no choice other than sending you to Calcutta on your own.'

'No! How can you even think of that?' Debu exclaimed. 'How can I go there all alone? I want to stay here in Shillong with all of you. I want to stay in my school, with my friends. I won't go to Calcutta. Never. You can't force me to go there.'

'Listen Debu,' Mrs Dutta said gently. 'Your father and I have been discussing this for a while now. And it hasn't been an easy decision for us. But the way things are going in this place, you may not be able to complete your school in time if you continue to stay here. You are in the middle of class nine now. Your board exams are coming up soon. This is the most crucial stage of your life. God only knows how long the schools and colleges will remain shut. It has been two months already and there is no sign of re-opening.'

'No! I won't go!' Debu shouted. He blinked hard to push back the tears threatening to burst out any moment. 'How can I leave you and Baba and my friends and my school and everything and just go away to Calcutta?'

'But how long can you afford to stay on here like this, Debu? Bandhs, curfews, school shutdowns, blackouts, people being killed, being thrown out of their homes. How long can things go on this way?'

'But things are still going on!' Debu screamed. 'People are still living here. Everyone is not running off to Calcutta.'

'People who have a choice have already left. Only those who don't have anywhere to go to are still hanging on here.'

'And where do I have to go to in Calcutta?' asked Debu.

'Why, your Phool Pishima's house, of course,' Mrs Dutta replied.

'I spoke to her some days back,' Mr Dutta said. 'She has agreed to let you stay in her house if you get admission into a school in Calcutta.'

'No, I won't go there. I will never go there. I hate it. I hate it!' he was crying openly now.

'Do you think I would ever dream of sending you away from home if there was any other way?' Mrs Dutta pulled Debu to herself and gently stroked his head.

He pushed her away. 'I will never go there! Do you hear me? Never! I hate you! I hate you all!' he screamed as he lurched down the cobbled garden pathway and ran out of the house.

'Debu come back!' Mrs Dutta cried.

Mr Dutta laid a hand on her shoulder. 'Leave him alone,' he said. 'He's upset. He needs some time to absorb this shock.'

'Poor boy,' she said. 'How I hate what I am doing to him. But what else can I do?' she looked up at her husband, her eyes glistening. 'Do you think I am cruel, a bad mother?'

Mr Dutta wrapped her hands in his and pressed gently. 'No, you are a very good mother. Much better than I am a father. You did the right thing to bring up the Calcutta topic. Things are going from bad to worse here. He needs to be mentally prepared in case he has to leave. We all have to be mentally prepared.'

'I don't know how I will stay in this house with Debu not being around. It's going to be so lonely, so empty.'

'Same here. But we'll cross that bridge when we come to it. The first thing is to find a decent school in Calcutta that will admit him in the middle of the academic year. It won't be easy, I'm sure. All sorts of strings will have to be pulled. I will ask Phool-di if she can help us. She is well connected.'

'I will pray for it to happen. Although it will kill me the day Debu goes away. So far from us and at such a young age too. He's still just a child,' her voice cracked. 'But it's better for him, better for us. Better to go than to live with this constant fear and uncertainty.'

Mr Dutta nodded. 'I never thought I would say this, but I have to agree with you. I will write to Phool-di today itself.'

* * *

The prospect of being deported to Phool Pishima's house in Calcutta petrified Debu. He didn't know what he was more scared of—the City of Dreadful Night or the Aunt of Dreadful Disposition. Few people in this world had been more inappropriately christened than Phool Pishima—there was nothing flower-like about her. Tall, reedy, a disapproving frown permanently etched on her brow, and piercing eyes that missed nothing—she had a way of making most adults, and all children, feel like they had done something wrong, even when they had done nothing. This was a result of long years spent as the principal of a prominent girls' convent school in Calcutta. The arduous task of moulding generations of unruly children into socially acceptable adults had resulted in a personality that was composed primarily of steel and ice.

Because of her imposing persona and equally impressive height, the extended Dutta clan was always looking up to Phool Pishima for advice on matters both great and small. This she provided with relish, for she had strong views on most things. She herself was a spinster with no children of her own. But when it came to other people's children, she had no hesitation in teaching them the same three principles by which she ran her school—Discipline, Discipline, and More Discipline. Recently, her counsel had resulted in one of Debu's cousins being packed off to a Sainik School somewhere in rural Bihar. The boy had been caught bunking classes to watch movies.

There were many such stories of Phool Pishima. Over the years, they became part of the family folklore. Debu had heard them and was in no doubt that his life would be finished if he was exiled to her house. One evening, he overheard snatches of a conversation between his parents, which only ratcheted up his fears.

'Phool-di has replied to my letter,' Mr Dutta was saying. 'She says that she will speak to the Principals of St Lawrence and St Joseph's soon about Debu's admission.'

'That's good news. I will pray for Debu,' Mrs Dutta said.

'But she also thinks that getting admission in the middle of the academic year may be difficult. We may have to wait until May–June next year for the new academic session to begin. But she will start trying right away.'

'May is not too far. Just a few months. Do you think we should tell Debu about this?'

'Better not. It will only make him more depressed. Besides, let's see if things become better here. If the schools reopen then maybe he can complete his class ten from Shillong and then shift to Calcutta for his eleven and twelve.'

Debu's heart sank. It looked increasingly likely that, sooner or later, he would be deported to Calcutta. It was only a matter of time. The one ray of hope was if the situation in Shillong improved. Until only a few days ago, he had welcomed the school shutdown. Now, he prayed fervently to Lord Shani to reopen them, pledging to sacrifice two years' pocket money for a grand puja—if he didn't have to go to Calcutta.

But this time, Shani Dev was less gullible. Things only went from bad to worse. The school shutdown continued, bandhs were called every other day, the demonstrations against foreigners intensified and incidents of violence became routine.

In an attempt to keep the peace, an old colonial law of the Indian Penal Code now began to be frequently invoked by the police—Section 144 of the CrPC, or 'CRP', as it was popularly called. Whenever there was a flare-up in the city, police jeeps would fan out into the streets, loudspeakers blaring: UNDER SECTION 144 OF THE CRPC, PUBLIC ASSEMBLY OF 4 OR MORE PEOPLE IS STRICTLY PROHIBITED.

Within a short time, 144 CRP became a part of everyone's lexicon. It signalled trouble—gulmaal. The mere mention of it could trigger a mass Pavlovian response amongst people, who would immediately drop whatever they were doing and scamper back to the safety of their homes.

Most of the Pavlovian pooches were non-tribal. The tribals, however, did not regard 144 CRP with any fear. In several areas of the city, it was a custom more honoured in the breach than observance. The mass closure of schools and colleges by the USF had resulted in an entire generation of young boys and men with plenty of time on their hands. Several of them freely roamed the streets in their localities and beyond, with scant regard for the strictures of 144 CRP.

A few among them took it upon themselves to prove the truth of Phool Pishima's favourite maxim: *An idle mind is the devil's workshop.* They reasoned that since college was closed and they were not learning anything, they might as well start earning something. And this was easily done. All they had to do was to periodically call upon a few non-tribal shopkeepers in their locality and threaten to beat them up—unless they coughed up some money.

It was a simple but effective business model. The investments were low (a knife, a chain perhaps, and a few rough-looking pals to gang up with) and the returns were excellent. Almost overnight, a whole new industry sprang up in town—extortion.

* * *

As with any sunrise industry, everyone wanted a piece of the action—the police, the politicians and an increasing number of militant groups who were gathering in the shadows. The new currency of the tribal agitation became money. The ranks of the extortionists swelled as their hunger for money grew. To satisfy their burgeoning greed, they pressed into action a new weapon—a piece of paper that went by the innocuous name of 'Trading License'.

The Trading License was a permit issued under state law, which had to be mandatorily obtained by any non-tribal wanting to run a business in Shillong. In the past, getting the license was little more than a simple formality. But now, the extortionists had realized that it was a potential goldmine. But to dig out the gold, they needed help from unusual quarters—the traditional Khasi village assembly, known as the Dorbar Shnong.

Historically, the chief duty of this centuries-old gram-panchayat-like institution had been to maintain peace and harmony in its locality. And for years, it had done just that. It was usually headed by a venerable gentleman of the neighborhood, who bore the honourific title of Rangbah Shnong or Headman. These headmen were more like kindly headmasters and their exertions were limited to rapping the odd mischief-monger on his knuckles. They had no real powers except one—the authority to recommend whether a Trading License could be issued to a non-tribal businessman, or not. In the earlier days, they usually did. But now, encouraged by the extortionists, several headmen did not recommend the trading licenses to non-tribal businessmen—unless a substantial sum of money was paid under the table. Refusal to pony up would lead to the cancellation of the license and curtains for the non-tribal's business.

The transformation from headman to godfather was smooth and swift. Soon, money began streaming out of the tills of non-tribal businessmen and flowing into the pockets of the extortionists who, more often than not, had the tacit support of the headmen. The extortionists roamed the streets like packs of wolves, and the wheels of their mint turned quietly and smoothly.

Mr Dutta had not been harassed by the Dorbar or the extortionists yet. But the Trading License for his medicine shop was due for renewal soon, and he feared the moment of its arrival. All around him, people were being forced to pay up exorbitant sums of money. Those who could afford to do so, managed to survive. Those who couldn't, had to shut shop and leave—never to return again.

The Trading License had become for Shillong what the Salt Tax had been to colonial India—a powerful weapon in the hands of the indigenous tribal population against the foreign invaders. But the extortionists were no Gandhis, and the path chosen by them was to end in Shillong's tragedy.

In shop after shop, the lights went out and the shutters came down. The usual flurry of busy shoppers was replaced by the shadowy figures of extortionists, flitting through the streets in search of fresh prey. Without the bustle of commerce, the ringing of school bells and the grumblings of disgruntled office-goers, an eerie silence descended upon the hills.

Shillong became a city of ghosts—the souls of its people crushed beneath the weight of a thousand blackouts, curfews and intimidations.

A MACHCHLI-VELLIAN MOVE

BUT AMONG THE ghosts, there still remained a few bold spirits who believed it was high time for the non-tribals to strike back. Most of them lived in the Bengali stronghold of Jail Road. They started holding secret meetings to decide upon a possible course of action. More often than not, they ended in more talk than action. But over a period of time, two different factions began to emerge with divergent views on the path forward—the Militants and the Moderates.

The Militants were fewer in number, mostly hot-headed young men full of sound and fury. They were of the view that the only form of defense was offense. The fight had to be taken right into the enemy camp, blood had to be revenged with blood. The most aggressive of them proposed frontal tactics. They wanted to form heavily armed vigilante squads, who would attack Khasi-dominated localities and strike the fear of God into them. Others, more cautious, advocated guerilla warfare. They suggested hit-and-run strategies such as beating up the odd Khasi on the streets and making a run for it.

The Moderates were more circumspect. They pointed out that the Bengalis were just a tiny island of non-tribals in the middle of a sea of hostile tribals—at the mercy of powerful waves that could sweep them into oblivion at any moment. And when that happened, there would be no one around to throw them life-jackets. By now, it was amply clear that the local politicians and police were indifferent, and even hostile to their welfare, while most of the bureaucrats and politicians in New Delhi were oblivious of their very existence—routinely confusing Shillong with Ceylon. They were in this war alone, their lives expendable, said the Moderates. The foolish misadventures proposed by the Militants were surefire recipes for disaster.

Like the founders of the Indian National Congress had done over a century ago, the Moderates advocated a prayer-and-petition strategy. The first and most critical thing, they said, was to end their isolation. They needed to draw national attention to their plight and intensify their appeal to the central authorities to step in and rescue them. Not everyone was pleased with such a genteel approach. It was not worthy of the sons of Subhash Bose and Aurobindo Ghosh, they muttered darkly. But in the end, it was the Moderates who prevailed.

A flurry of paperwork now commenced. Letters were written to the editors of national newspapers, and petitions sent to the Governor, President, Prime Minister and Home Minister. Signatures were collected, local newspaper reports of violence against non-tribals were collated and letters pleading the government of India to come to the aid of the non-tribals were dispatched. But the greatest hope of the Moderates rested upon the man who was once known as 'Sarboharar Neta' or Leader of Those Who Had Lost Everything—Jyoti Basu, the Chief Minister of West Bengal

They sincerely believed that if there was one person in the world who would understand their plight and have the power to do something about, it was Jyoti-babu. After all, he was just like them—the quintessential Bengali gentleman, a bhadrolok, highly educated (in London, no less) and fond of Rabindra Sangeet and Scotch. Besides, it was well known that Jyoti-babu and his comrades were deeply sympathetic to the causes of oppressed peoples from all over the world. Wasn't it his party who had stormed the streets of Calcutta, shouting the slogan: *Amaar naam, tomar naam, Vietnam, Vietnam* (Your name, my name, Vietnam, Vietnam)? Hadn't they protested against American atrocities by renaming Harrison Road the Ho Chi Minh Sarani—the road on which the US Consulate stood?

If the Communists of Bengal had such deep sympathies for the people of the Far East, then surely they would understand the agony of their own brethren in the Northeast. Appeals

for help were sent out and appointments were sought with
Jyoti-babu. A secret delegation of Moderates even managed
to land up in Writers' Building to meet the Great Helmsman
of Bengal. But to their chagrin, it turned out that Jyoti-babu
and his Communist comrades recognized only class and not
community. Saigon was closer to their hearts than Shillong. It
is not known what exactly Jyoti-babu said to the delegation
from Shillong. But it was short and presumably went along
the lines of *Sorry. Just parlam na* (Just can't do anything).

The Bengalis were now back to square one. The militant
voices grew strident once more but their schemes fizzled out
after a few incendiary speeches. The fact of the matter was
that no one was willing to beard the lion in his own den. In
the end, there was only one plan of action to which everyone
agreed—The Machch Moratorium.

A proposal was made for all Jail Road Bengalis to stop
buying fish from the Khasi fishmongers who came down to
Jail Road Bazar every evening. The idea was received with
great enthusiasm. It would hit the Khasis where it hurt most—
their livelihoods. It would be poetic justice for the denial
of Trading Licenses to the non-tribals. Best of all, it was a
risk-free plan—the fishmongers were the perfect soft target.
There were about twenty of them, all women. They were poor,
decent folks, too busy trying to make ends meet to have any
interest in politics. Boycotting these fishwives was much less
dangerous than trying to beat up the odd Khasi youth.

The Machch Moratorium Movement got off to a good
start. In an impressive act of collective willpower, the Bengalis
proudly strutted about the Jail Road fish market, ignoring
the pleas of the fishwives to buy their fish. It gave them great
pleasure to see the Khasis begging for help as they imperiously
swept past them without a second glance.

But no hilsa is without its bones, and no silver lining
without its cloud. As the days went by, the Bengali babu
began to realize the torment of a fish-less existence. Though

he endured this trauma bravely, compensated by the pleasure of revenge. Despite the unpleasant, hollow feeling inside their stomachs, the Bengalis of Jail Road felt as if they had rediscovered their long-lost spines. The men huddled in the street corners congratulating each other that, for the first time in many years, they had finally got the better of the Khasis.

But there were a few voices of dissent as well. Mr Dutta's was one of them. He had been an old-time customer of all the fishmongers (except two, who had tried palming him off with rotten fish once too often). He had known them for years and enjoyed the banter that accompanied the ritual of selecting and haggling over the day's catch. The fishmongers knew that he had a pharmacy and sought his medical advice for their ailments from time to time. And so, over the years, a companionable relationship had developed between them. Even at the height of the gulmaal, Mr Dutta could not think of them as the enemy, nor they him.

Mr Dutta had never been in favour of the Machch Moratorium. He had voiced his protest against it from the moment it had been first proposed. In his view, it was a cowardly attack on a bunch of impoverished, innocent villagers who were only trying to make a living. But on being overruled by the majority, he reluctantly agreed to join the boycott in the interest of Bengali unity. In any case, he thought, the moratorium would fizzle out in a few days and the fishmongers would not suffer too much. But days became weeks and soon, a month had gone by. The fish sellers were in real distress now. Their income had ground to a halt, their savings were being depleted fast and it was becoming difficult for them to even have two square meals a day. Mr Dutta was deeply anguished to see their plight.

By now, it was customary for the politically active Bengalis to meet every Sunday morning in the Jail Road Puja Mandap to take stock of the situation, and discuss matters of self-preservation. It was during one of these meetings that Mr Dutta decided to raise the issue of the fish boycott.

'It is over a month now that the boycott has been going on,' said Mr Dutta. 'I think we have made whatever point we wanted to make. These people are suffering. We should stop now.'

'Stop now?' retorted Mr Ghosh. He was Mr Dutta's next-door neighbour, a plump, swarthy man with thick lips that were always stained red with kwai. He owned a stationery shop in Anup Chand Lane and there were rumours that he had recently been threatened by the extortionists. 'Mr Dutta, for the first time we have these fellows by the balls and you are saying that we should let them go now?'

A chorus of voices rose in his support: 'The boycott must go on! No stopping. No surrender.'

'If we stop now, they will think we are weak.'

'We have to hit them where it hurts.'

'Well said! Screw the Khasi bastards!'

Mr Dutta waited for the clamour to subside and said, 'I am sorry, but I can't agree with you. These people have been coming here to Jail Road Bazar for years. All of you know them well. You know that they have never done us any harm. They are innocent.'

'Innocent?' Mr Ghosh sneered. 'What about Shibani and Sanjeeb Purkayastha? What about Lahiri and so many other people? Were they not innocent? Or have you already forgotten about their deaths.'

'I have forgotten nothing Ghosh-babu. I was among the first to say that we should fight back—with arms if necessary. But two wrongs don't make a right. What we are doing is wrong.'

'Please Dutta-babu!' Mr Ghosh popped a kwai into his mouth. 'Don't give us big big lectures as if you are Gandhi-ji's grandson. First you say that we should fight back and the moment we start doing it you want us to stop? Do you want us to sit at home, like we have always done, wearing bangles on our wrists? Don't you have any pride as a Bengali?'

'I have no pride in hurting some poor, illiterate fishwives

who have done nothing wrong. I know these people. Most
of them are mothers just trying to keep their homes going—'
    'They are Khasis. That's all that matters!' an angry voice
cut in.
    'They are the only breadwinners in their homes! The
husbands are mostly alcoholics. You know that as well as I
do. If this goes on for much longer, whole families will starve
to death.'
    'Good riddance!' the gathering shouted. 'We don't care.
Let them all go to hell.'
    'Very well then,' said Mr Dutta. 'Then go and do whatever
you want. But I do not wish to have any part in this. Goodbye.'
He marched out of the meeting, ignoring the jeers and jibes
that followed him.

* * *

One evening , a few days later, when a sliver of yellow moon
was floating large and low over the horizon, Mr Ghosh spied
a woman furtively entering Mr Dutta's house. Mr Ghosh, who
had a healthy interest in the affairs of his neighbours, took a
close look at the visitor. Her face was turned away from him,
but he could see, even in the gloaming, that she was wearing
a black and red tartan shawl and a jainsem. More collusion
with the enemy, thought Mr Ghosh, as he hid behind a large
hydrangea bush.
    The woman was tip-toeing down the gravel path that led
to the front door of the Duttas' house. Casting quick, nervous
glances about her, she bent over the doorstep and carefully
placed a large oblong parcel upon it. Even as Mr Ghosh was
trying to figure out what she was up to, she bolted back the
same way she had come and, in a trice, vanished into the
darkness.
    A frightened Mr Ghosh immediately raised the alarm:
'Bomb! Bomb! Mr Dutta—there's a bomb in your house,'
he screamed.

Mr Dutta threw open the front door and rushed out. In his hurry, he failed to notice the parcel and his foot struck against it. It flew out into the garden, landing with a thud near the boundary wall that stood between the two houses. Mr Ghosh jumped out from behind the hydrangea bush as if suddenly impaled by a red-hot poker. Covering his head with his hands, he dashed for cover. 'Run, run! That bomb is about to explode. Run for your lives everyone!'

By now, the families of both houses had arrived at the scene. At Mr Ghosh's words, they froze in their spots. Hearts pounding, they braced themselves for the ear-deafening blast they thought would blow them to smithereens. Seconds passed, then minutes. But there was no explosion. Everyone slowly straightened up, jerking out of their awkward, terrified postures like marionettes being pulled up by strings.

Mr Dutta was the first to recover his wits. He darted inside the house and returned carrying a pail of water in one hand. With the other, he seized a long bamboo pole that was propping up a young hibiscus plant and cautiously approached the parcel. A flurry of warning cries broke out.

'Don't take the risk, Dutta babu,' said Mr Ghosh hopping nervously in the safety of his verandah.

'Don't go there! Are you mad?' Mrs Dutta screamed. 'We don't know what that thing is. Call the police, call the fire brigade.'

'How should I call them? We don't have a telephone,' replied Mr Dutta. 'And even if I could, do you think they would come just because I asked them to?'

'Then stay inside the house until it explodes. Why are you unnecessarily risking your life?' said Mrs Dutta.

'Not only yours, ours too,' Mr Ghosh added. 'You should listen to your wife, Dutta-babu.'

'Will everyone please calm down?' Mr Dutta said. 'I don't think it's a bomb. If it was, it would have exploded by now,' he advanced a few more steps. 'Now, let's see what this thing is. Everyone get inside the house, please.'

Standing as far away as possible from the mysterious object, Mr Dutta heaved the bucket back, pouring out a stream of water over it. There were no ominous hissing sounds, no fizzes, nothing. He tapped it gingerly with the bamboo pole. Still nothing...

'It feels soft and squishy,' said Mr Dutta, as he gave it a harder poke. 'It's definitely not a bomb.' He stepped forward and went down on his knees to examine the package more closely. A moment later he stood up, chuckling loudly. 'Hah! So much fuss for nothing!' he said.

'What is it?' asked Mrs Dutta.

'Nothing to worry about,' Mr Dutta chuckled. 'It's only a fish.'

'What!' Mr Ghosh exclaimed. 'A fish? Not a bomb? Are you quite sure?'

'Not even a cracker,' Mr Dutta replied. 'Just a fish—bowal by the looks of it.'

Mrs Dutta came forward to take a look. 'Oh god!' she gasped. 'It's true. It is a fish. Oh dear god, what will happen to us now?'

'What do you mean, what will happen now? Nothing. It was just someone's idea of a practical joke, I suppose,' Mr Dutta said. 'It's over now.'

'No, you stupid man! It's not a joke!' Mrs Dutta exclaimed. 'Don't you understand? Someone is trying to do black magic on us.'

'Black magic?' Mr Dutta's eyebrows shot up.

'Of course,' Mrs Dutta replied. 'It must be. Otherwise, why would anyone throw a rotten fish into our house? Someone wants bad things to happen us.'

'Your missus is right, Dutta babu,' Mr Ghosh chimed in from across the wall. 'This is definitely black magic. The woman who threw it was Khasi. They are known to be experts in such matters. Surely you know how they cut locks of hair from little children as sacrifice to their snake goddess.'

'What nonsense! That's just a stupid rumour,' Mr Dutta snorted. 'There's no black magic here,' he pointed at the offending object. 'Look at it. It's a perfectly good fish. Fresh and clean.'

'You don't know anything about these things,' Mrs Dutta retorted. 'My mother once told me of a crooked moneylender in our village in Assam, whom everyone hated. One morning, he woke up to find a rotten fish lying outside his door. A red swastika symbol had been drawn on its stomach with sindoor. It looked fresh from the outside but the moment it was touched, the fish's stomach burst open and hundreds of maggots came crawling out of it. The stench was unbearable, my mother told me.'

Debu had been observing everything with great fascination. 'What happened next?' he asked.

'That same afternoon, the man caught a fever,' his mother replied. 'He was a rich man. They called the doctors. He was given the best possible treatment. But nothing worked. The fever kept rising and in three days' time, he was dead.'

'Wow!' said Debu. He glanced fearfully at the fish to see if there was a swastika symbol on it.

'Don't believe everything you hear, Debu. These are just village tales,' his father said. He prodded the fish hard in its stomach with the bamboo stick. 'Look, it's perfectly alright, just like I said. There's nothing to worry.'

'That's what you say. But I can't take any chances,' his mother said. 'I'm not letting that fish come anywhere near the house. Go and throw it away somewhere. And after that come inside and take a bath. Debu, you first. Go on, quickly now. I don't have time. I'm going to have to wash the whole house with Ganga-jal now.'

'Good idea, Mrs Dutta. That is the right thing to do,' said Mr Ghosh. He had walked across and was now peering curiously at the fish. 'But Dutta babu—I don't understand something. Why would a Khasi woman take the risk of coming all by herself into Jail Road to leave this fish in your house? It's very strange.'

By now, several other people from the nearby houses had started trickling in. 'Yes, Dutta babu, why would someone leave this beautiful, fresh bowal fish in your house? A nice, big one too—at least three kilos I'm sure,' said a neighbour.

Mr Dutta shrugged. 'I have no idea,' he turned to Mr Ghosh. 'You say you saw her. Any idea who she is?'

Mr Ghosh was about to reply when he was interrupted by the sound of a scuffle. A beefy young man pushed through the gathering. He was dragging a Khasi woman behind him, squirming helplessly in his grip. Debu recognized him as Babul, an unemployed man in his late twenties who spent his days either strutting around Jail Road Bazar looking self-important, or playing cards in Arun Restaurant near the bus stand.

'What are you doing here, Babul?' Mr Dutta asked. 'And who is this woman?'

'I caught her running down the steps leading to Wahingdoh,' Babul replied. 'There was a guilty, scared look on her face. There was something about her that did not seem to be right. I guessed that she was up to no good. I stopped and asked her what she was doing in Jail Road after dark. She tried to run away from me, but I caught her and brought her here,' he looked around with a smug smile and said, 'Just doing my bit to keep the locality safe, you know.'

'That I can see,' Mr Dutta said drily. His nose wrinkled as he caught the stench of cheap whisky on Babul's breath. 'Why have you brought her to my house?'

'She keeps saying she knows you,' said Babul. 'I wanted to make sure.'

'Knows me?' said Mr Dutta as he peered at the woman.

The woman let out a wail: 'Bah Dutta, it's me. Tell him to let me go. I haven't done anything wrong.'

'Oh, Kong Jenny! It's you?' Mr Dutta said in a startled voice. 'What are you doing here so late in the evening?' He turned to Babul. 'Let her go. I know her. I am sure she hasn't done anything wrong.'

Mr Ghosh sidled up to the woman and stared at her. 'Wait a minute—I know her too. She sells fish in Jail Road Bazar, isn't it? I used to buy at her shop sometimes.'

'Yes. Now let her go for god's sake,' said Mr Dutta.

'Oh, so she must be the one who left the fish on your doorstep!' Mr Ghosh said. 'Why did you do that? Trying to do Khasi black magic tricks is it, you witch?'

Frightened gasps went up amongst the gathering.

'Speak up!' Babul gripped her hand and twisted it roughly. She squealed in pain. 'Tell us if you were trying to do black magic on us. Otherwise, we'll give you the thrashing of your life!'

'Let her go, Babul!' Mr Dutta grasped Babul's hand and prised it loose. 'Don't you know how to behave with a woman?'

'She's no ordinary woman,' someone yelled. 'She's a witch. She came to do black magic in our homes. Give her a good hiding!'

The woman was sobbing. 'Please let me go. I haven't done any harm,' she whimpered. 'I just came to give the fish to Bah Dutta, nothing else. Bah Dutta, you know why. You please tell them.'

'What is this all about Dutta-babu?' Mr Ghosh asked.

All eyes were now on Mr Dutta. He shuffled uncomfortably for a few moments before saying, 'I think Kong Jenny was only trying to repay me. That's all.'

'Repay you?' asked Babul.

'Yes. I...I have been giving her some money now and then over the past few weeks,' Mr Dutta mumbled. 'Ever since the stupid fish boycott started.'

'I'll tell them, babu,' Kong Jenny said. 'It's all my fault. I was desperate. There was no food to eat at home. I asked...I begged Bah Dutta to buy some fish from me. Otherwise we'd starve. But he said he couldn't do that because of the boycott.'

'Instead, I said that I could lend her some money from time to time, until the boycott was over,' said Mr Dutta. 'She could pay it back whenever she could manage.'

'But I didn't want the money for free. I thought I could repay it with my fish. It must have been a long time since you had any. It's your favourite—bowal,' Kong Jenny smiled wanly at Mr Dutta. 'I knew that you couldn't have taken it from me in the market in front of everyone. So, I thought of leaving it in your house. I'm sorry. I am really very sorry for the trouble I've caused.'

The neighbours muttered darkly amongst themselves as Babul turned to Mr Dutta. 'So Dutta-babu, you have been giving her money is it?'

'What could I do?' Mr Dutta replied. 'She has four children. The husband is a drunkard. She told me she was running out of money. She needed my help.'

'Chhee, chhee,' Mr Ghosh shook his head in disgust. 'How could you betray our cause? How could you betray your own brothers?'

'How could I refuse,' Mr Dutta said. 'I've known her for years. I felt sorry for her...for them.'

Babul grabbed Mr Dutta by the collar of his shirt. 'Dutta-babu, it's only because of people like you that we Bengalis get screwed. You are a coward and a traitor. And you will have to answer for this. We will show you soon. But first we'll show this Khasi bitch what it means to mess with a Bengali. Come with me!' he shoved aside Mr Dutta and seized the fishmonger's hand. She struggled to free herself from his clutches, but he was too strong and dragged her as if he was hauling a sack of potatoes.

'Leave her alone,' came a voice, cold and hard as a razor's edge. It was Mrs Dutta. Her face was set in granite. Two spots burned bright red on her cheeks as she planted herself in front of Babul, a bamboo pole gripped tightly in her hand, the knuckles turning pale from the pressure. 'Leave her alone, I said,' she repeated.

'What are doing, boudi? Please step aside,' said Babul.
'Let go of her, I said!' Mrs Dutta raised the bamboo pole.
'Otherwise I will break your bones. I swear to god that I'll
do it.'
'Have you gone mad?' Babul said. 'This woman—' he broke
off and staggered back as Mrs Dutta lifted the pole high and
brought it down on him. Cries of panic cry broke out, but
to everyone's relief, the pole jolted to a halt a fraction of an
inch above Babul's head.
'The next time I won't stop,' Mrs Dutta said. 'If you don't
let her go at once, I will break your head.'
'Now, now—just calm down,' Mr Dutta said.
'You keep quiet,' Mrs Dutta snapped. There was instant
silence. 'As it is, you have caused enough trouble. Now
everyone listen to me very carefully—I will not stand by and
watch an innocent woman being attacked by a jobless, drunk,
loose character and a bunch of shameless cowards who are
not fit to lick the boots of this good man,' she looked up at
Mr Dutta. 'My mister may have his faults, but he is a good
man, a kind man. Who he gives money to and who comes to
his house is his business and I will not stand for him being
abused in his own house. Do you understand?'
Babul slowly released his grip on Kong Jenny. She
whimpered quietly as Mrs Dutta draped an arm over her
shoulder and said, 'Let me tell you one more thing. Kong
Jenny will walk out of this house now. None of you will lay
a finger on her. If anything were to happen to her today or
any other day, I will personally identify each one of you to
the Khasi boys in Wahingdoh. Then we will see how brave
you all are. Understand?'
'Yes,' said Babul in a strangled voice. The others nodded
obediently, like little children being ticked off by the class
teacher.
'Now go!' Mrs Dutta commanded. 'Out all of you! Get out
of my house. Otherwise I swear I will really break someone's
head today.'

'Right, right. We'll just get going then,' the neighbours mumbled and hastened away. Babul was the last to leave, throwing murderous looks at the Duttas as he slouched past.

Mrs Dutta waited until they were all out of sight, before lowering the bamboo pole. She walked back slowly to the verandah and sank into a chair, ashen-faced and trembling. Mr Dutta stared at her as if he was seeing a ghost.

'Baap re baap! What just happened to you there?' he asked in bewilderment.

'I don't know myself. I think I must have gone a little mad,' Mrs Dutta lowered her head. 'But what was going on wasn't right. If you had tried to do anything smart, then Babul might have beaten you up too. That's all.'

Kong Jenny had been standing by the gate like a block of stone. She now hobbled across to Mrs Dutta and took her hand. 'Thank you,' she sobbed. 'Thank you for saving me today.'

'It's all right,' Mrs Dutta said.

'I'm really sorry for—' Kong Jenny said.

'No need to be sorry,' Mrs Dutta cut in. 'It wasn't your fault. It was very kind of you to come here to give us the fish. And very brave too. Thank you.'

'It's the least I could do. I'm really sorry for the trouble,' said Kong Jenny.

'It's okay,' Mrs Dutta said wearily. 'You should go now. And one more thing—please take the fish with you. We can't eat it. I hope you understand?'

Kong Jenny nodded. She shook Mrs Dutta's hand, patted Debu on his head and left. Debu had no idea what had come over his mother that night. He could scarcely recognize the bamboo-pole-wielding nemesis of bullies and cowards as his own mother. But he felt immensely proud of her.

* * *

News of this incident spread fast. Within no time, everyone in Jail Road came to know that not only had Mr Dutta boycotted the fish boycott, but he was actively trying to sabotage the movement. And that hellcat of a wife of his was hand-in-glove with him. They deserved to be taught a good lesson, was the verdict.

And so, from being one of the most popular families in the neighbourhood, the Duttas suddenly found they had become pariahs. People stopped talking to them. Those who earlier used to drop by home to have a chat or watch TV stopped coming. Mr Dutta bore the brunt of their ire. *Traitor, Khasi lover, coward, fish addict,* they would jeer at him whenever their paths crossed. The Bengali shopkeepers in Jail Road Bazar would look through him, or pretend that they had just run out of whatever provisions he was looking for. Invariably, he would find a few rotten vegetables slipped into his shopping bag. And one evening, he returned home to find a dead rat lying outside the front door. He was lucky, Mr Dutta thought, that he had his own house to live in. If he was staying in a rented place, he would surely have been evicted by now.

Even Debu was not spared. His cricketing friends in Jail Road started giving him the cold shoulder. Debu was a fairly good batsman and would usually come in at number two or three. But suddenly, he found himself relegated to number eight. When he asked the captain about the reason for his demotion, he was told that it was to give the other batsmen a chance. The captain was an older boy whom he liked, and Debu did not make a fuss about it. But other things started to happen as well. His usual fielding position was in the slips, close to the other players, where he was a part of the general chit-chat that continued alongside the play. But now, he found himself banished to the third man boundary, isolated from everyone else. During the breaks, the other boys would huddle together, chattering amongst each other, only to clam up when he approached. In the beginning, Debu thought it was just his imagination that something was wrong. But soon,

it was impossible not to feel the undercurrent of animosity
directed at him.

'Have I done something wrong?' he asked one day. 'Why
is everyone behaving like this with me?'

'At least we are still letting you play with us,' the captain
replied. 'Be grateful for that.'

'Be grateful for what? You're letting me play because I'm
a good batsman.'

'If you're so good, then go and play with your other friends
no? Your Khasi friends,' another boy cackled.

'What Khasi friends?' Debu's face went red. He hadn't told
anyone about Clint or Audrey.

'You think we don't know?' the captain said. 'Your history
teacher, Mr Chakraborty is a relative of ours. The other day
he told us all about your new friend. Clint—that's his name,
right?'

Damn, thought Debu, why did Chakraborty have to have
relatives in Jail Road? 'He's not a friend. Just someone I met
at tuitions,' he lied and immediately felt small resorting to
this deceit. But along with the shame, a small spark of anger
flared up inside him. Granted that they were his friends, that
he had known them for many years now, but what right did
they have to poke their noses into his personal life?

'Stop lying, sala,' the captain said. 'We know exactly what
you have been up to. Chakraborty told my father everything.
When I told the others, they wanted to throw you out that
day itself. But I said that you had been playing with us for a
long time and we should give you another chance.'

A chorus of angry voices surrounded him from all sides.

'We don't want people like him in our team. Throw him
out.'

'Yeah, my father said that I should stop mixing with his
family.'

'Same here. They are traitors. His father buys fish from
the Khasis.'

'Get out and don't show your face here again.'

Someone pushed Debu roughly from behind. He staggered and nearly fell down. They advanced upon him, their eyes angry, accusing. He shrank from them but they had encircled him and there was nowhere to go. He felt trapped, helpless.

'Like father, like son,' a boy said, taller and brawnier than the rest. 'If you like these Khasi fellows so much, why don't you get out of Jail Road and go live with them?'

'Yeah, go and lick their boots, like your father,' jeered another.

A white-hot rage seared through Debu. He hurled himself at the boy and grabbed him by the collar. 'I'll break your bloody bones if you talk about my father like that,' Debu screamed and drove a fist into the boy's midriff. He let out a gasp, doubling up in pain.

With a roar of anger, the other boys pounced on Debu, kicking and punching him. A blow caught him on the chin and he crumpled to the ground. Luckily, everyone was trying to hit him at the same time and what might have become his funeral, turned instead into a confused melee—a swarm of flailing arms and legs that, more often than not, missed their target and struck each other. Debu somehow managed to crawl through the thicket of limbs and break free from the clutches of his assailants. He scrambled to his feet and made a run for it. A few boys pursued him but he was too fast and, after a while, they gave up the chase.

'Go back home and eat your rotten fish,' he heard them yell, as he fled down the steps that led to the safety of his home.

The same fear that he had felt a few months ago, on the steps of Jacob's Ladder, now surged through him. It occurred to him that he had become a dkhar once again—but this time, amongst his own people.

COUNTRY ROADS

LIFE HAD BECOME unbearable for Debu. He couldn't go out to play. He couldn't go to school, which continued to remain shut because of the USF agitation. He no longer had any friends in the neighbourhood and his mother forbade him from visiting his school friends elsewhere, saying that it was neither necessary nor safe. She advised him to stop cribbing about being bored and instead spend his time studying for the Board Exams.

So all Debu could do was potter around at home and study or read books. In fact, Mr Dutta had stopped buying new books for him in an effort to cut down on expenses. Out of desperation, Debu started browsing through his father's collection. This was distributed over two shelves of a small steel and glass cabinet. The lower shelf was packed with slim paperbacks with deliciously enticing titles like *The Villain and the Virgin*, *This Way for a Shroud*, and *The Case of the Strangled Starlet*, which had been written by a James Hadley Chase. Next to the Hadley Chases was a stack of novels featuring the adventures of one Nick Carter Killmaster, which sounded equally exciting. But to Debu's chagrin, this shelf was under lock-and-key. His father refused to open it for him, saying that he was too young to read such books. Instead, Mr Dutta pointed him to the upper shelf (which was unlocked), and suggested that he try reading something serious for a change. It would be good for his character.

The pride of the upper shelf was a massive green hardbound tome called *The Complete Works of William Shakespeare* and three volumes of something called *Das Kapital*. Next to them stood an array of thick novels written by a bunch of bearded Russians with intimidating names like Solzhenitsyn, Sholokhov and Dostoyevsky. Shakespeare and *Das Kapital* were clearly non-starters, so Debu took a stab at a couple of the Russian novels. But he found them slow and depressing...he could not go beyond a few pages.

In short, Debu was as miserable as Freddie Threepwood, the son of Lord Emsworth in the Wodehouse novels, whom the great author had once described as experiencing 'the sort of abysmal soul-sadness which afflicts one of Tolstoy's Russian peasants when, after putting in a heavy day's work strangling his father, beating his wife, and dropping the baby into the city's reservoir, he turns to the cupboards, only to find the vodka bottle empty.'

In the middle of this gloom, there was but one faint ray of hope that made his own abysmal soul-sadness seem a little more bearable. It was a letter from Clint. Professor Bose had handed it over to him in the last tuition class, informing him at the same time, that Clint would no longer be coming in for tuitions. Debu was deeply disappointed by this news. Now he wouldn't be even able to meet one of the few remaining friends he still had, he thought. But as soon as he read the letter, he cheered up. It said:

Hey Debu,
It's been a long time since we met. I was hoping that I would be able to see you at Audrey's birthday party. But after discussing it with her, we both felt that it wouldn't be safe for you to come to her house in Nongrim Hills. That's why we didn't invite you finally. So yeah, sorry about that. But it was for your own good.
Anyway, we are getting really bored these days with all these stupid bandhs and curfews and whatnot. So we thought it's about time we had some fun. That's when Audrey got this great idea of going to the Sacred Forest in Mawphlang for a picnic. We want you to come with us. I guess you've never been there. It's an amazing place. You should see it. It'll be super fun. We'll have whisky and food and music and everything.

*Now for the date—we plan to go there next week on
Wednesday. It's a little far from Shillong, but if we leave
early we should be able to get back to the city before it's
dark. Anyway, we'll be with my friends and you don't
have to worry about anything—meaning you'll be safe.
So this is the final plan—I'll pick you up in a jeep at Police
Bazar in front of the newspaper stalls at 9 in the morning
on Wednesday next week. We drive down to Mawphlang,
do the picnic and get back to Shillong by 4 PM. Be there
okay? We'll be waiting for you—so don't ditch and don't
be late.
Bye and see you,
Clint
PS: Hope Bose gives you this note when you come for
your classes.
PPS: I'm not going to be taking classes with Bose for
anymore. No point. My father says it's just a waste of
money going for tuitions, when no one knows when the
schools will open again. For once I agree with him!*

Debu read the letter several times. A picnic in the sacred
forest with Clint and Audrey! After weeks of being holed up
inside the house with only tragic Russian heroes for company,
it sounded like manna from heaven. But as his excitement
rose, his mind was bogged down by the dead weight of that
eternal, insuperable question—how to escape from his mother's
clutches? And that too for one full day, when he had neither an
excuse nor permission to go anywhere except tuition classes.

There were other questions that troubled him as well.
Where was this Mawphlang place? How long would it take
to get there and back? Was it safe? What if Clint's jeep broke
down on the way and he was stranded in the middle of
nowhere? As Wednesday drew closer, he fell into an agony of
indecision. In the end, unable to bear it anymore, he decided
to make a few discreet enquiries with his father.

'Baba, how far is Mawphlang from here?' he asked.

Mr Dutta looked up from his newspaper. 'Mawphlang village you mean? It's quite far from here, twenty-five kilometres or so. Why do you ask?'

'Just like that. Is there a forest there?' Debu said.

'Yes, a very big one. They call it 'The Sacred Forest'. When we were young we used to go there for picnics,' his father smiled. 'It's a strange place—ancient, unspoilt, untouched by human hands for centuries. You can almost feel the presence of dinosaurs lurking behind the trees.'

It thrilled Debu just to hear his father speak of the place. A desire to go there and see it for himself flared up inside him like a flame caught in a gust of wind.

'Haven't been there in ages,' his father was saying. 'Wish I could see it again sometime.'

'So why don't you? Even better, why don't we all go there together?'

'Not safe. It's a hundred per cent Khasi area,' Mr Dutta said with a sigh. 'Any non-tribal going there would be taking a big risk,' he glanced at Debu. 'But why the sudden interest in Mawphlang? I hope you're not thinking of going there?'

'Oh, of course not,' Debu lied. 'A friend was talking about it the other day and it sounded interesting—that's all.'

'That's good. It's a pity you can't go there. It's certainly worth seeing. Maybe I'll take you there once things get better. But right now, it's impossible. Shillong is far too dangerous these days. You must have noticed that I don't go anywhere without my khukri. It's sad, but what to do,' his father said and returned to his newspaper.

* * *

It took many hours of agonizing before Debu reluctantly concluded he would have to turn down the picnic invitation. Firstly, like his father said, it was just too risky going to a place like Mawphlang. Secondly, he could not think of a single good reason to convince his mother that he had to be out of the house for a whole day. She could smell a lie from a mile away, and would almost certainly see through whatever stories he came up with. And if, by any chance, she came to know that he had been picnicking in Mawphlang with a bunch of Khasis, then he would be instantly packed off to Calcutta—no questions asked. That much he was sure of.

Having made his painful decision, he was now faced with the equally painful task of communicating it to Clint and Audrey. And the only way he could do that was to meet them in Police Bazar at the appointed hour. Otherwise they would be waiting for him and, if he didn't show up, then they would get really pissed with him. And he had no desire to piss off the few remaining friends he had.

So, on the morning of the picnic, Debu convinced his mother that he had to go over to a friend's house in the morning to copy some notes. She asked the usual Whos, Whats, Whys and Whens, but he had anticipated her inquisition and come prepared with a plausible story.

He heaved a sigh of relief when she finally bought it and said, 'Okay, go if you have to. But come back home by eleven. Not a minute later, you hear?'

'Yes Ma, of course,' Debu said and dashed out of the house. At the stroke of nine he was at the newspaper stalls in Police Bazar just like Clint had instructed in his note. A few minutes later, an open Willys jeep rumbled up the road and screeched to a halt in front of him. Clint was in the driver's seat, Audrey beside him. She was wearing a pair of dark oval sunglasses and a red beret perched on her head at a cheeky angle. Debu thought she looked just like a movie star. His heart hammered out a few extra beats.

'Hola Dabboo,' Audrey waved at him. 'Good to see you after so long.'

'Yeah, you too,' Debu's lips stretched out into a daffy grin.

'What are you waiting for?' said Clint. 'Hop in.'

The moment of reckoning had arrived. He was sorely tempted to cast all caution to the wind and jump into the jeep. But he drew upon every drop of willpower inside him and said, 'Umm…I'm sorry guys. But I can't come with you.'

'What the hell man!' Clint exclaimed.

'What's the problem Dabboo?' asked Audrey. 'This is just not done.'

'I'm sorry,' Debu hung his head. 'But there are some problems. I just can't come today. I—'

'Oh come on! Don't be such a spoilsport,' said Audrey.

'Yeah, seriously,' Clint added. 'What *is* the problem?'

'I'm not feeling well,' Debu lied. He didn't want to tell them about his mother's inquisitions and his father's warnings, and the hundred other fears and doubts that were gnawing at him. 'Not feeling well' was the simplest excuse that could think of.

But Clint wasn't having any of it. 'Not well? No problem,' he reached into a bag resting on the rear seat and fished out a bottle of whisky. 'Here—have a shot of this. You'll feel great,' he thrust the bottle at Debu.

Debu shrank back, a bubble of panic ballooning inside his stomach. The last thing he wanted was to be seen anywhere near a whisky bottle at nine in the morning in the middle of Police Bazar. 'Will you put that bottle away? People are watching us. Someone might see me.'

'Oh, so that's what's really bugging you, hna?' Audrey lowered the sunglasses to the tip of her nose and tilted her head at him. 'You're ashamed of being seen with us?'

Debu's cheeks went red again. He cursed himself for his insufferable blushing and mumbled, 'No, of course not. That's not what I meant. I would love to come with you guys. I really would. But I told you—I'm not well. Besides I can't be out of home for a whole day.'

'Why not?' asked Clint.

'Well—you know…parents and all that…' Debu mumbled.

Audrey clapped her hands and let out a hoot of laughter.

'Ohhh, now I know what the real problem is. He's scared. Poor little baby is scared of his momma. I always knew he was a mama's boy.'

Debu's face went beetroot red. 'I am NOT a mama's boy, okay?' he shouted. 'And I'm not scared!'

'Oh yes, you are,' Clint said. 'You're a real scaredy crow mama's boy.'

'Mama's boy! Mama's boy! Dabbo is a mama's boy!' Audrey chanted in a sing-song voice.

'Mama's boy! Mama's boy!' Clint joined in, drumming his fingers on the steering wheel.

Debu banged his fist on the bonnet of the jeep. 'Stop it, will you! This isn't fair.'

'Then stop making excuses and come,' said Audrey.

'Listen if it helps—we'll wrap up early, okay?' Clint added. Debu wavered. 'Early? Like by when?' he asked hopefully.

'Let's see,' Clint glanced at his wristwatch. 'It's nine now. One hour to get there, one hour to come back. We'll spend four hours there and be back in town by two o'clock. Okay with you?'

'Get your maths right, Clint,' Audrey said. 'If we spend four hours there, we'll be back by three, not two. Is that okay with you, Debu?'

'No, no! That's far too late,' Debu protested. 'I have to be back home by one latest.'

'Make it two,' Clint said.

'No, one,' Debu said.

'What's with you boys?' Audrey exclaimed. 'Haggling like a pair of fishwives. We'll get back into town by one thirty and that's that. Okay with everyone?'

'Fine by me,' Clint shrugged. 'Debu, you?'

'Ummm, just give me one minute please,' said Debu. It was tempting, very tempting. If he could be back home by late afternoon, he might just be able to get away with it. Of course, Ma would be mad at him but he felt he would be able to cook up some suitable excuse.

'What are you thinking so much about?' Clint asked.

'I've planned this for so long. It'll be great fun. Come on Debu! Don't be such a bore,' Audrey said.

This was the last straw. There was no way he could let Audrey think that he was a mama's boy *and* a bore. Besides, she was asking him so nicely. He made his decision.

'Okay. Let's go,' he said.

'That's like a good boy,' said Clint as Audrey nodded in approval. 'Get into the jeep.'

* * *

Half an hour later, they had left the town behind and were speeding down the highway towards Mawphlang. Clint inserted a cassette into the car's tape deck. A song began to play:

Almost heaven, West Virginia
Blue Ridge Mountains
Shenandoah River...

Clint and Audrey crooned along with John Denver, belting out the refrain:

Country roads take me home,
To the place I belong...

Debu hadn't heard this song before. But its melody was infectious and he soon found himself singing along with Clint and Audrey. The full-throated voices of the three young friends soared into the cool, pine-scented air that greeted them as they climbed up the winding highway leading to the sacred grove of Mawphlang.

'You guys can have some whisky if you want,' Clint said. 'It's inside that bag.'

'Wait till we get there at least,' Audrey said. 'We don't want to become alcoholics like you.'

'What alcoholic? Can't you see? I don't drink when I drive,' Clint said. 'I only thought *you* guys might want to get the party started.'

'I wouldn't mind some whisky,' Debu said. Speeding down the open road with the wind rustling through his hair and the sun full on his face, he felt like a bird released from its cage after months of captivity. He reached for the whisky bottle and took a swig. It burned down his throat but not as much as his first drink at Kalsang. He took another nip. The warmth spread though his veins like liquid fire. It felt good. Life felt good.

'I'm so happy I came,' Debu said. 'Wouldn't have missed this for anything. Thanks for dragging me along.'

'Cool. Glad you could make it,' said Audrey.

'Anyone else coming?' Debu asked.

'A couple of my friends,' Clint replied. 'But they are coming separately in their own car.'

It was curious, Debu thought, how Clint and his friends all seemed to have cars. He wondered whether he should mention it, but he had a feeling that Clint would rather not talk about it. Instead, he took another sip of whisky and asked, 'What's so special about this sacred forest?'

'You've stayed so many years in Shillong. You still don't know?' Clint smirked.

'I only know that it's very old and you can't touch anything inside it,' Debu said.

'That's the problem with you guys,' Clint said. 'Not interested in what's there right outside your own homes. Only know what's there in Delhi and Calcutta.'

'Hey, it's easy for you to talk like that!' Debu said angrily. 'You're free to go wherever you want to, whenever you want to. But I can't. My home is in Jail Road. That's where I stay and that's where I have to keep staying all the time—stuck inside the one-kilometre radius of Jail Road Puja Mandap,' Debu retorted. 'So don't give me your bull-crap about not knowing anything about my own home, as you call it.'

'Shut up, both you guys,' Audrey said. 'Don't start a fight now.'

'He started it. Not me,' Debu said.

'Then you finish it,' Audrey said.

'Okay fine,' Debu sulked. 'But he has to say sorry first.'

'Sorry first,' Clint said. 'Happy? Man, you're so sensitive!'

'There—he said sorry. You can stop sulking now,' Audrey said.

'Okay,' Debu said grumpily.

'You still want to know what was so special about the sacred forest?' Audrey asked.

'Yeah, I guess,' Debu said.

'According to legend, the sacred forest in Mawphlang is the home of U Ryngkew, the guardian spirit whom the god U Blei sent down to earth to protect mankind,' Audrey said. 'You have to be very careful in the sacred forest, because the spirit of U Ryngkew still roams there, protecting the land from any harm. Once inside, you cannot cut a tree or a branch or even pick a blade of grass. You cannot take anything from it, not even a pebble. Nor can you leave anything behind. You must leave it exactly as you found it. If you don't, then U Ryngkew will get angry with you and then all sorts of horrible things will happen to you.'

'Like what?' asked Debu, fascinated by her account.

'Who knows,' Audrey shrugged. 'Maybe pestilence and plague, frogs and locusts—like it says in the Bible.'

'What has the Bible got to do with our sacred forest?' Clint said. 'It's U Ryngkew's land. He has his own special punishments.'

'Like what?' Debu asked again.

'I heard that people who don't obey his laws get their necks twisted so that their heads get turned backwards, facing their butts,' Clint said.

'Wow,' said Debu, trying to picture what that would look like.

'Anyway bad things are supposed to happen to people who don't respect the sacred grove,' Audrey said.

'And so for centuries, the sacred forest has lived and grown, uncontaminated by human touch. It's a strange place—where time does not flow like a stream, but stands still, like a pool of water.'

'Ooh,' said Debu. 'You're quite a poet.'

'Yeah, a bad one at that,' Audrey said.

The jeep came to a halt. "Okay, Bad Poets' Society,' said Clint as he switched off the ignition. 'We've arrived. Here it is—the sacred forest.'

THE SACRED FOREST

A THICKLY WOODED expanse stood in front of them. They walked towards it and soon were inside the forest, their feet sinking slightly into the damp carpet of leaves below. A sudden hush fell around them, like the lowering of a curtain upon a stage, cutting them off from the world of men and ushering them into the realm of the forest gods. A tunnel of green awaited them. Ancient trees, gnarled and thick as the limbs of some petrified giant, stood on either side of a narrow pathway, the creepers snaking up the moss-covered trunks like veins of green blood. Above them arched a canopy of leaves that gleamed amber and green in the sunbeams filtering through the high branches. Tiny sounds oozed through the silence—the abrupt crooning of a barbet, the rustle of leaves as a lizard darted at an unsuspecting dragonfly, the murmur of water trickling in some hidden stream.

They walked noiselessly, the stillness of the forest seeping into them. Presently, they arrived at a small clearing. A cluster of rock monoliths, faintly reminiscent of the menhirs in the Asterix comics, stood in the centre. Their rocky surfaces were covered with lichen and moss. Debu was about to sit on top of one of them when Clint grabbed his shoulder and pulled him away.

'Don't do that,' Clint said. 'That's a holy place. Those stones are the memorials of our ancestors.'

'I'm sorry. I didn't know,' Debu said.

'I told you. You have to be careful in this place,' said Clint.

'Stop pestering him, Clint. How would he know about such things?' Audrey said. 'So Debu, what you think?'

'It's amazing. It looks like some prehistoric forest,' Debu said. 'Everything is so old, untouched.'

'Yeah, it's a little eerie, no?' Audrey said. 'Looks like it's been here since the beginning of time.'

'It's as if the droplets of time trickled into the trees and the earth and the rocks, and are now trapped inside forever,' Debu said.

'Oooh!' Audrey clapped her hands softly. 'Look who's the poet now.'

'Sorry...I'm just blabbering,' Debu said with an embarrassed smile.

'No, no, it's a good start. Go on,' Audrey said.

'Hey, why don't you guys go ahead and take a look around?' Clint said.

'What about you? Aren't you coming?' Audrey asked.

'I'll have to wait here until the others arrive,' Clint replied. 'Don't know why they are late. If we get in too deep, they won't be able to find us,' Clint said.

'Okay, we'll go ahead then. Otherwise we won't have much time to see the place. See you soon, Clint. Let's go, Debu,' said Audrey and the two of them headed into the forest.

Audrey softly hummed a familiar melody while Debu ambled by her side, the whisky jostling pleasantly inside his stomach. The lines of a poem sprang unbidden to his mind. He could not recall its name or where he had read it, but for some reason, the verses of the opening stanza had stayed with him.

A book of verses underneath the bough,
A jug of wine, a loaf of bread—and thou
Beside me singing in the wilderness—
O, wilderness were paradise enow!

In spite of not having a book of verses or a loaf of bread with him, the poem seemed to be a perfect description of his present situation. After days of captivity inside the four walls of home, the wilderness of Mawphlang truly felt like paradise. A feeling of bliss overcame Debu and he gratefully took in deep breaths of the pure, clear air. He couldn't remember the last time he had felt so peaceful and happy.

'This is such an amazing place,' Debu said. 'Thanks a lot for inviting me. It was really very nice of you.'

'Don't be silly. Glad you could make it,' Audrey replied. But every Eden has its snake, goading its inhabitants to pry into matters better left alone. One such snake now reared itself inside Debu's head.

'Can't help wondering why though?' he asked.

'Why what?' Audrey frowned.

'I mean why did you invite me?' Debu asked. 'I mean I am sure you guys are pretty popular. You must have plenty of other friends.'

'Oh god! Stop fishing for compliments, Debu,' Audrey said irritably.

'No seriously, why me?' Debu persisted.

'Because we enjoy your company, that's why. Now stop asking these dumb questions,' Audrey said.

But fuelled by the whisky and the wilderness, Debu persisted. 'I never could understand why a cool girl like you would bother hanging around with someone like me?'

Audrey rolled her eyes. 'You are really beginning to get on my nerves now, Debu. Just shut up and walk,' she stomped off, leaving him behind.

'I'm only being frank. What with me being Bengali and all that?' Debu said as he followed her.

She came to a halt and spun around to face him, her eyes blazing. 'What the hell man! Why did you have to bring that up now, in the middle of such a beautiful place? Can't we take a break from this Khasi-Bengali crap for one goddamned minute?'

'Hey, look…I didn't mean to…I'm sorry,' Debu stammered, taken aback.

'Why do you have to screw up everything? Don't you understand anything, you dumbfuck? That's exactly why I wanted to come here—to the forest, to nature. Because I wanted to get away from it all. To get away from the crap that's going on…the curfews and bandhs and killings and the rest of the shit. Don't you get that?'

'I'm really sorry.'

'It sickens me—this whole tribal/non-tribal business. As if we are nothing more than our stupid tribes. For god's sake, why can't we just be ordinary, decent people first?'

'Sorry.'

'And will you stop saying sorry! It's driving me nuts. It's not your bloody fault, you idiot! It's the fault of the bloody politicians. They are behind everything,' she sat down on the grass and lowered her head. 'I'm going mad staying in this place—no school, no work, nowhere to go, nothing to do. Just fighting and killing and sitting around at home.'

Debu shuffled uncomfortably on his feet. All he could think of saying was sorry, but he decided against it. He felt like kicking himself for screwing up what had until now, been a perfect day.

It took a while before Audrey had calmed down a little. 'Sorry for ranting. Mind if we sit here for a bit?' she said.

'Sure,' said Debu and sat down beside her. She moved away, avoiding his gaze. No one spoke for a while. Unnerved by the silence, Debu fished out a pack of cigarettes from his pocket. Audrey cocked an eyebrow.

'A whole pack? I didn't know you smoked that much,' she said.

'It's increased lately. Too much tension at home.'

'How many per day?'

'About four or five,' Debu replied. This was a wild exaggeration. At best, he would filch the odd cigarette once in a while from his father's stocks—just to stay in touch. Recently, to make life easier for himself, he had flicked a whole pack. Not that he enjoyed smoking much. It made his throat rasp and he coughed sometimes when inhaling. But he thought he looked cool with a cigarette dangling from his lips and had started carrying the pack with him, just in case the opportunity presented itself.

'You're really dumb if you smoke so much,' Audrey said.

'And I saw you gulping down the whisky in the car. What's with all the boozing these days?'

'Nothing. I like the taste,' Debu retorted.

'Yeah, right,' Audrey said. 'The taste! Don't bullshit me. You're just trying to copy Clint.'

'I'm not,' Debu said. 'Now *you* are beginning to bug me. Let me just have a peaceful smoke, okay?' He struck a match and lit the cigarette. Because of their bickering, he had failed to notice that it was a filterless Charminar. He took a deep drag and immediately broke into a paroxysm of coughing.

Audrey watched him, amused. 'What happened stud boy? I thought you were smoking half a pack every day?'

'I was...I mean...I am,' Debu croaked as he wiped the water streaming out of his eyes. 'It's just that...this cigarette is really strong,' he stubbed it out with the heel of his shoe.

'Don't throw that cigarette butt there,' she said sharply. 'You're not supposed to leave anything behind in the forest.'

Debu stuck out his tongue. 'Ooops! I'm so sorry. Forgot about that completely. I'll take it with me when we leave and throw it outside.'

'Why do you even try to smoke when clearly, you can't? I don't think you even like it much.'

'But I do,' Debu protested.

'My foot you do! You guys are all the same. Always doing dumb things to impress girls.'

'I'm not trying to impress anyone,' Debu lied. 'I just happen to enjoy the flavour of tobacco.'

'Happen to enjoy the flavour of tobacco,' she mimicked him in a sing-song voice. 'What a silly little boy you are. Just like Samrat.'

'Who?'

A brittle smile appeared on Audrey's lips. 'A guy called Samrat Ghosh,' she said. 'He was three years senior to me. Used to live next door to us. Had been staying there ever since I can remember. There weren't too many other young people in the neighbourhood. So, we were always hanging around together, inseparable almost. We practically grew up together. I was an only child. He was like the brother I never had.'

This brother-business sounded ominous to Debu. He had never considered his relationship with Audrey, such as it was, to be of the fraternal variety. He hoped that she didn't think of him as his rakhi brother or something. Luckily, she wasn't a Bengali girl or this might have been a distinct possibility...

Audrey was speaking softly, as if to herself. 'He wasn't very interested in football or cricket or other boy-stuff. Had his nose inside his books all the time. We use to chat together for hours in his house. He's the one who got me hooked to Asterix and Holmes and Poirot and—'

'And dog carts and menhirs and strychnine?'

'Exactly. Didn't know much of the world except for what was inside his books. Always trying to impress the girls in the neighbourhood, and mostly failing. It was quite touching,' she tossed her beret at him. 'Just like you, as I said.'

Debu ducked. The beret landed on the grass. 'So where is he these days?'

Audrey shrugged. 'Don't know. He left Shillong two years ago, along with his family. One day, they were there and the next they had gone.'

'Why?'

She got up and wandered about. 'They were staying in a rented house,' she said. 'One fine day, their landlord asked them to vacate the place. They had nowhere to go and asked for a little time, just a few days to find a new house. But they weren't given even that much. The next day the landlord brought in a bunch of goons and had them thrown out on the streets. That was the last I saw of Samrat. It's been two years now. I don't think I will ever see him again.'

'Khasi landlord?'

Audrey bit her lip and nodded. 'Yeah.'

'This Samrat...he never contacted you after he left? Never wrote a letter even?'

'Nothing. And quite frankly, I'm not surprised.'

'Why?'

Audrey looked away. There was a long pause before she said, 'You see Debu, the landlord was my father,' she said, the words coming out unevenly. 'He thought I was becoming too friendly with a non-tribal,' she buried her face in her hands. 'Too friendly...can you believe it? We were only twelve and fourteen, for god's sake. Just two kids who happened to like each other.'

Debu didn't know what to say. He listened quietly as Audrey went on, 'In the beginning, I didn't even know what had happened. I thought they had gone off on a holiday or something. I was very hurt that Samrat hadn't even bothered to wish me goodbye. It's only later, when I accidentally overheard some neighbours gossiping, that I realized what had happened. I hated my father for what he had done. I had a huge showdown with him. I kicked and screamed and said all sorts of things to him. But who cares what a twelve-year-old says? They had gone for good—just like that,' she snapped her fingers. 'God knows where they are, what they are doing these days. Samrat's father was a small-time businessman. Never had much money. It must have been tough on them.'

'Try not to worry too much about it. The same thing has happened to lots of other people here. People get by somehow. They survive. I am sure they will be fine,' he said with a buoyancy he did not feel.

Audrey did not seem to hear him. 'I feel so horrible. I keep thinking that in some way it was my fault. Maybe if I hadn't been so friendly with him, it would never have happened. It just eats me up sometimes,' her voice splintered. 'I miss him so much. I wish I could meet him once more. Just to say sorry, to say how very, very sorry I am.'

The intensity of her emotions made him feel inadequate, helpless. But it was painful to see her sobbing quietly without doing anything. He edged towards her and gingerly placed his arm over her shoulder. Much to his relief, she did not stiffen at his touch or push him away. 'It's not your fault,' he said and held her close.

After a while she looked up, eyes red and swollen, damp smudges on her cheeks. 'Sorry. Don't know what came over me suddenly. I'm a total jerk for spoiling your picnic like this.'

'No problem,' Debu said. He hadn't moved a whisker in the last few minutes and his arm had gone numb. But his senses tingled from the soft warmth of her body pressed against his, the mild fragrance of soap and eau-de-cologne and the rise and fall of her breath. He ignored the dull ache in his arm and stayed as unmoving as a rock.

'Got a handkerchief?' she asked. She had collected herself and her tone was brisk. Debu rummaged through his pocket and was happy to discover one. She took it from him and blew her nose hard into it. 'Thanks,' she passed it back to him.

'Umm—that's fine, you can keep it,' said Debu. He liked her and all that, but he drew the line at nasal fluids.

'Okay, that's so sweet of you,' she gave his hand a squeeze. 'And thanks for putting up with my mood swings.'

'No problem,' Debu said shyly.

'I keep getting them all the time these days. It's like, one minute I'm all super excited and high on life and the next moment, I'm down in the dumps. Don't know whether it's because of all the crap that's happening around us these days or because of my damned periods. You guys don't know how lucky you are to not have menses.'

Debu's cheeks turned brick red. He had only the vaguest of notions about periods. His only sources of information were a few know-it-all classmates in school who were as ignorant as him. They spoke with such glib confidence on all matters female, that everyone considered them to be authorities on the subject. He had been able to gather from them that periods were a mysterious condition that affected women once in a month and had something to do with making babies. Audrey's casual candidness about such a loaded topic made his ears burn in embarrassment.

Audrey did not notice his discomfort. 'You know what I dream of these days?' she said.

'What?' asked Debu, hoping she wouldn't bring up another awkward topic.

'Getting out of Shillong and going off somewhere on my own. I'm so sick of the fighting and shutdowns and the pettiness all around. I feel like I don't belong here anymore. I don't want to stay here anymore.'

'Well...I don't like what's happening either. But I would hate to leave Shillong. I don't even want to think about it. It's still home for me.'

'Yeah, that's what I used to think as well. But I'm not sure anymore. I'm just waiting to finish school. After that I'm going to get the hell out of here.'

'And go where?'

Audrey shrugged. 'Dunno yet. Maybe Delhi. Or Bombay. Even Calcutta maybe, except that my Dad would never allow me to go there.'

'Ever been there?'

'Yeah, Calcutta once and Delhi a couple of times. Got a cousin who's studying there in St Stephen's. Of course, he can't wait to get out. He hates it there.'

'Why?'

'The guys in college tease him. Call him a Chink. Say he's a dumb tribal—you know the usual stuff. Plus, the heat drives him mad.'

'But you still want to go there?'

'Well, at least the colleges stay open. They have classes, good teachers. There are some career prospects. Why do you think people come from all over the country to places like Delhi and Bombay? For education, jobs, for a future. And that's what I want—even if they call me a Chink and pinch my butt on the buses. I want to go and study in a good college in a big city, get a good job, see the world. I've had it up to my eyeballs with these small towns with their small people and small minds.'

'Oh come on, I don't think Shillong's that bad. Although, my mother doesn't agree with me. She keeps talking about sending me to Calcutta. And I think my father has sort of come around to her point of view now. But I hate the very thought of leaving this place.'

'Don't be silly. Don't write off something without knowing anything about it. I agree with your parents. You should give Calcutta a shot. There's no future in this place—believe me.'

'So all of us should just leave Shillong and go off somewhere else?'

'Maybe.'

'And never see each other again?'

'Perhaps. Who knows?'

'If that happens…I'll…really…miss you.'

'Yeah, same here,' she took his hand and placed it against her cheek. He timidly edged closer to her. To his relief, she did not shy away from him. 'I wish life didn't have to be so complicated,' she said and nuzzled against him.

His mouth went dry from the tension. 'This is nice,' he managed to croak.

'Mmm,' she sighed languidly. She wrapped her arms around him, enfolding him in a tight embrace. He hugged her back, his heart now pumping furiously, the blood gushing into every part of his being. The fragrance of her perfume, the scent of her body mingled with his breath like an intoxicating draught.

Their lips brushed against each other.

His eyes closed in bliss. *Your first kiss*, a small, exultant voice whispered from somewhere inside his head. *Virgin no more*, it said to him. He knew he hadn't quite got there but he gladly believed it. They nestled closer together, every nerve of his body coming alive with pleasure and longing, when a harsh cry shattered the silence.

'Hey dkhar,' a voice said from behind them.

* * *

Wrenched out of his trance, Debu was flung back to the cold, damp reality of the forest. Two young men had appeared in the clearing. They were standing in front of them, arms akimbo. Something in their gaze suggested that they had been watching them for a while. As if they had been caught doing something ugly, an unreasonable shame passed through Debu and Audrey. They shrank away from each other, repelled by some invisible force that had suddenly sprung up between them.

The older of the two men swaggered towards them. He was an athletic fellow in his twenties, head shaven clean and a crucifix-shaped pendant dangling from his neck. 'What were you doing with that girl, dkhar?' he said.

'Nothing...I...we're just friends,' Debu mumbled.

'Friends, hna?' the man said. 'We saw what you were up to. Trying to mess around with our women is it, you fucking dkhar?'

'Let's teach the bastard a good lesson,' the younger man said. He wore the uncertain, wispy beard typical of late pubescence and seemed to have a scowl permanently stitched into his brow. He strode towards Debu, the twigs crunching beneath the tread of his heavy boots.

'Just leave him alone guys. He's a friend,' Audrey cried. She was shivering. Her face had gone white.

'You stay out of this,' the older man said roughly. He swung his hand back, catching Debu with a stinging slap square on the cheek. The sound echoed inside the clearing, like the crack of a whiplash.

Audrey hurled herself at the man, kicking and punching him. 'Stop it! Stop it! He's a friend. I told you he's a friend,' she screamed. The younger man grabbed her arms from behind and tossed her aside. She staggered and fell, cursing them at the top of her voice.

Debu's face burned brick red in shame. It was bad enough to be slapped in front of Audrey, but what really cut him to the quick was that it was she who had to come his rescue.

He was seething in helpless rage when he heard a familiar voice behind him.

'Hey, hey, hey—what's going on here?' said Clint, walking towards them, picnic basket in hand. 'What the hell is going on here, Pahara?' he asked the older man.

'This pylleng, this dkhar asshole was touching her, kissing her,' Pahara spat out in disgust. 'He needs to be thrashed, the bastard.'

'Shut your mouth,' Clint said. 'He's my friend. Leave him alone.'

'Friend? I see,' Pahara said. 'Funny friends you have these days.'

'I told you about him. You knew he was coming,' Clint replied.

'Yeah, but we didn't know he was trying to make out with Khasi girls,' Pahara said.

'Shut the hell up,' Audrey hissed. 'It's none of your damned business what we do.'

Clint lowered the picnic basket and sat down. 'Okay, everyone just calm down. We came here to have a picnic. So let's do that instead of fighting over nonsense.'

'This dkhar fucker is trying to steal a Khasi girl from under our very noses and you call it nonsense?' Pahara said. 'Isn't that what we are fighting against? Isn't that what our movement is all about?'

'He's my friend. Got it? That's all that matters,' Clint said.

'Yeah, I can see the sort of friends you keep these days,' Pahara threw a look at Debu which sent a chill down his spine.

The shame of being humiliated in front of Audrey was swiftly replaced by a new fear, as he realized that even if he somehow managed to escape this time, he was sure to have been marked. They would be on the lookout for him, they would catch him somewhere, sometime on some lonely street when there would be no Clint or Audrey to protect him—and this time they would surely finish him off. Thus would end the

inconsequential, farcical life of Debojit Dutta, the unlikely Don
Juan of the Bengalis, the infamous seducer of Khasi women.
'If you want to stay, stay. Otherwise get lost,' he heard
Clint say.

Pahara threw a small smile at Clint. 'Of course, we will
go, Bah Lyngdoh. It's your party after all. But don't think
of yourself to be such a big-shot just because you're the
headman's son, okay?'

'Oh shut the fuck up, Pahara,' Clint said. "Don't bring
my father into this. Especially when you know very well that
you guys are what you are only because of him!'

'Really?' Pahara smirked.

'Yeah, really! You dickhead! If it wasn't for my father,
you guys would still be fucking around on the streets, doing
jack-shit.'

'Yeah sure,' Pahara shrugged. 'But don't forget, he's the
headman because of us. Your dad would be nothing without
us. And neither would you.'

The younger man had been looking increasingly
uncomfortable with this turn of the conversation. 'Hey, forget
it, man. We know each other for so many years. Clint's a good
guy. His father is a good man. So, why are we quarreling
among ourselves? Let's go.'

'Yeah, let's go,' Pahara agreed. 'Who wants to stay here
anyway. Bye Clint, have fun with your new dkhar pals. We'll
see how you can manage without us.' He threw another
menacing look at Debu and the two men marched out of the
clearing. Within minutes they were out of sight, swallowed
by the forest.

* * *

For a while no one uttered a word. Audrey and Debu sat
motionless, faces turned away from each other, while Clint
fidgeted with the picnic basket.

'Anyone wants a sandwich?' Clint said after a while.

There was no response. Clint helped himself to a sandwich and munched on it.

Audrey glared at him. 'You're really disgusting,' she said. 'How can you eat at a time like this?'

'Well, at least you're finally talking,' Clint smiled. 'I thought you guys would never speak to me again.'

'Should we?' Audrey asked.

'Hey, look guys, I'm sorry,' Clint said. 'I'm really sorry for what happened.'

'How could you even think of inviting those two jerks?' Debu said hoarsely. His cheek was still smarting from Pahara's slap.

'I didn't invite them,' Clint explained. 'I just happened to mention to them some days ago that we were coming here for a picnic. They immediately jumped up and said they wanted to come as well. Said they were getting bored and wanted to have some fun. I couldn't refuse. I know them since we were kids. They're decent chaps. Believe me, I had no idea they'd behave like this. Don't know what got into their heads.'

'Assholes,' Audrey spat out. 'Their big fucking egos got hurt, I suppose, when they...saw me with Debu.'

'Yeah. By the way, what were you guys up to that made them so mad?' Clint asked, his eyes twinkling.

'Nothing,' Debu snapped. 'So, those guys are your friends?' There was an edge to his voice.

'Well...yeah...sort of,' said Clint. 'We live in the same neighbourhood. When we were kids we used to hang out together, play together. Nowadays, I don't mix with them much.'

'They said your father was a headman,' Debu said.

'Debu, that's enough,' Audrey said. 'What's the point of all this? We came here for a picnic. So let's just do that and—'

Debu raised his hand and cut her off. 'You stay out of this, Audrey. This is between him and me. He keeps lying to me. I'd like to know the truth for a change—from his own mouth. Clint, is your father a headman?'

Clint stood up, shifting uncomfortably on his feet. 'Yeah, he's the Rangbah Shnong of Mawpar,' he admitted.

'But earlier you told me he was a businessman.'

'Yeah, that as well. He's businessman, headman—both.'

'And these guys work for your father? You said they'd be on the streets if it wasn't for him?'

'Well...yeah...sort of. A headman needs all sort of people to get...umm...work done. And those guys are willing to do it.'

'What sort of work?'

'Oh, this and that,' Clint pulled out a blade of grass and nibbled at it.

'Don't try and avoid the question. What sort of work?'

'How should I know? It's my dad's work. Go and ask him if you're so interested.'

'I don't have to. I think I know. And now I understand why—' he paused.

'Understand what?'

'Why you've been so cagey about your family all this while.'

'Listen I—'

Debu cut him off. 'So do you work for your dad too? Beat up non-tribals?'

Audrey smacked him on the wrist. 'Just shut up, Debu! Clint isn't like that. You know he isn't.'

'I don't know who is what anymore,' Debu stood up and faced Clint. 'Maybe Chakraborty sir was right about you Clint,' he pointed a finger at him. 'Maybe you're only a goon, like he said. That's why you are friends with the goons who wanted to beat me up today.'

'Stop talking shit, Debu' Clint said. 'I'm not a goon. And neither are these people. They are my dad's people. I have to be with them, okay...even if I don't like them, sometimes.'

'Why?'

'What do you mean, why?'

'Why do you have to be friends with them even when you don't like them?'

'I told you man! Because they are my dad's people—that's why. Because he's my dad—that's why. He wants me to get along with the people that work for him.'

'And so you get along? Such an obedient son.'

'Yes, you little prick—so I get along! Because I don't have a choice, okay? He wants me take over his business after I pass out of school. So, I have to listen to what he says. Do you understand?'

'He wants to you take over his business? But I thought you wanted to become to become an artist?'

'Yeah, but you can't make a living only from art right? I've got to make some money as well. Dad's business gives me a chance of doing that.'

'And so you do whatever he tells you to do, whether you like it or not?'

'It's not so simple man! He's my father. I care for him, I respect him. He's giving me a home, he's giving me a ready business, money! He's even promised to set up my own art gallery if I take over his business!'

'Ah! Now I understand.'

'You understand shit, Debu. Can't you see? He's giving me a real chance to become an artist, to go after my dreams! How many parents do that much for their children?'

'Very few. I guess that justifies everything.'

'Stop talking crap. My father's a good person. He's done nothing wrong.'

'Apart from having a few goons in his keep? Burning houses, killing, extorting money? No, I guess not.'

'My dad doesn't do any such thing,' Clint shouted. 'You don't know anything about him. So just shut your goddamned fucking mouth!'

'He doesn't have to do anything,' Debu yelled back. 'His men do it for him. It's the same bloody thing, Clint. You Khasis, you're all the same—killers!'

'You fucking dkhar bastard!' Clint roared. He swung his

hand back and his fist came crashing on Debu's jaw. Debu staggered, his legs gave way and he collapsed.

Audrey gasped. Her hands flew to her mouth. 'Stop it! Just stop it, both of you!' she screamed.

There was a wet, salty feeling inside Debu's mouth. He realized he was bleeding, but not a whimper escaped his lips.

Clint walked across to Debu, his head hung low over his chest. 'I am sorry,' he said as he extended his hand to Debu. Debu pushed it away and lifted himself up.

All three of them sat on the grass, still and silent like the primordial trees that towered over them. After a while, Audrey got up on her feet and said, 'I think we should go back home.'

* * *

Not a word passed between Debu and Clint on the drive back from Mawphlang to Shillong. Audrey's attempts to make small talk fell flat, snuffed out by the wall of ice between Clint and Debu. They reached Shillong shortly after noon and halted by the newspaper stalls in Police Bazar to drop off Debu.

'Bye, Debu. We'll meet again sometime,' Audrey said.

'I don't think so,' Debu said, as he quickly climbed down from the jeep.

He sprinted away from them as fast as he could, the blood roaring in his ears. But even as he fled he could not help overhearing Clint's parting words.

'Yeah. Me neither.'

ALONE

BY THE TIME Debu reached home, it was one o'clock in the afternoon. Mrs Dutta was waiting for him by the front gate. He prayed that she would lay off him for once. He had been through a lot in the past few hours and his mind was in turmoil. He would just not be able to handle another one of her inquisitions. All he wanted to do was go to his room and be alone. But luck was not on his side.

The moment Mrs Dutta saw him, she pounced. 'Where have you been all this while?' she said.

'Sorry,' Debu said. 'It took a long time to copy all the notes.'

'Do you realize that you're two hours late! I've been worried sick. Another half an hour and I would have gone to the police station. When will you ever learn to be more responsible?'

'I told you no. I'm really sorry,' Debu said. A great weariness was coming over him. He couldn't take it anymore. If he had to answer even one more of her questions, he swore he would just run away.

'As it is there's so much tension everywhere,' his mother was saying. 'And here I am, all by myself, thinking all sorts of terrible things...and.... and...' her voice broke.

'What's happened Ma?' Debu asked.

'Just look at this,' she said and extended her hand. An irregular white object lay in the crook of her palm. It was a rock with a sheet of paper wrapped around it. Debu unfolded the paper and read the words scrawled across it in large, rough letters:

DOGS AND TRAITORS NOT ALLOWED IN JAIL ROAD!
KHASI LOVERS, LEAVE JAIL ROAD!

'Where did this come from?' Debu asked.

'They stoned our house this morning. Soon after you and

your father left. They must have been waiting for the house to empty out,' his mother replied. 'You see all these stones? They were throwing them at the roof, the windows. Broke them all,' she pointed at the shattered glass panes of the drawing room windows. 'That paper was wrapped around one of the rocks which landed inside the drawing room.'

'Who's they?' Debu asked, the anger rising inside him.

'I don't know,' his mother said. 'I was in the kitchen when it happened. I came running out to the garden when I heard the noise but they got away before I could get a look at them. I am sure it must be that Babul and his friends. Hooligans, cowards—the whole lot,' she shivered. 'Stones raining on the roof, glass shattering. And me, all alone in the house... it was so scary.'

'I'm sorry I wasn't there. I was...having problems of my own.'

'Fifteen years!' Mrs Dutta went on, her head shaking in disbelief. 'Fifteen years we've stayed in this locality. They are our own neighbours, our friends, people we have known for years. And this is what they do to us?'

'I guess people show their true colours only when there is a crisis,' Debu said.

Mrs Dutta looked up at him, startled. 'My little boy seems to have grown up all of a sudden,' she said and stroked his head gently. 'I wish you didn't have to grow up so much, so soon. I wish you could have had a more normal childhood.'

And then like the flicking of a switch, she snapped out of her reflective mood and was back to her usual brisk self. 'Anyway, what will be, will be. Life must go on. Come with me Debu—there's work to be done.'

Mrs Dutta armed herself with a broom and a dustpan, and began sweeping up the broken glass while Debu pasted old newspapers over the shattered window panes. They were in the middle of cleaning up when Mr Dutta arrived.

'Back so early?' Mrs Dutta asked. 'There's still a few hours to go before the curfew begins.'

'I closed the shop. It's been a bad day,' Mr Dutta said and sank into his favourite chair on the verandah. The newspaper-covered windows caught his eye. 'How did those windows break?' he asked. 'Playing cricket inside the house, Debu?'

Mrs Dutta explained what had happened and showed him the threatening note.

Mr Dutta gave a wry smile. 'Oh, I see. Now this too. Bad luck never comes in small doses, as they say.'

'What do you mean? Has something happened?' Mrs Dutta asked.

'Yes, trouble. Big trouble,' Mr Dutta lit up a cigarette. 'Got this notice today.'

'What notice?' Mrs Dutta asked.

Mr Dutta extracted a sheet of paper from his coat pocket and passed it to Mrs Dutta. 'This one here. It's from the local Dorbar Shnong. They say that they will not renew my Trading License. Which means that the pharmacy has to be shut down.'

'The pharmacy has to be shut down!' Mrs Dutta exclaimed. 'Who are they to say that? The shop has been running for years now.'

'Forty years,' Mr Dutta said. 'My father ran it for the first twenty. I was a young boy when I took it over from Baba. Now I'm an old man. It has been there for forty years. But they will shut it down in one day—unless my Trading License is renewed.'

'But...how can they do this?'

Mr Dutta blew out a cloud of smoke. 'There is no how or why. It's happening everywhere, with everyone. I was spared until now only because I've been there for so many years.'

'Surely there must be some way out?'

'This is India. There is always a way—the other way. It's all quite simple. If I can give them two lakh rupees in cash, they'll give me the license. There's nothing official about it, of course. But if I cough up the money, I'll get the license.'

'Two lakhs!' Mrs Dutta gasped. 'That's almost the cost of a house.'

'That's the going rate. I tried bargaining. But they wouldn't budge an inch.'

'But where will we get all that money from?'

'I don't know. It's a huge amount. Impossible to even think of—like Mount Everest.'

'Maybe…we should sell our house then?'

'And stay where? It's near impossible to find a house on rent in Jail Road these days. Or any other place that's safe for Bengalis. The demand is too high.'

'There is nothing we can do?'

'I will go to the police. I don't have much hopes but let's see what they have to say.'

'And if that fails? What will you do then?'

'What can beggars do except beg?' Mr Dutta said. 'I will have to beg them once again, and again. Like I'll have to beg our dear neighbours not to stone us anymore.' He looked grey and haggard, a frayed cardigan hanging loosely on his suddenly shrunken frame.

Debu had been listening quietly to them all this while. In the face of his father's troubles, his own seemed trivial, laughable even. He felt a little guilty about being so wrapped up in his own world until now. He got up and sat close to his parents.

Mrs Dutta gathered Debu into her arms. 'We are alone now, aren't we?'

'Yes, we are alone,' Mr Dutta said. 'But we are still together. We'll manage somehow.'

An eerie feeling passed through Debu, like someone had just walked over his grave.

* * *

In the days that followed, Mr Dutta did everything he could to save his pharmacy. He first visited the local police station to meet the officer in charge, Inspector Warjiri. The Inspector was a short, plump man in his late fifties, with small bright eyes that peeped out through the folds of fat on his round face. He was nearing retirement and intended to spend the rest of his working days playing solitaire over endless cups of tea and kwai.

He heard Mr Dutta with increasing impatience and finally said, 'Issuance of a Trading License is a matter of civil law, not criminal. The police can do nothing. You should meet the headman of the Dorbar.'

'I tried but he refused to see me. In any case, I don't think it will help. The Dorbar has already rejected my application to renew my Trading License without giving any reason whatsoever,' Mr Dutta said. 'That is why I have come to you, sir—for justice.'

The Inspector smirked. 'Justice eh? Whatsoever? Just because you know some big words in English you think you are a big man, eh? You think you can waste the valuable time of the police by filing some nonsense complaint?' He began shuffling a pack of cards.

'Nonsense complaint? What are you saying sir? I have been running my shop in Iewheh for twenty years now. And my father ran it for twenty years before me. For forty years there was never any problem in renewing our Trading License. What has happened suddenly?'

'There is always a first time for everything. If you have any complaint, please go to the competent authority.'

'But there is no competent authority!'

'Mr Dutta, I am a simple police inspector,' the Inspector said. 'How do you expect me to give answers about unanswerable agencies? In any case, it is a civil matter. I cannot help. Good day, Mr Dutta.' He began arranging the cards into neat columns on his desk.

'Is extortion a civil matter also? Three young men came to my shop last week demanding two lakh rupees for a Trading License. Is that also a nonsense complaint?'

'I see,' the Inspector threw him a sharp look. 'These young men—you know who they are? You have their names, addresses?'

'How can I? I don't know them. They were strangers. It is the job of the police to investigate who they are, isn't it?'

The Inspector banged his fist on the desk, sending the cards flying up. 'So now you will tell the police about their job, is it? You dkhars are all the same—you think you can just order us around. You have any proof of your statement?'

'No but—'

'You have no proof but you come in here and make false accusations against respectable people that they are extorting money from you?'

'I didn't say that. I said three unidentified men came and—'

'I heard everything you said. If you say one word more I will personally call the headman over here and he will take the necessary action against you for defamation.'

'Please sir. Hear me out,' Mr Dutta begged. 'I am a Shillong boy. I have been born and brought up here, sir. This is my home, my life. If my shop shuts down, my family will be out on the streets. For twenty years, my medicine shop has been serving the people of Iewheh, helping the sick. A doctor comes in twice a week and treats poor patients for free.'

The Inspector gave a crooked smile. 'First you cause the disease, then you sell the medicines and make money, hna? Please get out of here at once. I don't want to hear anything from you. Hey, someone get this man out of here,' he ordered and returned to his cards.

A constable marched in and escorted Mr Dutta out of the police station.

'Next time he comes here, throw him out,' he heard the Inspector say from inside.

* * *

Back home, the few remaining friends that Mr Dutta had in Jail Road advised him to pay up whatever the Dorbar was demanding. He wouldn't be able to fight them, they said. It was a big racket and everyone along the line was getting their share of the cut—the police, the politicians, the insurgents. Like everyone else, Mr Dutta would also have to pay up or shut down. There was no other option.

'Pay up, pay up—everyone says,' Mr Dutta said one evening at the dinner table. 'But how will I pay up? Where will I get two lakh rupees from?'

'We will have to get it—by hook or by crook,' Mrs Dutta replied. 'The shop has to be saved. How will we eat otherwise?'

With the typical Bengali nose-in-the-air disdain for business, Mrs Dutta had never much cared for her husband's shop. But now that there was a threat of losing it, like the Friar in 'Much Ado About Nothing', she realized 'the virtue that possession would not show' and her attitude underwent a sea change.

'You said you need two lakhs, right?' said Mrs Dutta.

'Yes. There's no way I can raise that amount of money,' Mr Dutta replied.

Mrs Dutta scribbled down a few figures on a scrap of paper. 'Let's see. If I sell my jewellery—'

'Please! Don't talk of such things,' Mr Dutta said.

'Why not? That's why people buy jewellery—for a rainy day.'

'But—'

'You can buy it back for me when things get better. Okay? Now please let me do the calculations in peace. So if I sell my jewellery, we will get thirty thousand, at least. Plus your savings—that's another thirty thousand. The scooter may get us another five thousand.'

'That's only sixty-five thousand. Long way to go.'

'That's all?' Mrs Dutta frowned and added up the numbers again.

'That's all. I might be able to borrow another ten thousand from Phool Di. Seventy-five thousand. Still over one lakh left to go. It's impossible.'

'Then offer them one lakh and see. Negotiate with them.'

'I've already done that. They refused point-blank,' Mr

Dutta exclaimed in irritation. 'I told you everything. But you never listen to me.'

'No, it's you who never listens to me!' Mrs Dutta retorted. 'I told you this day would come. I told you we should leave this place, while there was still time. But you just wouldn't listen to me. You never have. So for once in your life, listen to me!'

Mr Dutta grimaced. 'What do you want to say?'

'There is only way out,' Mrs Dutta said. 'Sell the house.'

'Sell the house? Are you mad? First of all, no Bengali will buy a house in Shillong in these times. And secondly, if we sell it, where will we stay? It's impossible to find a house on rent in Jail Road or any other safe locality. This house is our shelter from the storm and you are saying sell it?'

'You didn't understand. We sell the house and we go away. We leave Shillong.'

'And go to Calcutta? Even if we could somehow manage to sell the house, the money won't feed us for the rest of our lives. And who will give me a job at my age in a place like Calcutta. Anyway, you know what it's like over there. There are hardly any jobs.'

'Maybe I can get a job somewhere,' Debu piped in.

'Keep quiet, Debu,' Mr Dutta snapped.

'I was just trying to help, that's all!' Debu protested.

'I don't need anyone's help, okay?' Mr Dutta shouted. 'You people are driving me mad with your useless talk. I'll think of something.'

'Like what?'

'I don't know! Can you just leave me alone and let me think in peace! It's my duty to take care of all of you and I'm trying my very best—do you understand?'

'Fine! I was just trying to help that's all!'

'I don't want anyone's help! I just want to be left alone. Is that too much to ask for?' Mr Dutta shouted and stormed out of the house.

* * *

It hurt Debu to see his father in such a state. He wished he could do something about it. Apart from worrying about his father, his mind kept going back to the picnic in the sacred forest, and his fallout with Clint. A peculiar weariness gripped Debu. He did not feel like doing anything—neither reading, nor listening to music or talking to anyone. There were days when he felt unable to get out of bed.

Meanwhile, the arguments between his parents were becoming more heated with every passing day. One evening he overheard them talking.

'The Dorbar called me for a meeting today. They have finally agreed to come down to one lakh fifty thousand,' Mr Dutta said.

'Oh, that's good news,' Mrs Dutta replied.

'Yes, but I'm still short of about seventy-five thousand. And that is the lowest they will go. The headman told me not to come back without the full amount—in cash. I really don't know what to do now,' Mr Dutta's head sank into his palms.

'Should I meet him once? Maybe he will be more considerate towards a woman, a mother?'

'Don't be silly. You've been watching too many Hindi films. These are hard, business people. They won't even let you near them.'

As he listened to their conversation, an idea suddenly occurred to Debu. He kicked himself for not having thought of it earlier. He ran to his father and said, 'Baba, what is the name of this headman that you are talking to?'

Mr Dutta looked at him in surprise. 'The headman of Iewheh you mean?'

'Yes,' Debu replied.

'Raphaphang Marbaniang,' Mr Dutta said. 'Why do you ask?'

Debu's heart plummeted. 'Marbaniang? Not Lyngdoh?'

'No, not Lyngdoh,' his father replied shortly.

'Are you sure?' Debu persisted.

'Of course I am sure,' Mr Dutta exploded. 'It's Raphaphang Marbaniang. You think I don't know the name of the man who is out to shut down my business of forty years? Why are you bothering me with your stupid questions? Not a moment's peace in this house,' he said and walked away.

Debu was sorely disappointed. He had hoped that the headman who had been harassing his father would turn out to be Clint's father. In fact, he had counted on it. He could have swallowed his pride, apologized to Clint and asked for his father's help in getting the Trading License. But this Marbaniang character had flung cold water over his plans.

But the seed had been planted and the thought of approaching Clint's father to bail out Mr Dutta kept coming back. Debu reasoned that one headman probably knew the other. Perhaps this Raphaphang Marbaniang and Clint senior were even good friends. If Clint's father requested the headman of Iewheh, then there was a chance that it would be granted. It was a chance that had to be taken.

Excited by the idea, he started making his plans. He would first have to convince Clint to help him. But would Clint be even willing to meet him, let alone help, after what had happened at the picnic? There were other problems as well. How would he meet Clint when he didn't even know where his house was? All he knew was that he lived somewhere in Mawpar. But to go to a place like Mawpar alone in search of Clint's house was asking for trouble.

He thought about it for a while until at last, a solution presented itself. There was still one person whom he could count on, one person who he knew would be by his side. He was not alone—not yet. The very thought lifted his spirits and he began to plan his next move.

TRUCE

Debu had a small cardboard box in which he stored all his important belongings—a water pistol that looked like the real thing, a bookmark shaped like a sea-horse, a pen that could write in three different colours, and various other objects that were precious to him. Among his most prized possessions was the birthday invitation that Audrey had written to him. He picked it out of the box and glanced at the address written on it in her clear, confident hand. It said:

Audrey Pariat
C/O Neil Pariat,
Rose Cottage,
Nongrim Hills,
Near Post Office.

His mind went back to the day when Clint had given him the card in Professor Bose's class. Those were happier times, when they were still friends, when there were more adventures to look forward to. Now, it seemed like ages ago. He congratulated himself for having carefully preserved the card all this while, for without it, Audrey might also have been lost, like Clint.

Theseus-like, he held the skein of thread that would guide him through the maze of Shillong, leading him to her and then, onwards to Clint. He calculated that it would probably take him about two hours to pull off his plan. All he needed was his mother's permission to go out for some time. To his relief, she did not object when he trotted out his stock excuse of going to a friend's house to copy notes. He dutifully listened to her usual warnings and, with a prayer on his lips, embarked upon the voyage to Nongrim Hills.

Debu had never been to Nongrim Hills. It was at the other

end of town and had a reputation for being one of the most unsafe areas for non-tribals. So, he was greatly relieved when the bus dropped him right in front of the Post Office.

The street was empty, apart from a group of boys who were playing football. He could sense the change in their mood the moment they saw him—this stranger who had suddenly appeared before them. The game stopped. They watched him as he nervously scanned the surroundings for a Rose Cottage.

A football came flying at Debu. It was lucky that his senses had been on high alert, or he would not have been able to intercept the ball that was aimed directly at his face. It was a good strong kick. But Debu leaped up and trapped the ball expertly on his chest. He dribbled it and kicked it right back to the boys. They nodded their approval.

'Nice one, man. Great kick,' the boys said.

Debu sensed an opportunity. 'Excuse me, but would you know by any chance where Rose Cottage might be?' he asked in his most polite voice.

The boy who had kicked the ball at him walked over—a short, well-built teenager with a weather-beaten face peppered with freckles. 'Everyone knows where Rose Cottage is. It's Audrey Pariat's house. That one there,' he said, pointing at a small cottage with white-washed walls and a red roof behind a neatly trimmed hedge. 'You going there to meet her?'

'No. I mean—'

'You her boyfriend or what?' he gave a crooked smile.

Debu groaned. The last thing he needed was a hiding from a bunch of beefy footballers who thought of him as some sort of Lothario, out to seduce their women. He might even have accepted his fate, had there been a grain of truth in it. But to be beaten up for something that he clearly wasn't would be both painful and pathetic. More importantly, it would upset all his plans.

'No, no. Definitely not any boyfriend,' he protested. 'Hardly a friend, even. Just came here to return a book.' He fished out his physics textbook, hoping they would buy his story.

'It's okay, man, even if she's your girlfriend,' the boy patted him on the back. 'She's a nice girl. Have fun. Come back and play football with us once you're done.'

'Umm...okay...sure. Thanks a lot,' Debu mumbled.

He hurried down the road to Rose Cottage, pushed open the wooden gate and rang the doorbell. To his immense relief, Audrey opened the door. She stared at him as if she was seeing a ghost.

'What the hell are you doing here?' she hissed.

'I had to speak to you. It's urgent,' Debu explained.

'You stupid boy. Why did you come here? It's not safe,' she pushed him aside, away from the open door and drew the curtains.

'I had to meet you. Can I come inside please?'

'Are you mad? You can't.'

'Why not?'

'Don't you remember what I told you about Samrat? If Dad sees me with you, we'll both be in real trouble. You have to go.'

'I can't. I'm sorry, but I have got to talk to you. Can we meet outside somewhere?'

'Audrey, who are you talking to?' a man's voice came from inside the house.

'Oh hell! He's here. Get out right now. Wait for me at the Post Office,' she pushed him towards the gate. 'Now go!'

'How long will you take?'

'Dunno. As soon as I can. Have to make up some excuse.'

'Okay. I'll be waiting at the Post Office,' Debu said and darted out of the front gate into the street. The footballers were still at play.

'Whassup?' the freckle-faced boy called out to him. 'Back so soon? Had a fight with your girlfriend?'

'Well, you know...women...' Debu shrugged casually.

'Good. Come and play with us. Your team's goalpost is on that side, ours is on this side,' he indicated a line that had been scrawled across the street dividing it into two sections. 'Ready?' he said and kicked the football at Debu.

'Umm...okay,' Debu replied. He trapped the ball between his feet and joined the players.

It was unnerving to be surrounded by so many of them. But as they continued to play, his fears began to recede, and he soon found himself yielding to the pleasure of the game. For a few brief moments, he was no longer an outsider, but just another boy playing football in the soft sunshine of a Shillong morning.

'Debu!' he heard a voice call out.

'Your girlfriend's here,' said freckles.

'Oh, yeah. Sorry guys, got to go,' said Debu. He waved them goodbye and joined Audrey.

'Okay. Come back again some time,' freckles called out. 'Have a nice day.'

Audrey walked briskly down to the bus stop. 'Stay behind me,' she said to Debu in a low voice. 'I can't be seen with you.'

Debu followed her, maintaining what he hoped was a safe distance. 'Where are we going?' he asked.

'Kalsang. We'll talk once we are there. I hope the bus comes soon,' Audrey muttered.

A few minutes later a bus arrived. They boarded it separately, carefully avoiding eye contact. A brief ride later, they were at Kalsang.

Audrey ordered a plate of momos and said, 'How come you know those football guys?'

'I don't. They asked me to play with them. I couldn't say no. Why do you ask?'

'I hope they don't gossip about me. You know what people are like.'

'I don't think they will. Seemed to be pretty decent chaps.'

'Anyway, why did you come to meet me? What's the big problem?'

Debu told her. She listened quietly, nibbling at her momos. After he finished, she said, 'So let me get this straight. You want me to take you to Clint's house and ask him to help your father get his Trading License?'

'Yes, I guess you know where he stays?'

'Yes, of course I do—'

Debu rose to his feet. 'Then let's go there right away. I don't have much time.'

'Just hang on for one sec, Debu. I don't think Clint will want to meet you. He's really mad at you.'

'I understand. But I can't think of anything else. I'll do what it takes to make him less mad. But I have to see him.'

'You really think Clint's father will help you guys? I don't know a great deal about him, but he doesn't seem to be the type. You saw what his people are like.'

'I am praying that if Clint asks him, he will...otherwise...I don't know what we will do.'

'Honestly, I don't have much hope. But I can't think of anything else either. I guess we should give it a shot. Let's go and see if we can find Clint. You just keep quiet and let me handle it, okay?'

Debu nodded in agreement. They boarded a bus to Mawpar. Half an hour later, they were standing on the patio of Clint's house. Audrey knocked on the door. Almost instantly, Clint opened it, a cigarette dangling from his lips.

'Hey Audrey! What a nice surprise,' he gave a wide grin, when he noticed Debu standing behind her. The smile vanished. 'What the...why is this asshole here? I don't want to see him.'

'Stop talking like that Clint!' said Audrey. 'You are friends.'

'We were. But it's over,' Clint took a drag on his cigarette.

'It's never over. Debu came here to apologize to you. Debu—say sorry to Clint.'

'I'm sorry, Clint,' Debu said immediately. 'I shouldn't have said all those things to you. I...was being stupid, I got carried away.'

Clint looked at him quizzically. 'You came here just to say you're sorry?'

'That...and...well, there is something else too,' Debu replied.

Clint smirked. 'Of course. I knew it. There's always something, isn't there?' he said. 'So what do you want from me?'

'Can we come in first?' Audrey said.

'Well...okay,' Clint grunted. He led them into the drawing room. They sat down on a cane sofa and Clint listened impassively as Audrey explained the situation.

'So, basically—you want my dad to talk to the headman of Iewheh for renewing your dad's Trading License. Right?'

'Right,' Debu nodded.

Clint steepled his fingers and fixed his gaze on Debu. 'You are sure this is my dad that you are talking about Debu? The same guy who you said was a murderer? A dkhar killer?'

'Please Clint. I'm really sorry I said those things. I didn't mean it. We really need your help. If my dad doesn't get his license...we'll be finished.'

Clint shrugged. 'Yeah...well...bad luck man.'

'I told you I'm sorry. I really am,' Debu pleaded. 'Please help us.'

'Come on Clint,' said Audrey. 'Be a sport. Talk to your dad.'

Clint sauntered across to the long French windows and looked out. 'Sorry. But I can't.'

'Clint, you are being such a jerk,' Audrey spat. 'He's said he's sorry. He's begging you. What more do you want? Can't you see? He's in deep shit. You have to help him. You're friends.'

Clint continued to stare out the window.

'I thought you were different Clint,' said Audrey, her voice jagged, sharp as a sawblade. 'I thought you were a nice guy. But now I know better. You are just an asshole. An asshole with a small heart and a huge ego. Come Debu, let's go. We don't need this jerk's help. We'll figure out something else. And Clint Eastwood Lyngdoh—don't you ever dare to show your face to me again.'

Audrey grabbed Debu's hand and they marched out of the house. She slammed the door behind her as hard as she could and ran out into the street, cursing under her breath. Debu followed close behind, feeling more helpless than ever before. His grand plan had ended before it had even started.

They were halfway down the street when they heard Clint hailing them from behind.

'All right. All right. I'm sorry. Come back. I'll see what I can do,' said Clint.

Debu and Audrey stopped dead in their tracks. Huge grins broke out on their faces. They raced back to Clint. Audrey flung herself at him and gave him a hug.

'I knew it! I knew it! I always knew you were a nice guy,' she said.

Clint disentangled himself from her embrace and walked up to Debu. 'Hey, I'm sorry, okay?' he said sheepishly.

'No problems. I'm sorry as well. It was my fault,' Debu said.

'No, it was my fault,' Clint said.

'No, mine. I started it,' Debu said.

'All right, all right that's enough,' Audrey lifted her palms. 'Please don't start another fight now over whose fault it was. Go on, shake hands, you two.'

'Friends again?' Debu said and stretched out his hand.

Clint grasped it and pulled him into a bear hug. 'Yeah, friends,' he said.

Audrey rolled her eyes at them. 'Oh, you boys can be so silly. One moment you're at each other throats, and the next, you behave as if you want to get married.'

'Shut up Audrey,' the boys said in unison and instantly withdrew from each other.

'So Clint, will you ask your dad to speak to the Iewheh headman?' Debu asked.

'I will. But I don't know whether he will agree. After all, he doesn't like you Bengali guys much, you know,' Clint said. 'Anyway, it looks like we don't have any other option. So I'll give it my best shot.' He glanced at his watch. 'It's nearly ten now. He'll be leaving for work soon. Let me go and talk to him right away.'

They returned to the house. Clint led them into a small room and said, 'This is my room. No one will come in here. You guys close the door and stay inside until I come back. It's best that you're not seen.' He squeezed Debu's hand. 'I'll be off now. Try not to worry too much. I'll try my best.'

Debu nodded. 'Thanks a lot man. I know you will. Good luck,' he said as Clint headed out of the room.

JOHN WAYNE LYNGDOH

CLINT'S ROOM WAS sparsely appointed—a single bed, a straight-backed chair and a haphazard pile of books stacked upon a small study table. His hygiene and neatness policy was one of laissez-faire. The room was in a complete mess—a mound of unwashed clothes heaped upon the bed, papers strewn on the floor, a patina of dust on the table and cobwebs hanging from the rafters above. All of it would have been uninviting without the paintings covering the walls from corner to corner. Most of them were landscapes of Shillong—hills, waterfalls, an empty street in the moonlight, the view from Shillong Peak, among others. Their warm, vibrant colours lit up the dishevelled room and seemed to bring the world outside into the confines of its four walls.

'He paints beautifully, no?' Debu said as he gazed at the paintings.

'Yeah, I really hope he gets to become an artist and open his own gallery someday,' said Audrey.

'Same here. But what a mess this place is,' Debu wrinkled his nose. 'My mother would have killed me if I kept my room like—' he stopped. 'I'm sorry. I forgot he doesn't have a mother.'

'Make sure you don't say such dumb things when he's around,' Audrey said.

They waited in silence, the tension snuffing out any possibility of small talk. Their eyes kept darting to the clock, as one moment ticked inexorably into the next. After what seemed like an eternity, Audrey asked the question that was gnawing at them both. 'Why is he taking so long?'

'Yeah, it's over twenty minutes already. I hope everything is okay,' Debu said, when the heavy tread of footsteps sounded outside. The door flung open and a man barged in, followed closely by Clint. Debu recognized him at once. He was the older of the two men who had attacked them in the sacred forest. He felt a familiar lurch in his stomach and, in spite of the sudden chill inside the room, beads of perspiration formed on his brow.

'Just as I thought, Bah Lyngdoh. It's him!' the man said, pointing an accusing finger at Debu. 'I told you, I thought I saw him enter the house, just half an hour ago, with the girl.'

A third man had entered the room. He was in his fifties, attired in a brown corduroy jacket and a pair of grey woollen trousers. A pipe was clamped between his teeth and the ends of his greying moustache were stained yellow from nicotine. He looked like an older version of Clint and there was no doubt this was John Wayne Lyngdoh, father of Clint Eastwood Lyngdoh. He puffed on his pipe as his gaze swept over Audrey and Debu.

'You are Debojit Dutta?' he asked.

'Y...y...yes, Mr Lyngdoh,' Debu replied, his teeth chattering in fright.

Clint stepped forward and placed himself between Debu and his father. 'He's my friend,' said Clint.

'You didn't think twice before bringing a dkhar into my house?' said Mr Lyngdoh.

'I told you. He's my friend,' Clint replied.

'And what about me? Am I not your father? Don't you know better than to bring a dkhar into my home? That too on an official matter? You think this is some children's game?'

'I thought you could help him, that's all,' said Clint.

'Help? Why should I help these people? They keep coming here in their thousands, taking away our jobs, our properties, our women. They keep coming, more and more of them, taking more and more, until they will take our very Shillong away from us. And you want me to help these people? How could you bring him here? How could you even think that I would break the rules of the Dorbar to help his father? I'm ashamed to even call you my son!'

'It's my fault sir, not his,' Debu mumbled hesitantly. 'Clint didn't want to meet me. I came here by myself—'

'You will speak when I ask you to,' Mr Lyngdoh cut in. 'It's good that Pahara here told me what was going on, otherwise I might not even have known what my son was up to these days. Thank you, Pahara.'

'You're welcome, Bah Lyngdoh,' said Pahara. 'Do you want me to take care of him?' he nodded towards Debu.

'There's nothing to take care of,' Audrey said. 'We'll just be off. Sorry to have disturbed you, Bah Lyngdoh. Come Debu,' she said. She grabbed his hand and made a dash for the door.

'Wait, wait, what's the big hurry?' Pahara said, quickly stepping forward to block their path.

'Let us go,' Audrey demanded, her eyes flashing.

'You see, Bah Lyngdoh?' Pahara said. 'How she speaks up for him. Didn't I tell you? This dkhar bastard is trying to steal our women.'

'Steal your women? I'm only fourteen for god's sake,' Debu exclaimed.

Audrey's face went red. 'Bah Lyngdoh, this man is speaking rubbish. There's nothing between us. We are just friends.'

Pahara spread out his palms. 'You see? He's already hooked her.'

'Just shut your dirty fucking mouth Pahara,' Clint snarled. 'One more word of crap from you and I'll break all your bloody bones.'

'You see, Bah Lyngdoh,' said Pahara. 'This is what your son has become. He would attack his own brother for the sake of a dkhar.'

'Yes. I can see. Things have indeed gone too far,' Mr Lyngdoh said.

'I wonder what the Dorbar will have to say about this,' Pahara said. 'The headman's own son...' he clucked his tongue softly.

Mr Lyngdoh waved his arms with the air of someone having

reached a decision. 'They will say nothing. My son will get the punishment he deserves. So will the dkhars,' his eyes drilled into Debu's. 'You tried to misuse your friendship with my son. You tried me to get me break the Dorbar rules. You tried to take advantage of my official position. But I don't blame you. It must have been your father who put you upto this—'

'He didn't. I swear he didn't,' Debu shouted in panic.

'Keep your mouth shut,' Mr Lyngdoh snarled. 'You expect me to believe that a young boy like you would have thought of this by yourself? Dutta Pharmaceuticals—that's your father's shop, right?'

Debu lips clenched into a thin tight line. A great dread gripped him as he listened speechlessly to Mr Lyngdoh. 'Must be. After all, how many Duttas own a pharmacy in Iewheh market? I've seen the shop. It's been there for many years. Too many years perhaps,' Mr Lyngdoh turned to Pahara. 'You know the place?'

'The one opposite the bus stand, right?' Pahara asked.

'That's the one. Get some boys ready. We have work to do.'

'Got it, Bah Lyngdoh,' Pahara grinned. 'What about him?' he nodded at Debu.

'Keep him locked up somewhere safe until we are done. Your house maybe?' Mr Lyngdoh said. 'We don't want him getting in the way.'

'Sure. I'll take care of it,' said Pahara. He advanced upon Debu who stood there helplessly, panic turning his legs into blocks of stone.

'Run Debu, run!' Clint cried as he flung himself at Pahara. Pahara lurched and crashed against the study table. In a flash, Clint was upon him, pinning his arms down on the table. 'Run Debu, run! Get out of here,' he cried.

For a moment, everyone was too stunned to move. Then Debu found his feet and darted for the door. But he found his path blocked by Mr Lyngdoh. The old man grabbed him by the neck and pressed hard, nearly choking the breath out of him. 'My own son dares to defy me because of you? Because of a dkhar? I'll show you!' Mr Lyngdoh snarled.

Debu tried to prise himself free from Mr Lyngdoh's grasp. But the man was too strong for him. He was finding it difficult to breathe, his vision swimming. But panic lent him courage he did not know he possessed. He swung his leg back and slammed his knee right into Mr Lyngdoh's pelvic area. The old man howled in agony and released his grip on Debu's throat.

'Shih kmei! Stut liah!' he gasped as he bent double, clutching his genitals.

'Sorry, sir. Didn't mean to hurt you,' Debu said as he hurtled out of the house and onto the street.

'They'll be coming for him,' he heard Clint call out from inside. 'Tell your father that they'll be coming for him. Run, Debu, run.'

Debu ran. He didn't stop until the house of John Wayne Lyngdoh was far behind him.

THE ATTACK

HE BOARDED THE first bus that came along. Luckily it was headed for Police Bazar. He was relieved to find an empty seat, for his legs were on the verge of folding up. His breath came hard and fast, the panic nearly overwhelming him. He willed himself to calm down before the consequences of his disastrous misadventure began to sink in. *I screwed up big time! What will happen to Baba now? Oh god! What have I done?* he thought, the guilt swelling inside him like a malignant growth. For all he knew, John Wayne Lyngdoh and his band of cowboys were already out to get his father. And he was responsible for it.

He had to do something, he had to make amends for his stupidity. Clint had told him to warn his father that they were coming for him. They knew where the shop was and, in all likelihood, they would be waiting for him there. He would somehow have to stop his father from going to the pharmacy. He glanced at the wristwatch of the person sitting next to him. It was nearly eleven. He heaved a sigh of relief. Mr Dutta usually left for the shop at noon. He had just enough time to get back home, confess his misdeeds and warn his father of the danger that awaited him.

He waited impatiently as the bus chugged slowly up GS Road to Police Bazar. He disembarked and raced home. His mother was in the drawing room, nodding her head to the beat of a Hindi film song crooning on the radio. She looked relaxed, happy—happier than Debu had seen her in a long time.

'Ah, here you are at last,' she looked up with a smile as Debu careened into the house, panting like a race-horse at the finish line. 'I've been waiting for you. There is some wonderful news. Looks like our luck is finally turning.'

Deb was out of breath. Unable to speak, he stood there

gulping in great mouthfuls of air as Mrs Dutta gave him a
bemused look. 'Why must you always be in such a hurry?
Panting like a fish out of water?' she asked. 'Anyway, like I
was saying, there is some good news.' She waved a postcard
at him and said, 'Your Phool Pishima writes to say that
she has managed to get a mid-year admission for you in St
Lawrence School.'

'Oh,' Debu gasped.

'It's one of the best ICSE schools in Calcutta. And she has
agreed to let you stay in her house until your Board Exams are
over,' she joined her palms and lowered her head in front of
an invisible god. 'Isn't it wonderful? I can't even begin to tell
you how happy I am. You don't have to stay here anymore.
You don't have to lose a year. You are saved Debu.'

'Ma, where is Baba?' Debu asked.

But Mrs Dutta's mind was elsewhere. 'Whatever happens,
happens for the best, like I always say. This is the best time
for you to go to a big city like Calcutta. There you will be
able to prepare for the competitive exams so much better.
We will miss you, of course. But it's only a few years. And
Calcutta is not so far from here. You will come here during
the holidays. We will go there—'

'Ma, I have to see Baba!' Debu cut her off. 'Where is he?
It's urgent.'

'Yes, yes always in a hurry. Aren't you excited by the news?'
Mrs Dutta looked miffed.

'I am Ma. But right now I have to talk to Baba. Where
is he?'

'Gone out.'

'Gone out? Where, when?'

'I'm telling you everything. Just learn to be patient. I told
you, no? Our luck may finally be turning. I am hoping he will
come back home with some more good news.'

'Where has he gone for god's sake?'

'To meet the headman of Iewheh Dorbar. The man has
finally agreed to meet your father. Can you believe it?'

Debu's stomach turned into a block of ice. 'The headman? You're sure?'

'Of course, I'm sure. One of the boys from the shop came home to inform us that the headman has asked your father to meet him immediately at the shop.'

'Baba's gone to the shop?'

'Can you imagine?' Mrs Dutta went on happily. 'After all these days of trying so hard to get an appointment and now suddenly—'

'HAS BABA GONE TO THE SHOP?'

'I'll give you one tight slap, Debu, if you shout at me like that again. What is wrong with you? Of course he has gone to the shop. I told you, the headman is coming there to meet him. He left about fifteen minutes ago on his scooter.'

Debu shot out of the house. 'Where are you going, Debu?' Mrs Dutta called out in alarm as she scurried after him. 'At least take your sweater. It's cold outside. Ufff! What a boy!'

But Debu was already gone, racing down the streets back to the Police Bazar bus stand. He boarded the first bus headed for Iewheh, praying that he wasn't too late.

* * *

Half an hour later, he was standing in front of Dutta Pharmaceuticals. The shutters were pulled down. It appeared to be closed. But a small crowd had collected outside the shop, the bystanders talking excitedly amongst themselves. It was clear that something had happened. Debu pushed through the gathering and entered the shop.

The sight that lay in front him made him gasp in shock. It looked as if the pharmacy had been struck by a hurricane. The shelves had been ripped out, the medicine cabinets torn apart. Tablets, capsules, pills and powders were scattered all over the shop. Shards of glass were strewn across the floor, now slick with malodorous syrups trickling out of hundreds of broken bottles. An irregular red patch was slowly spreading near the cash counter. It looked like blood. Debu's bowels twisted in fear. Dear god! Please let Baba be safe, please let Baba be safe, he prayed.

'Baba, are you there?' Debu called out.

There was no reply. Debu crunched across the broken glass up to a tiny cubicle at the rear of the shop. It was his father's office. He pushed open the door and to his immense relief, Mr Dutta was sitting inside, hunched over the table, head sunk into his hands.

'Baba?' said Debu. 'Are you alright?'

Mr Dutta looked up, older and wearier than Debu had ever seen him. 'What are you doing here?' he asked in a startled voice.

'Oh, I've been so worried that something had happened to you.'

'You shouldn't have come here. It's not safe.'

'But I...I thought, I thought...' Debu couldn't go on.

Mr Dutta gathered him into his arms. 'Hush, hush! It's okay. I'm fine.'

'I'm sorry. I'm so sorry for what happened,' Debu cried. 'The shop...they've destroyed everything. They could have hurt you. It's all my fault. It all happened because of me.'

'What are you talking, Debu?' Mr Dutta said kindly. 'You have nothing to do with this. A bunch of thugs attacked the shop this morning.'

'I know. And it's all my fault. What if they had killed you?' Debu blubbered.

Mr Dutta went down on his knees so that he was face to face with Debu. 'Look at me Debu. See? Nothing's happened to me. I'm alive and kicking.'

'But the...blood?' Debu pointed to the crimson patch near the cash counter.

'It's not mine. It could have been but it wasn't. I escaped. But that poor boy wasn't so lucky.'

'Which poor boy?'

'The strange young boy who saved my life this morning. It's his blood. It was a bad blow, I only hope he's still alive.' A new fear gripped Debu. 'Who...what are you talking about? I can't understand anything.'

'I'm telling you,' said Mr Dutta as he lit a cigarette. 'This morning, I was informed that the headman of Iewheh wanted to meet me at the shop. I rushed here as quickly as I could and was waiting for the headman to arrive when suddenly, four men barged into the shop. They were shouting slogans, cursing. The usual ones—foreigners, dkhar dogs, etcetera. I tried to pacify them but they shoved me aside. Then they started breaking everything in sight with their iron rods and shovels. I begged them to stop but it was useless. I stood by helplessly as they tore through the shop,' Mr Dutta's voice trembled. 'This little shop of mine, which I have built for over twenty years, with my own hands, with my blood and my sweat and my love. This shop which for twenty years has provided for me and my family, which has given me everything that a man could need—food, a house, a scooter, your school fees. I couldn't just stand by and watch while they destroyed it in front of my own eyes. I went mad with anger. And then I did a really stupid thing.'

Mr Dutta took a drag on his cigarette and said, 'I remembered that my khukri had been kept in the bottom drawer of the cash counter. The first chance I got, I grabbed it and faced the attackers. Get out of here, I said to them, otherwise I will cut you to pieces.

'Three of the men surrounded me. The fourth, a much older man, stood watching. I didn't know him but I learned later that he was the headman—one Mr Lyngdoh. "What shall we do with him?" the other three asked him. Get him, Lyngdoh ordered. One of the men raised his shovel and was about to bring it down on me when all of a sudden, a young boy appeared out of nowhere. He leaped forward and grabbed my attacker from behind, trying to pin his arms down. But the man was too strong for the boy. He wriggled free and blindly swung his shovel at the boy.

'"Stop! Stop!" the old man shouted.

'But it was too late. Everything was happening so suddenly...so fast...before I could grasp what was going on, I saw the shovel hit the poor boy's head. A red gash opened up on his head and...blood...blood...started spilling out of it,' Mr Dutta shivered. 'The poor boy gave a moan and rolled over. It was horrible. The headman rushed forward, crying. He cradled the boy in his arms. "Clint? Can you hear me? Clint?" he said. But there was no reply. The boy was unconscious.'

'You're sure Mr Lyngdoh said Clint?' Debu asked hoarsely, although he already knew the answer.

'Yes, Clint. His own son, I believe. When I saw that poor boy lying there in a pool of blood, I thought they would surely finish me off. "Kill the dkhar, kill the dkhar," they started shouting. The man with the shovel was about to strike me once again, when the strangest thing happened. Lyngdoh grabbed his hands and stopped him. "Why are you stopping me?" the man asked angrily. "Look what's happened to your son because of him."

'"It's because of my son that I am stopping you. Because my son risked his own life to save this man." Mr Lyngdoh turned to me, an odd expression on his face. "I don't know why he did it but I want him to tell me himself. And he will tell me. Until then no one is to touch this man. We have had enough bloodshed for one day."

'He ordered everyone to clear out and rushed Clint to the hospital. They carried him out and drove off in their jeep,' Mr Dutta took a deep drag. 'And that's how I escaped with my life today. All because of this boy, this Clint.'

'Yes, you did. I can easily believe Clint doing something like that.'

'Who is he? How did he come here? Why did he do it?'

'I'll tell you all that later. Where is he now?'

'They said they were taking him to the hospital.'

'Which hospital?'

'Must be Roberts.'

'Sure?'

'I would think so. Roberts is the nearest from here. I can only pray that he is okay. Head injuries can be very dangerous,' he said, when he realized that his son was no longer there. He rushed out to see Debu racing down the road. 'Debu? Where are you going?' he called out.

But Debu was already out of sight.

THE SINS OF THE FATHERS

HALF AN HOUR later, Debu was at Roberts Hospital. He walked up to the reception and asked, 'Has a Clint Eastwood Lyngdoh been admitted here?'

'Yes, he's here,' a voice replied. Audrey was standing behind him, her head lowered. Debu could see that she had been crying.

'How is he?' Debu asked. A lump had formed in his throat. He was finding it difficult to speak. She avoided his gaze. 'What? Say something. Is he...' he could not bear to bring the word to his lips. Someone placed a hand gently on his back. He turned to see Mr Lyngdoh beside him, the lines on his face taut as a wire stretched till breaking point.

'No, he's alive,' Mr Lyngdoh said. 'They took him to the operation theatre a while ago.'

'Operation? For what?'

'He's had a brain haemorrhage,' Mr Lyngdoh replied. 'There is internal bleeding. Quite a lot I believe. The blow caught him at a bad place on the head, a very bad place.'

'Oh no! Mr Lyngdoh, will...will he be okay?' Debu asked.

'The doctors are doing everything they can. But everything depends on the operation. We can only hope.'

The fears that had been bubbling inside Debu over the last few hours now breached the limits of his endurance. He broke into a rasping sob. 'I'm sorry. I'm so sorry,' he whimpered. 'If only I hadn't gone to your—'

Mr Lyngdoh enfolded him in his arms. 'Shhh...shhh. Don't say that,' he comforted Debu. 'You did nothing wrong. It is us adults who are responsible. We dragged you children into our fights, our stupid power games. And now my son...my poor motherless son...is paying the price for my sins, my greed. If something happens to him...I will...I don't know what I will do.'

'Don't be so hard on yourself, Mr Lyngdoh. It was an accident,' said a voice.

Mr Lyngdoh looked up in surprise. 'Mr Dutta!'

'Yes, I guessed that Debu was coming here, so I followed him,' Mr Dutta replied. 'How is your son?'

He listened gravely as Mr Lyngdoh told him about the operation. 'I am to blame for this, Bah Lyngdoh,' he said. 'If only I hadn't attacked your men with the khukri, then this would not have happened.'

'Don't make me even more ashamed of myself by saying that, Mr Dutta. I don't know how I will ever be able to look myself in the mirror again,' Mr Lyngdoh's face had gone pale. 'This wasn't the way things were supposed to have turned out. I swear to you that we didn't want to hurt you. We had only planned to damage your shop and scare you. But things just went out of control...it's my fault, all my fault!'

'Bah Lyngdoh, Mr Dutta?' said Audrey.

'Yes?' they replied together.

'Can we please forget what happened?' said Audrey. 'It's over and done with. What matters now is Clint's life.'

'Yes, that is true,' Mr Dutta said. 'Mr Lyngdoh, your son is the bravest, most selfless person I have ever known. If there is a god above, then he will live. You must not lose hope.'

'Will all of you pray with me? For Clint?' Audrey said. She held out her palms. Mr Lyngdoh, Debu and his father joined their hands with hers. The four held on to each other, their lips moving in silent prayer for the boy who had brought them all together.

They were still deep in prayer, when the surgeon approached them. Mr Lyngdoh beseeched him in mute appeal.

'The operation has been successful,' said the surgeon. 'We have managed to stop the bleeding. He will live.' The four of them broke into a collective sigh of relief.

'But unfortunately, he has slipped into coma,' the surgeon continued.

'Coma?' said Mr Lyngdoh.

'Yes, his vitals are normal, but he is in an inert state,' the surgeon said. 'Right now, he is unable to see, or speak, or move.'

'How long will he be like that?' Mr Lyngdoh asked.

'Difficult to say. Comas are tricky things. Some people come out of it in a few hours, others take days. Sometimes even longer.'

'Longer? How much longer?'

'In some cases, it could go on for a month, sometimes several months. Unfortunately, we can't say. But try not to worry too much, Bah Lyngdoh. He's a young, fit boy. I am hopeful that he will make a good recovery.'

'Will he be alright, doctor?'

'That we can say only after he comes out of the coma. Unfortunately, the damage to the brain was quite severe. There are likely to be after-effects.'

'What sort of after-effects?' Mr Lyngdoh asked.

'We don't know right now. But it is unlikely that he will ever be the same again,' the surgeon replied.

CALCUTTA

19th June
Calcutta
Dear Clint,
How are you? It's been six weeks now since we moved to this hell-hole that goes by the name of Calcutta. I came to visit you in the hospital every day until we left Shillong. But I guess you wouldn't know that because you were in a coma. Even at the best of times, you were pretty much brain dead, right? Ha ha.
Hey, sorry for that. But Audrey wrote to me saying that you are finally able to talk AND walk—more or less normally. So I thought I'd pull your leg a bit. At least it will move now.
But jokes apart—WOW! I mean just WOW! That is such awesome news. Baba and Ma were thrilled to hear this as well. You gave us all a real scare, you know. After what the doctor told us, we were terrified that you would be like a vegetable for the rest of your life. THANK GOD that's not happening.
Yeah, I know that life is not all peaches and cream yet. Audrey tells me that your right arm continues to remain paralyzed. Bad...guess it really sucks not to be able to paint. But you know what? Things will become better. I KNOW they will. I KNOW you will get back to painting very soon. You just HAVE to keep hoping and do your exercises and stuff. It WILL happen, okay? So please don't get depressed and start drinking and all after you get out of hospital.
I know you must be feeling miserable. In case this helps—so am I. I've joined a school here in Calcutta. And boy, does it suck! The kids here are so weird. They do nothing but study night and day for some engineering entrance exam called JOINT which is still like YEARS AWAY!! And

*Calcutta itself! Oh my god! It's so dirty and crowded...
and the heat! It's like living inside a boiler wearing thermal
underwear all the time. But more of that in my next letter.
So as you can see life sucks—BIG TIME! We are still
staying at my aunt's place. And she is like Indira Gandhi
and Hitler combined. It's DO this and DON'T do that—
from morning to night. Baba is also getting quite sick of
it and wants to move out, into our own flat. But the rent
in Calcutta is pretty steep and we can't really afford it
right now.*

*Baba had to spend most of the money we got from selling
the house in Shillong for setting up a medicine shop here.
It's a small one, on the outskirts of the city—some place
called Garia. He keeps saying that the business here is
bad—like really slow. Not like it was in Shillong. Funny,
isn't it? I would have thought that people here would be
falling sick all the time with the crazy heat and the pollution.
Speaking for ourselves, we have all been going pretty crazy
trying to adjust to our new lives here. I guess it's been
the hardest for Baba. He's gone all quiet. Hardly speaks
much and looks worried all the time. Hardly ever laughs
anymore. In Shillong, he used to laugh all the time. He's
become like a stranger these days. I miss the old him.
Like I miss the old days. Like I miss you and Audrey and
Shillong so so badly.*

*Sometimes when I think back on those days, I can't help
thinking that whatever happened was my fault...*

*You remember our picnic in the sacred forest when Audrey
and I had gone for our walk? I had lit up a cigarette and
had stamped the butt into the ground. It was a stupid
thing to do. I was planning to pick it up and throw it
outside when we were leaving. But as you know, all sorts
of things started happening just after that and the cigarette
completely slipped my mind. I guess it's still lying there
somewhere. A half-burnt, man-made Capstan cigarette
from the twentieth century, polluting a prehistoric forest.
I guess I had defiled holy ground. I came in with my mess*

and fouled up a place that was so beautiful, so pure.
Who knows if the spirit of U Ryngkew got really mad at
me...at us. Maybe that's why all this bad stuff happened
to us. Who knows?
Anyway, got to go now. Ma's calling me. Now that you are
up and about, I will write to you—every week, I promise.
But you have to do your exercises and GET THAT HAND
MOVING again so you can start painting again! Please
tell Audrey that I miss her and I will write to her soon.
Don't know when I can come to Shillong again. But
then again, I haven't really left it, have I? It's there inside
me—all the time.
Lots of love,
Debu

Debu read through the letter once, corrected a few mistakes
and inserted it into an envelope. He was licking the postage
stamp when he heard his mother calling him.
'Yes Ma, what is it?' Debu asked.
'Ah, here you are,' his mother parted the curtains and
popped her head in. 'There's a letter for you,' she said and
handed him an envelope.
Debu tore it open. It contained a crayon sketch of three
stick figures. They were standing at the foot of a rectangular-
shaped pedestal upon which was mounted a fourth stick figure
that seemed to have an oval halo around its head.
Below the sketch, there appeared a few words in a near
illegible scrawl like that of a child who has just begun to
write. It said:

To the patron saint of youths, juvenile delinquents and
magicians.
We seek your blessings. They are long overdue.
Amen,
Clint

A smile broke out on Debu's lips. For the first time in
many months, he felt happy.

ACKNOWLEDGEMENTS

My sincere thanks to:

Preeti Gill—for believing in the idea of this book when it was only an unfinished graphic novel, and representing it to the best publisher that I could have hoped for.

Mitra Phukan, Murli Melwani and Ankush Saikia—fellow writers from the Northeast, for your support at a time when the future of this book seemed uncertain.

Hansda Sowvendra Shekhar—for agreeing to read the final manuscript and providing his very generous quote.

Anindya Chatterjee—for Open Tee Bioscope, which nudged me to embark upon my own explorations of childhood and its memories.

Adil Hasan and Reshmi Mitra—for being my first readers and for your invaluable feedback and thoughtful suggestions.

Kartikeya Jain—for killing a few of my darlings but letting most of them live.

Anurag Basnet—editor extraordinaire, guide, critic, cheerleader and friend, without whom this journey in search of lost time would neither have begun nor ended.

Pampa and Sumedha—for everything, always.